SCORPION SHARDS

THE STAR SHARDS CHRONICLES
BOOK 1

SCORPION SHARDS

Neal Shusterman

SIMON & SCHUSTER BFYR

NEW YORK LONDON TORONTO SYDNEY NEW DELHI

SIMON & SCHUSTER BFYR

An imprint of Simon & Schuster Children's Publishing Division

1230 Avenue of the Americas, New York, New York 10020

SIMON & SCHUSTER BFYR is a trademark of Simon & Schuster, Inc.

For information about special discounts for bulk purchases,

please contact Simon & Schuster Special Sales at 1-866-506-1949

or business@simonandschuster.com.

The Simon & Schuster Speakers Bureau can bring authors to your live event.

For more information or to book an event,

contact the Simon & Schuster Speakers Bureau at 1-866-248-3049

or visit our website at www.simonspeakers.com.

Also available in a SIMON & SCHUSTER BFYR hardcover edition

Book design by Hilary Zarycky

The text for this book is set in Granjon.

Manufactured in the United States of America

First SIMON & SCHUSTER BFYR paperback edition May 2013

2 4 6 8 10 9 7 5 3 1

The Library of Congress has cataloged the hardcover edition as follows:

Shusterman, Neal.

Scorpion shards / Neal Shusterman.

(The star shards chronicles ; book 1)

Originally published by Tor, 1995.

Summary: Six teenagers, each tormented by what seems to be an exaggerated
adolescent affliction, come together to try to stop the "beasts" that threaten
to destroy them and the world.

ISBN 978-1-4424-5836-9 (hardcover)

[1. Supernatural—Fiction. 2. Horror stories.] I. Title.

PZ7.S55987

[Fic]—dc20

2012049166

ISBN 978-1-4424-5114-8 (pbk)

ISBN 978-1-4424-5116-2 (eBook

For Anne McD., a star-shard of the highest order,
and for Mike and Christine,
who now shine like a double sun

ACKNOWLEDGMENTS

SCORPION SHARDS BEGAN AS A SMALL IDEA, BUT RAPIDLY EVOLVED INTO a trilogy, this being the first of three books. Along the way there were a great many people whose support and expertise made this book possible.

First, I'd like to thank the regional and scientific experts I met online through Prodigy, who lent an air of authenticity to the story. In Alabama, Matt Dakin, David Camp, Louis Davis, and R. D. McCollum. In the Midwest, Vicki Erwin and Tammy Hallberg. In Boise, Marilyn Friedrichsmeyer and Bradford Hill. In the Northwest, Rick Reynolds, Kim Guymon, Carol Hunter, and Jerry Morelan. And the astronomy and scientific experts John Winegar, Laura L. Metlak, Frank Sheldon, Charles Mielke, Stephen Kelly, and Paul Erikson.

Thanks also to Kathy Wareham, Diane Adams, and Scott Sorrentino, whose comments on early drafts helped to shape the story.

My deepest gratitude and admiration to Kathleen Doherty, who believed this book into existence in its initial Tor Books publication; and to my sons, Brendan and Jarrod, who, when they were young, made me a whole boxful of Creepy-Crawler scorpions, to paste on copies of the book; and thanks to their mother, Elaine, who was of great support and encouragement while this book was being written.

The new and improved incarnation of the Star Shards Chronicles could not have been possible without the support of my agent, Andrea Brown, as well as David Gale and Justin Chanda at Simon & Schuster, who are great luminous souls themselves, and saw fit to breathe new life into these books. They have always been among my favorite books. I'm thrilled that Simon & Schuster are getting them to a new audience!

My only disclaimer is that the star Mentarsus-H does not really exist. But if it did, then this might be what happens . . .

CONTENTS

Part I
American Dregs

1. THE DESTROYER

A SHATTERING OF GLASS.

A monstrous crash echoing through the glass-domed restaurant—and then a second sound so horrid and final it could have meant the very end of the world. The way thunder must sound to a man struck by lightning. The ear-piercing rattle of breaking glass, combined with the deep wooden crunch that followed, pinned the high and low ends of human hearing, and what remained between were dying dissonant chords like that of a shattered—

—piano?

The restaurant's maitre d' could not yet believe his eyes. He stood dumbfounded, trying to figure out what on earth had happened.

The final tinkling of ruined crystal fell from the ornate glass roof of the Garden Court Restaurant—the pride and joy of the Palace Hotel—the most beautiful restaurant in all of San Francisco. Until today. Today shards of the crystal ceiling were stabbing the plush Victorian furniture to death.

And it *was* a piano—or what was left of it, lying like a shipwreck in the center aisle.

Is God dropping pianos on us today? thought the maitre d'. *I should have called in sick.*

The restaurant was closed, thank goodness—Sunday brunch did not begin until eight—but workers and early-rising guests had already gathered to gawk.

Of course it must have been the piano from the new Cityview lounge, up on the top floor, but how could it have come crashing down seventeen floors, through the glass roof?

"Should I notify security?" asked one of the waiters, but somehow the maitre d' was sure security had already figured out there was a problem.

IN LIKE A FLASH and out in the blink of an eye.

The boy called Dillon Cole was in the street in an instant and vanished into the foggy morning. The streets were not crowded, but there were enough people for Dillon to lose himself among unknown faces. He wove through them, brushing past their shoulders, leaving a wake of chaos behind him. The souls he bumped into lost their concentration and sense of direction—a woman stopped short, forgetting where she was going; a man lost his train of thought in the middle of a conversation; a girl, just for a moment, forgot who she was, and why she was even here . . . but then Dillon passed, and their thoughts returned to normal. They would never know that their confusion was caused by Dillon's mere touch. But Dillon knew. He wondered if believing such a thing was enough to send him to the nuthouse. If that wasn't enough to have him locked away, certainly the other things would do the job.

Things like that business with the piano. For all the commotion it had caused, it had been an easy enough stunt. It was a simple thing to get into the deserted top-floor lounge on a Sunday morning. Since the grand piano was on wheels, it hadn't been that hard to ease it across the floor, out onto the patio. As he moved the piano, his fury had grown along with

the burning, screaming need to finish this act of destruction—
a need that ate at his gut like an uncontrollable hunger.

A wrecking-hunger.

Adrenaline coursed through his veins, giving him incredible strength as he heaved the piano onto the ledge—but all he could feel was that wrecking-hunger, forcing him on like a hot iron drilling down to his very soul. He hoisted the heavy beast of a piano onto the ledge, where it balanced for a moment, floating between possible futures, and then it disappeared, taking the railing with it.

One second. Two seconds. Three seconds.

The impact came as a deafening scream of dying crystal as the great glass roof seventeen floors below was shattered . . . and the wrecking-hunger was instantly quelled. That pressure deep inside was released by some invisible escape valve. Dillon took a deep breath of relief and didn't spare the time to look at his handiwork. He got out.

Wearing a bellhop uniform he had taken from a storage closet, Dillon took the elevator to the lobby and left without anyone giving him a second glance—and why should anyone suspect him? He was fifteen, but could pass for seventeen; he was an attractive, clean-cut, redheaded kid who simply looked like one of the kids the bell captain was training. So no one noticed him as he slipped out into the street, where he quickly took off his bellhop jacket and vanished into the morning.

Now, the hotel was far behind him and, in front of him, the stairwell of a BART station descended into darkness. Fog swirled around it as if it were the mouth of a black cave, but to Dillon it was a wonderfully welcome sight.

Once he was down the stairs and heard the approaching train that would carry him away, he knew he was home free. He dropped the bellhop jacket in the trash as he hurried to

4 ·   NEAL SHUSTERMAN

catch the train. He was not caught. He was never caught.

The train stopped, Dillon found a seat, and it rolled on. Only now, as the hotel fell farther and farther behind, did he relax enough for the worries to fill his head.

Please, he begged. *Let no one be hurt. Please let no one be hurt.* The restaurant was closed—but what if a waiter had been setting tables? What if a housekeeper had been vacuuming the rug? Dillon was always careful—he was always good at predicting exactly how his little disasters would unfold, and so far there had been no major injuries . . . but he was starting to slip—the wrecking-hunger was making him careless. When the hunger to destroy came, it was all-consuming and didn't allow him second thoughts. But now in the aftermath of his horrible deed, when his spirit seemed to hang like that piano on the edge of its drop, he could clearly see the ramifications of these awful, awful acts.

People could have died! And I won't know until I see the news. The weight that now burdened his soul was truly unbearable . . . yet it was more bearable than the hunger, which always came back, making him forget everything else. He would fall slave to it again, and the only way to escape was to destroy something. Anything. Everything. The bigger the better. The louder the better. And when it was done the pressure would be gone. The hunger would be fed, and the relief would be rich and sweet like a fat piece of chocolate melting in his mouth.

But the wrecking-hunger had been getting worse lately. It didn't come once a week anymore. Now it came almost every day, pushing him, pressing him, demanding to be fed. Even now as he sat on the train, he felt the hunger again. How could it be? So soon! Wasn't the piano enough? It was the biggest, it was the loudest, it was the worst he'd done yet.

What more did he have to do to be free of this terrible hunger?

The woman sitting next to him on the train eyed him with a look of motherly concern—a look Dillon hadn't seen for the entire year he had been out on his own. She glanced at his shaking hands.

"Are you all right?" asked the woman.

"Sure, fine."

And then she touched his hand to stop it from shaking.

"No!" said Dillon, but it was too late. She had touched him. Her face became pale and she shrank away.

"Ex . . . excuse me," she said in a daze, and she wandered off to find a seat far away from Dillon. Then she sat down to begin the task of unscrambling her mind.

"WHAT ARE YOU AFRAID of, Deanna?"

"Everything. Everything, that's all."

Deanna Chang's pale hands gripped the arms of her chair as if the chair were the only thing keeping her from being flung into space. The room around her was painted a hideous yellow, peeling everywhere like flesh, to reveal deep red underneath. The place smelled musty and old. Faces on fading portraits seemed to lean closer to listen. The walls themselves seemed to be listening. And breathing.

"I can't help you, Deanna, if you won't be specific."

The man who sat across the old desk shifted uncomfortably in his chair. *I make him nervous,* thought Deanna. *Why do I even make psychiatrists nervous?*

"You *can't* help me, okay?" said Deanna. "That's the point." He tapped his pencil on the desk. The eraser fell off the end and rolled onto the stained floor.

I hate this place, thought Deanna. *I hate this room, I hate this man, and I hate my parents for making me come here to hear the same questions the other shrinks have asked, then give the same answers, and have nothing change. Nothing. Ever.*

A woman's voice wailed outside, and Deanna jumped. She couldn't tell whether the sound was a shriek, or a laugh.

"I'm afraid," said Deanna. "I'm afraid of dying."

"Good. That's a start."

Deanna began to rub her pale, slender arms. Behind her and beneath her, the springs within the padding of the chair poked and threatened her through the fabric of the worn upholstery. "At first I was just afraid of walking outside alone. I thought it would end up being a good thing, because it made my parents move us to a better neighborhood—but it didn't stop when we moved. I started to imagine all the terrible things that could happen to me." She leaned forward. "That was two years ago. Now I see myself dying every day. I see my body smashed if our house were to collapse. I see a man with a knife hiding in the closet, or the basement, or the attic in the middle of the night. I see a car with no driver leaping the curb to pull me beneath its wheels . . ."

"You think people are out to get you?"

"Not just people. Things. Everything."

The shrink scribbled with his eraserless pencil. Somewhere deep within the building a heater came on, moaning a faint, sorrowful moan.

"And you imagine these awful things might happen to you?"

"No!" said Deanna. "I *see* these things happening to me. They happen, I feel them—I see them—It's REAL!" Deanna reached up and brushed cool sweat from her forehead. "And then I blink, and it—"

"And it all goes away?"

"Sometimes. Other times the vision doesn't go away until I scream."

The shrink in the cheap suit loosened his tie and put his finger beneath his collar. He coughed a bit.

"Stuffy," he said.

"I'm not safe going out," said Deanna. "I'm not safe staying in. I'm not safe here—because what if the stupid light fixture above my head right now is slowly coming unscrewed and waiting for the perfect moment to fall and crack my skull?"

The shrink looked up at the fixture, which did, indeed, seem loose. He leaned back, unfastened his collar button and took a deep breath, as if the air were thinning. He was becoming frightened, Deanna noted—just like everyone else did when they were near her. She could feel his fear as strongly as her own.

"I think I might drown," Deanna said. "Or suffocate. I always feel like I'm suffocating. Have you ever felt like that?"

"On occasion." His voice sounded empty and distant. He seemed to shrivel slightly in his chair.

Deanna smiled. Feeling his fear somehow made *her* fear begin to diminish. "I give you the creeps, don't I?"

"Your mother is very concerned about you."

"My mother can take a flying leap, if she thinks *you* can help me."

"That's not a healthy attitude."

"You know what? *I* think you're gonna screw me up worse than I was before. Can you guarantee that you won't? And are you sure this stuff is *all* inside my head? Are you *certain*? Are you?" Deanna waited for an answer.

If he said he was sure, she would believe him. If he swore up and down that he could take away the darkness that shrouded her life, she would believe—because she wanted to believe that it was a simple matter of her being crazy. But he didn't answer her. He couldn't even look at her. Instead, he glanced down at his watch and breathed a sigh of relief.

"Is my time up?"

"I'm afraid so."

"FORGIVE ME, FATHER, FOR I have sinned."

"Tell me what your sins are, my son." The priest on the other side of the confessional sighed as he spoke. He must have recognized Dillon's shaky voice from the many times Dillon had come to confess.

"I've done terrible things," said Dillon, cramped within the claustrophobic booth.

"Such as?"

"Yesterday I broke a gear in the cable house—that's why the cable cars weren't running. This morning I shattered the glass roof of the Garden Court Restaurant."

"Dear Lord." The priest's voice was an icy whisper. "I can't give you absolution for this, Dillon."

Dillon stiffened, suddenly feeling as if the booth had grown smaller, tighter, pressing against him. "Please," he begged, "no one was hurt—the news said so—*please!*"

"Dillon, you have to turn yourself in."

"You don't understand, Father. I can't. I can't because it wouldn't stop me. I would find a way to escape and wreck something else—something even bigger. It's not like I want to do this stuff—I *have* to. I don't have a choice!"

"Listen to me," said the priest. "You're . . . not *well*. You're a very sick boy and you have to get help."

"Don't you think my parents tried that?" fumed Dillon. "That kind of help doesn't work on me. It only makes me worse!"

"I . . . I'm sorry, I can't absolve you."

Dillon was speechless in his terror. To go without forgiveness for the things he was forced to do—that was the worst nightmare of all. He gripped the small cross around his neck, holding it tightly, feeling the silver press into his palm.

"But I'm not guilty!" Dillon insisted. "I have no choice—
I'm *poisoned*! I'm *cursed*!"

"Then your penance is taking this confession to the
police."

"It's not their job to absolve me!" screamed Dillon. "It's
your job. You're supposed to take away my sins, and you can't
judge me! You can't!"

No answer from the priest.

"Fine. If you won't absolve me, I'll find a priest who will."

Dillon flung the cherrywood door out so hard, it splintered
when it hit the wall. A woman gasped, but Dillon was past
her, and out the door as quickly as his anger could carry him.
The wrecking-hunger was already building again, and he
didn't know how much longer he could resist it. He had half
a mind to throw bricks through the stained glass window of
the church, but it wasn't God he had a gripe with. Or was it?
He didn't know.

He had told the priest his name a week before in a moment
of weakness, and now it could very well be his ruin. Would
this priest betray the secrecy of the confessional and point a
finger at Dillon?

Dillon didn't want to find out. He would have to leave
tonight and find a new place to wreak his havoc. He had
worked his way up from Arizona without getting caught,
and there were still lots of places to go. There was a freedom
in feeling completely abandoned by life, Dillon tried to convince himself. It was easy to keep moving when every city
was just as lonely. When every face in every crowd was just
as uncaring.

But there had to be one more feeding—just one more
before he left. It would need to be something grand and

devastating—something that would put the wrecking-hunger to sleep for a while.

Are you proud of me, Mom and Dad? he thought bitterly. *Are you proud of your little boy now?* He thanked God that they were dead, and hoped they were far enough away from this world not to know the things he had done.

NOT FAR AWAY, DEANNA Chang climbed a steep sidewalk, trying to forget her appointment with the psychiatrist. She didn't dare to look at the people she passed—they all eyed her suspiciously, or at least it seemed that they did—she could never tell for sure. It made her want to look down to see if her socks were different colors, or if her blouse was bloody from a nosebleed she didn't even know about. Now that she was outside, her claustrophobia switched gears into agoraphobia—the fear of the outside world. It wasn't just that her fears were abnormal—they were unnatural, and it made her furious. She had had a warm, loving childhood—she had no trauma in her history—and yet when she had turned twelve, the fears began to build, becoming obsessions that grew into visions, and now, at fifteen, the world around her was laced with razor blades and poison in every look, in every sound, in every moment of every single day. The fear seemed to steal the breath from her lungs. So strong was the fear that it reached out and coiled around anyone close to her; her parents, the kids who had once been her friends—even strangers who got too near. Her fear was as contagious as a laughing fit and as overwhelming as cyanide fumes.

As she reached the corner, her fear gripped her so tightly that she couldn't move, and she knew that she was about to have another waking-vision of her own death. That it was only in her mind didn't make it any less real, because she felt every measure of pain and terror.

Then it happened: Confusion around her, loud noises. She blinked, blinked again, and a third time, as she tried to make the horrific vision go away. But the vision remained. The driverless car leapt from the curb, and it swallowed her.

DILLON WATCHED FROM THE top of the hill, his horror almost overwhelming the wrecking-hunger in his gut. His eyes took it in as if it were slow motion.

The truck was hauling six brand-new Cadillacs to a dealership somewhere. A few minutes ago, Dillon had jaywalked across the street. He had searched for the chains that fastened the last car onto the lower deck of the truck and picked the locks with the broken prong of a fork. Another human being could have spent all day trying to figure out how to pick those locks—but chains, ropes, and locks were easy for Dillon. He was better than Houdini.

He had clearly anticipated the entire pattern of how the event would go, like a genius calculating a mathematical equation. The car would spill out of the transport truck; the bus driver behind it would turn the wheel to the right; the bus would jump a curb; cars would start swerving in a mad frenzy to get out of the way of the runaway car; many fenders would be ruined—some cars would be totaled . . . but not many people would get hurt.

Maximum damage; minimal injury. This was the pattern Dillon had envisioned in his unnaturally keen mind. What Dillon did not anticipate was that the driver of the bus was left-handed.

Dillon walked up hill and watched as the truck lurched forward, got halfway up the steep hill, and then the last car on its lower ramp slid out and down the hill. Horns instantly began blaring, tires screeched, the escaping Cadillac headed straight for the bus . . .

. . . And the bus driver instinctively turned his wheel to the left, instead of the right—*right into oncoming traffic.*

That simple change in the pattern of events altered everything. Dillon now saw a new pattern emerging, and this time there would be blood.

Horrified, he watched as car after car careened off the road into light posts and storefronts. People scattered. Others didn't have the chance.

Dillon watched the driverless car roll through the intersection and toward a corner. A man ran out of the way, leaving a solitary girl directly in the path of the car—an Asian girl no older than Dillon, who stood frozen in shock. Dillon tried to shout to her, but it was too late. The driverless Caddy leapt the curb, and the girl disappeared, as if swallowed by the mouth of a whale.

For Dillon Benjamin Cole, it was a moment of hell . . . and yet in that moment something inside him released the chokehold it had on his gut. The hunger was gone—its dark need satisfied by the nightmare before him. Satisfied by the bus that crashed deep down the throat of a bookstore; and by the ruptured fire hydrant that had turned a convertible Mercedes into a fountain; and by the sight of the girl disappearing into the grillwork of the Cadillac. Dillon felt every muscle in his body relax. Relief filled every sense—he could smell it, taste it like a fine meal. A powerful feeling of well-being washed over him, leaving him unable to deny how good it made him feel.

And Dillon hated himself for it. Hated himself more than God could possibly hate him.

A HOSPITAL WAS AN indifferent place, filled with promises it didn't keep, and prayers that were refused. At least that's how Dillon saw it ever since he watched his parents waste away in a hospital over a year ago. The doctors never did figure out what had killed them, but Dillon knew. They had held their son one too many times . . . and they died of broken minds. Insanity, Dillon knew, could kill like any other disease. Dillon had watched his parents' minds slowly fall apart, until the things they said became gibberish, and the things they did became dangerous. In the end, Dillon imagined their minds had become like snow on a television screen. With thoughts as pointless as that, sometimes a body knows to turn itself off and die.

Now, as he stepped into the private hospital room with a bouquet of flowers, Dillon barely recognized the girl in the bed. He had only seen her from a distance—before the Cadillac had taken her down, and then in the aftermath of his awful accident, when she was whisked into an ambulance and taken away. How could he expect to recognize a face he had seen so briefly? And yet he had seen that face long enough for it to haunt him for the rest of his life unless he paid this visit.

Her name was Deanna; he had found that much out. She was half-Asian; an only child. The nurse at reception had asked if he was family, he told her he was a cousin. Once inside the room, he told her mother that he was a classmate. He sat beside the mother, chattering lies about a school and teachers he had never heard of, and then the mother got up to make some calls, leaving Dillon alone to keep a vigil for the girl. For Deanna.

DEANNA FLOATED DEEP IN the void, hearing nothing but her own heartbeat. She opened her mouth to scream, but no sound came out. She felt far away, beneath an ocean, for she could not breathe at all. She forced herself up and up, toward the light at the surface, her head pounding, her chest cramping, until finally she broke surface, into the light of—

—a room. A hospital room. Yes. Yes, of course. The driverless car of doom. How terrified she had been of it. She had seen it before. Only this time it had been real. It was not just there to terrify her—it was there to kill her—and it could have, too—but she wasn't dead. She wiggled her toes—she wasn't even paralyzed. She moved her right arm and felt a searing pain shoot through her wrist that made her groan.

"You're all right," said someone next to her. The voice of a man. No—a boy. She lazily turned her head to face him, and her eyes began to focus. He was her age—fifteenish, with red hair but eyes that were dark and so frighteningly deep that she couldn't look away. *Soulful,* her mother would call those eyes.

"Your wrist is sprained," he said. "You've probably got a concussion too, but still you're pretty lucky, considering what happened."

"Who are you?" she asked.

"No one important," he replied. "My name's Dillon." She still could not look away from his eyes, and what she saw there told her all she needed to know. His eyes poured forth his guilt, and she knew that somehow he had done this to her. He had sent the terrible driverless car.

"You bastard," she groaned, and yet she felt strangely relieved. This time it *had* been real, not just another vision—and yet she wasn't dead. In its own way, it was a relief.

Dillon leaned away, unnerved. "I didn't want to hurt you." He said anxiously. "I didn't want to hurt anybody. . . . It's just that . . ." He stopped. How could he hope she could ever understand?

"No, tell me," she said and grabbed his hand. Dillon gasped and tried to pull his hand back; but even in her weakened state, she held him firmly . . . and he was amazed to discover that his touch didn't scramble her mind. She did not shrink away from him.

How was this possible? Everyone he touched was affected—*everyone*.

"Your hand is warm," she said, then looked at him curiously. "You're not afraid! I don't make you afraid!"

"No," he said. She smiled, keeping her eyes fixed on his, and in that moment a brilliant light shone through the half-opened blinds—a sudden green flash that resolved into a red glow in the dark sky.

Whatever that light was, it seemed to make the rest of the world go away, leaving the two of them floating in a hospital room that was floating in space.

This, thought Deanna, *is the most important moment of my life* . . . and she immediately knew why.

"You're like me!" she whispered. "You're just like me!"

Dillon nodded, his eyes filling with tears, because he too knew it was true. In this instant, he felt closer to Deanna than he had ever felt to anyone. *I almost killed her*, he thought. *How horrible it would have been if she died, and we had never met.* He marveled at how the strange light painted a soft glow around her charcoal hair, and he felt a sudden reverence for her that was beyond words. The only words that he could speak now that would make any sense would be his confession.

"I destroy everything I touch," said Dillon.

"You don't destroy me," answered Deanna.

"I'm a monster," said Dillon.

"That's not what I see," she answered. It was the closest thing to forgiveness Dillon had ever felt. Then Deanna began to cry and began a confession of her own.

"I'm afraid," she said.

"Of what?"

"Of this place. Of my life. Of everything inside and out. I'm terrified."

Dillon gripped her hand tightly. "Then I'll protect you," he said. "I'll make sure nothing out there can hurt you."

Deanna smiled through her tears, because she knew that this boy who had almost destroyed her now meant to protect her with all his heart. He held her hand with a delicate intensity, as if having her hand in his was a miracle of the highest order. In this instant, she trusted him more than she had ever trusted anyone.

"No," she answered. "We'll protect each other."

2. 'STONE GETS COOTIES

ON THAT SAME NIGHT, THE DARK SKY OVER ALABAMA WAS punctuated by a million stars. Still, those stars were not bright enough to shed light on the ground, and since the moon had not yet risen, the ground was left darker than the space between the stars.

Winston Marcus Pell lay in his lightless room, wiggling his fingers, trying to see them. His dark skin could have been painted fluorescent yellow, and still he'd have seen little more than a vague shadow.

A night this black was either a good omen or a bad one—depending on which set of superstitions you chose to believe—and Winston had to keep reminding himself that he didn't believe in that silly stuff. Educated people like him didn't have superstitions—that was left to the poor folk still trapped deep in the Black Belt, tilling its cruel dark soil. People who didn't know any better.

So why, then, was Winston so afraid on nights like tonight?

The wind came and went in great and sudden gusts that rattled the windows and tore off leaves before their time. Those yellow October leaves, orphaned by the wind, would shatter against the side of their big old house, sounding like scampering mice. When the gusts had passed, there was silence as empty as the night was dark. This was wrong, Winston knew. It was terribly wrong.

There are no evil creatures out there, he told himself. Those were stories told by old folks to keep kids from wandering out into the dark—but the silence—it was all wrong!

There are no crickets.

That was it!

The realization made Winston's neck hairs stand on end and made him want to shrink even smaller beneath his blanket. There were *always* crickets, chirping all night long out here in the country—even in October. When they'd moved out from Birmingham, it was weeks before Winston could sleep because of the crickets.

What had shut the crickets up tonight?

Winston cursed himself for being so stupid about it. Damn it all, he was fifteen—no matter how he looked on the outside, he was fifteen *inside*, and shouldn't be worried about what crickets choose to do on this night. On this dark night. On this dark creepy night.

Winston knew why he was afraid, although he didn't want to think about it. He was afraid because, apart from the local superstitions, he knew there were stranger things in heaven and earth than he could shake a stick at.

Like the strange and awful thing that had been happening to him for almost three years now. Of course no one talked about that to his face anymore. No one but little Thaddy, who was just too dumb to know any better.

Winston clenched his hands into fists, wishing he had someone to fight. Well, maybe he was afraid of a night without crickets, but if something were out there, he was mad enough to beat the thing silly. He'd paralyze it and leave it helpless on the muddy ground, no matter how big it was.

A gust of wind ripped across the silence, then a thin ghostly wail flew in from the next room followed by the sound of running feet.

Thaddy was in Winston's room in a terrible fright. He

smashed his shin against Winston's wooden bed frame, and his wail turned into a howl.

"Hush up!" ordered Winston. "I don't want you waking Mama."

"There's a monster outside, 'Stone," cried Thaddy. "I seen him! He was at my window gonna rip my guts out, I know it." Thaddy wiped his eyes. "I think it was Tailybone."

Thaddy made a move to jump into bed with Winston, but thought better of it. Instead he just grabbed Winston's blanket off of him and curled up with it on the floor.

"You had best give that back, or you'll be sleepin' with no front teeth." But Thaddy didn't move.

"It's out there, 'Stone, I saw it. It was drooling on my window. I swear it was. We gotta get the rifle."

"We ain't got a rifle, you idiot!"

Winston slipped out of bed and touched his feet to the floor. In the silence, the floorboards creaked.

"Where are the crickets?" asked Thaddy.

"Hush yo' ass, or I'm gonna paralyze your lips till morning."

"No! I'll be good. I promise. No more talking," which was like a wind-chime promising to be quiet through a hurricane.

Winston glanced out of his window. In normal moonlight, he could see the yard and beyond, all the way through the neighbor's field. Tonight, he could barely see the fence—and just beyond the fence, the cotton seemed to roll like beasts in the shadows. Tigers and big fat alligators.

"I can smell it out there," mumbled Thaddy. "It's got a dead smell, like somethin' back from the grave."

"Quit trying to scare yourself," said Winston. He didn't smell it the way Thaddy did, but Winston knew that Thaddy was right—something *was* out there—he could sense it.

Winston grabbed his baseball bat from beneath the bed and headed toward Thaddy's room with Thaddy close behind. No reason to wake their mother up until they knew for sure.

"It's Tailybone, I know it!" whined Thaddy.

"There's no such thing, that's just a dumb old story," Winston said, for himself as much as he did for Thaddy.

Then Thaddy made an observation. It probably wasn't true, but it bothered Winston just the same. "You're shorter today, 'Stone," he said. "Reckon now you've got so short you can't whoop a grave-monster."

Winston threw Thaddy an evil look and put his forefinger up, just an inch away from Thaddy's mouth as a warning. Even in the dark, Thaddy could see the silhouette of the finger about to touch his lips.

"No! No! 'Stone, I'll shut up. I promise."

Little Thaddy was ten years old—a full five years younger than Winston—but Winston was two inches shorter. Winston was, in every way, the size and shape of an eight-year-old.

It hadn't always been that way. He had grown like a weed until the time he was twelve or so. Then, when his friends started sprouting legs and knobby knees, Winston stopped growing up . . .

. . . and started growing down.

The way he figured, he'd have the body of kindergartner again when he was eighteen.

"I wish *I* could grow backward," Thaddy had once said, when he outgrew his favorite bike. But as he watched his big brother become his little brother, Thaddy's thoughts on the subject changed. Thaddy made no such wishes anymore.

The door to Thad's room was ajar, and Winston pushed it all the way open. Its hinges complained with a high-pitched creak as the door swung open to reveal . . . an open window. If there was a thing out there—it could be in the house now! It could be anywhere!

"Thaddy, was your window open before?"

Thaddy stuttered a bit.

"Think! Was your window open or closed?"

Thaddy couldn't remember.

A gnarled branch hung just outside the window, coiled as if fixing to reach in and grab something. In the tree, a rag fluttered in the breeze.

"It's my shirt," said Thaddy. "I threw it at the thing. Maybe I scared it away, maybe."

Winston stood at the threshold of the room for the longest time, not daring to go in. He squinted his eyes and looked at the tree. The light was so very dim that he could barely see the tree at all, and the more he looked the more he thought he saw a face in it. A big old twisted face. A goblin with a head the size of a pumpkin leering into the window.

"It's just the tree," explained Winston, breathing a silent sigh of intense relief. "Your fool head is playing tricks on you again."

"But what about the smell, 'Stone?"

"Dead possum, maybe—under the window, like last year," said Winston, but the smell didn't catch him the way it caught Thaddy.

Thaddy clung to this explanation, and climbed into bed. Winston tucked his brother in, making sure to touch only the blanket.

"Thank you, 'Stone," said Thaddy. "And I'm sorry about what I said before about you being too small and all. I think it's great that you're small."

"Quit talking about that!"

Winston didn't want anyone talking about it ever. The very

first sign of trouble came about three years ago. Not only had it become apparent that he had stopped growing, but something else just as alarming began to happen. It was the way Winston's touch could make a person tingle. Carpet shocks, his parents called it. Didn't think much of it. Then they had taken Winston to the doctor for a simple flu shot. The doctor noticed his height was half an inch shorter than a year before. Didn't think much of it. Must have been a mistake. A few months later, they knew it was no mistake. He was a whole inch shorter. Four doctors later, and they still didn't know what to make of it—and none of the doctors would acknowledge the strange effect Winston's touch was beginning to have on people. Vitamin deficiency, they said. Genetic fluke. One doctor named Guthry wanted to called it Guthry's Syndrome and tried to send him up to the Mayo Clinic where they'd study him like a rat.

So they stopped seeing doctors.

It was the crazy old sisters down the road who called it "Growing Down." They called Winston a witch child, and it made his dad furious. Mr. Pell had been a man of science—a pharmacist—but more than that—a scholar. He was an educated man with educated friends; he had moved back from the city to set an example and help the small town he grew up in. Those two old sisters were everything he hated about growing up black, poor, and ignorant in the Deep South.

When Winston's dad died of a heart attack, the sisters spread word that it was Winston who did it, by putting "a stunt" on his daddy's heart, the way he had put a stunt on their little vegetable garden, where nothing grew larger than the size of a finger. For all Winston knew those toothless old crones were right.

Of course, people didn't really believe he had killed his

father, but the thought was always there—and by then, Winston's touch could numb people's arms, making them tingly, like when your foot fell asleep. The family had stopped going to church soon after, because Baptists saw God or the Devil in everything. It wasn't exactly comfortable being the center of attention on Sunday. Still, Winston often wondered . . . if he could stunt vegetables, numb flesh, and grow backward, was that science or magic? God or the Devil?

Winston finished tucking Thaddy in nice and tight, just the way he liked it.

"The window, 'Stone. Gotta shut out the rotten possum smell."

Winston went to the window, and remembered Thaddy's shirt hanging in the branch, just out of his limited reach. Before closing the window, Winston leaned out into the night to get the shirt . . .

. . . and the monster, sitting in the tree limbs beside the window, hissed like a python.

Winston screamed!

The hideous thing was less than a foot from Winston's face. It was going to kill him. It was going to rip his guts out like Thaddy said. Why, of all times, did Thaddy have to be right about something *now*!

It leapt deeper into the tree, and the tree limbs clattered like bones as the thing hurried to the ground.

"It's Tailybone!" screamed Thaddy, half out of his little fool mind. "It's Tailybone!" And he screamed for their mother.

Winston pushed himself back into the room and fell to the floor. A light came on downstairs.

"Thaddy, are you all right? What's going on up there?" Winston headed downstairs with the baseball bat, and Thaddy fell in line close behind, still whimpering about Tailybone.

"Shut up!" Winston commanded his brother. "There ain't no such thing, there never was and there never will be!"

"Then what was that?"

"I don't know, but it wasn't no Tailybone. It was a some*one*, not a some*thing*," Winston was sure of that now, because the face of the beast had something very human about it. Maybe it was something that escaped from someplace. A carnival. An asylum.

"Maybe it's an alien, maybe," said Thad. "It was so UGLY!"

"What was so ugly?" shouted Mama. They passed her room downstairs, on the way out the back door. She was already scrambling out of her bed and into her wheelchair.

"Don't worry, Mama, I'll check it out."

"Don't you go out there, Winston, if it's a prowler, we'll call the sheriff!"

But nothing she could say would stop him now. At first he had been terrified, but the terror was quickly boiling itself into full-blown fury. He had his fighting fury up, and no one messed with 'Stone Pell when he was in a fighting frenzy.

The kids around town knew that you didn't fight that little freak 'Stone, unless you wanted to be laid out by the count of five—because now Winston's touch was more than just numbing. Every punch Winston threw was guaranteed to paralyze whatever it hit. First your right arm would go sense-less, then your left, then your chin, then your gut, and before long you were lying on the ground, your body limp and useless for hours—maybe even till morning. Maybe longer.

It left Winston with no one to fight, and that was a horrible thing, because lately all Winston wanted to do was fight.

Winston and Thad raced through Mama's stunted garden, hopped the fence, and followed the thing out into the pasture at the edge of a field ripe with cotton.

The moon was on the rise now, making the cotton shine

like snow. There was enough light to see the shape of the thing as it lumbered behind the octopus tree, an ancient live oak with a dozen limbs perfect for climbing. The thing tried to get up into the tree, but Winston swung the bat. He missed, but the creature slipped on some Spanish moss, and fell to the ground. Thaddy pushed at it once, and then ran to hide behind the octopus tree.

"Paralyze it, 'Stone," yelled Thad. "Paralyze it good!"

Winston threw the bat down and cornered it against a hedge thick with sharp thorns. He moved in for hand-to-hand combat.

The beast wasn't as big as he had thought—but it was certainly bigger than he was. Winston dove on the thing, fists flying. It struggled, and Winston grabbed onto its arms—but the thing pulled away, and they both fell over the fence into the cotton. He couldn't paralyze it, no matter how hard he tried. All he could do was fight it, and so Winston and the beast rolled in the cotton, fighting one another, until the beast spoke.

"Stop it," it screamed in a voice that was wet and raspy, but still not evil enough for a nightmare beast. "Or I'm really gonna have to beat you silly!"

The thing threw Winston off, and he landed hard against a fence post with a thud.

By now Thaddy was scratching his arm—the one that had touched the thing.

"Why aren't you paralyzed yet?" Winston demanded. "What the hell are you?"

"I'm a freak," it said. "I'm a freak like you."

Winston took a good look at its face. It was pocked and cratered, like the face of the moon—full of peeling sores and swelling boils, as if it had been bathing in nuclear waste. It was what Winston imagined leprosy might be like—only worse.

That's when Thaddy made an amazing observation.

"I think it might be a girl," he said.

A girl? Winston regarded the grotesque face. It was hard enough for Winston to figure what color its skin was, much less its sex. The straight blond hair gave away that it was white, but the fact that the hair was short and matted didn't reveal what sex it was, if any.

"Are you a boy or a girl?" demanded Winston.

"A girl," it said, disgusted.

By now, Thaddy was scratching his arm like crazy.

"What did you do to him?"

The she-thing smiled. "He shouldn't have touched me. Guess I gave him cooties."

Thaddy looked at Winston and the pizza-faced girl in horror, as if to say *You mean there really is such a thing as cooties?* He turned and ran back to the house, screaming for Mama.

"He'll get a rash on his arm," said the girl. "Probably come down with a bad fever for a week or so, but then it'll go away . . . he shouldn't have touched me."

"Winston?" called his mother from the porch. "What's going on out there?"

"Just some girl, Mama," said Winston. "Thaddy fell in some poison ivy—better tend to him." This was far easier than trying to explain to her the truth.

When his mother had rolled back into the house, the girl-thing told Winston her name was Tory, short for Victoria.

"What's wrong with you?" Winston asked Tory.

"Acne," she said. "Ain't you ever seen acne before?"

Winston looked closely. If this was acne, it was acne gone

mad. There was a human being down there, but it was hidden far beneath an oily layer of zits built on zits. If you spread all those blemishes across ten faces, each face would still be painful to look at.

"You're damn ugly," observed Winston.

"Gee, thanks for noticing, Mighty Mouse. It just so happens that I know who you are. I've been watching you ever since my aunt and me moved here last month. Are you really a witch midget? A devil-dwarf?"

"Go to hell!" shouted Winston, and he leapt at her. So what if she was a girl? No one called him things like that.

They rolled and fought, and even though Winston wasn't really winning, it felt good. It felt wonderful to actually have someone to fight who didn't fall to the ground the second he touched them.

"You possum-rot pus-head," shouted Winston.

"You pin-headed voodoo troll!" shouted Tory.

"Slime-drippin' cesspool explosion!"

"Baby-brained diaper butt!"

"Fusion-face!"

"Shrunken head!'

"Elephant girl!"

Tory delivered a punch to the nose that was right on the mark. It hurt pretty bad, and Winston had to stagger off, collapsing by the fence.

"Why can't I paralyze you?" he asked weakly.

"I don't know," she said. "Why don't you get sick when I touch you?"

They looked at each other like boxers in separate corners.

"Sorry I hit you so hard," said Tory. "It's just that the elephant girl thing is a sore spot. It's what they used to call me when I lived in Florida."

28 •   NEAL SHUSTERMAN

"Where'd you live, the Everglades?" jabbed Winston. "Are you a swamp thing?"

Tory didn't answer. Even in the dim light Winston could see her puffy eyes filling with tears.

"Okay," said Winston. "Truce?"

"Truce," echoed Tory, rubbing the tears from her eyes before they had a chance to fall. *Tears would probably make her face sting*, thought Winston.

"You always go looking in people's windows at night, scarin' 'em half to death?" he asked, wiping his bloody nose.

"Sun's bad for my delicate complexion," said Tory, "so I do all my exploring at night. People don't see me that way. Suits me just fine."

"Does your face . . . hurt?"

"All the time." She leaned a bit closer to him, whispering. "Is it true you're growing backward?"

"What do you care?" snapped Winston.

"I came looking for you because I heard what people said about you. I wanted you to touch my face . . . paralyze it so I couldn't feel it at all, and maybe it would stop hurting."

Winston shook his head. "But you don't paralyze like the others. . . . Why?"

Just then their faces were lit by a light in the sky, shining brighter than the crescent moon. The cotton around them glowed green for a moment and then pink. At first Winston took it to be the sheriff's spotlight, but the color was wrong— and it was too high up.

They stood up to get a better look. It was an uneven ball of light, maybe a fourth the size of the moon. It hurt their eyes to look at it.

Winston backed up to a fence post, leaning on it for balance. The light had triggered something inside of him, and he thought he might pass out. All at once, his brain was firing like crazy, and he was filled with an overpowering sense of wonder and confusion, as if all his life he had been sleeping and was just waking up. But of all the confused feelings and thoughts that rocketed through his head, the most overwhelming feeling of all was the sense that this light in the sky, whatever it was, was meant for him.

"It's incredible," said Tory. "I've never . . . *felt* anything like it."

Winston looked over at Tory and could see in her rapid breathing and wonder-filled eyes that she was hit by the same devastating wave of emotion that he felt. She had the same revelation that this odd light in the sky did not just hit their eyes, it ignited their souls.

It made Winston furious!

Whatever that light was, it was for him and him alone. He didn't want to have to share such a special thing with this hideous girl beside him. It would mean that they didn't meet tonight by accident—they were drawn together—somehow bound like soul mates. Winston found the thought unbearable.

"I . . . know you, don't I? asked Tory. "We're the same age, you and me!" She said it with such excitement, it made Winston cringe.

"We might both be freaks," growled Winston, "but I ain't nothin' like you! We got nothin' in common, do you hear me?!"

It was then that Winston noticed the noise. It had been growing all around both of them since the light had appeared in the sky, and now its volume grew and multiplied until it buzzed in the brush like an air-raid siren. Winston knew right then that the sound was aimed at the two of them, and no one else in all of Alabama—and he knew that it was a sign he could not deny. The sound was nature itself, screaming out to tell him that this torturously ugly girl was more his sister than anyone born to his family. More like him than anyone he had known.

"What is it?" asked Tory, holding her ears. Winston tried to squeeze out the sound as well, but couldn't.

"Crickets," answered Winston. "Millions of 'em."

3. A PLANETOID, THE FULL MOON, AND THE SCORPION STAR

EARLIER THAT SAME DAY, AND A THOUSAND MILES NORTHEAST, the south fork of eastern Long Island was set upon by an unseasonably warm fog. It brooded dense and round on the weather maps like a gray cataract—an unseeing eye surrounded by cold, clear skies. Shrouded in the center of the fog stood Hampton Bays High School, where things had been normal until third period. That's when the chase began for Lourdes Hidalgo.

It started in the science lab, and the chase spread through the school as Lourdes tried to escape from the teachers who chased her. She had lost them by ducking into a broom closet, and now she descended the south stairwell, hoping that everyone would be thrown off track just long enough for her to burst out into the foggy October and freedom.

As Lourdes lumbered down the worn metal stairs of the old school, the stairs rang out in dull, heavy tolls, like an ancient mission bell. The bolts creaked, and the steel steps themselves seemed like cardboard, ready to give way under her immense weight.

Lourdes, however, had grown used to that. She was used to chairs buckling beneath her when she sat. She was used to the way her hips would brush past both sides of a door frame when she entered a room, as if the entire room was a tight pair of pants she was trying to squeeze her way into. But she would never get used to the cruel teasing.

Now Lourdes was bounding down the metal stairs, two steps at a time, running from teachers, the guidance counselor, and the principal. Ralphy Sherman had deserved what Lourdes had done to him, and so she fought back her tears, and fought the remorse that was trying to take hold of her.

Ralphy had been whispering lies about Lourdes in science lab, as if he himself believed they were true. *Did you hear that Lourdes was offered ten grand to join the circus? Did you hear that Lourdes donates fat to the Southampton Candle Factory? Did you hear they found some loose change and a TV remote in Lourdes's belly button?* Lourdes tried to control herself. She bit her tongue and gritted her teeth, but there's only so much abuse a person can take. She wanted to hurt him as much as he hurt her—as much as they all hurt her, and so she pushed Ralphy up against the wall, held her hand firmly on his chest, and felt his chest begin to crush inward. Ralphy tried to scream, but couldn't. His face turned red, purple, then blue. By then the teacher had taken notice and come running, so Lourdes stepped away from the limp blue kid, and he fell to the floor. Lourdes ran.

Now, as she lumbered down the stairs, she cursed the steps and the way they rang out every time her bursting orthopedic shoes hit them.

It was at the first floor landing that Lourdes encountered Mrs. Conroy, the principal of Hampton Bays High.

"Hold it right there, Lourdes." She stood ten steps beneath Lourdes, and her voice was well trained to wield power—power enough to stop the grossly obese girl in her tracks. Lourdes swayed just a bit, and the steps creaked like the hinges of a rusty door. There wasn't any sympathy from anyone in school this year—not even the principal. It was as if sympathy and understanding were limited to a certain waist size, and if a person grew beyond that limit, they were fair game for all forms of cruelty.

"You are coming to the office," said Mrs. Conroy, "and we're calling your parents. What you've done is very serious, do you understand?"

"Of course I understand," said Lourdes. "I'm fat, not stupid." Her voice was thick and seemed to be wrapped within heavy, wet layers of cotton. When Lourdes spoke, it sounded as if she was shouting from inside the belly of a whale.

"I didn't kill him, did I?" asked Lourdes.

"No," said Mrs. Conroy, "but you could have."

Lourdes was relieved and disappointed at the same time.

"This school has had about enough of you," growled Conroy.

"Does that mean I'm expelled?"

"We'll talk about it in my office."

"Fat chance," said Lourdes. She took one step at a time as she descended slowly toward her principal.

Boom! The steps rang out as Lourdes planted her swollen feet on them.

Boom!

In a moment she eclipsed the stairway lights, and Conroy's face was lost in shadow.

"I'm warning you, Lourdes . . ."

Boom!

As Lourdes approached, Mrs. Conroy seemed smaller and less powerful. Why, she was just a wisp of a woman after all, thought Lourdes.

Boom!

"Lourdes, I won't let you past me."

"So try and stop me."

Boom!

As Lourdes continued her descent toward the frail principal, Conroy unconsciously gripped the rail, already feeling

Lourdes's pull—her *gravity*, for Lourdes did have a gravity about her. When she was in a room, it was difficult not to find oneself leaning in her direction. If a breeze blew in through the window and scattered papers, they would all stick to Lourdes until she peeled them off. If you threw a paper airplane at her, it would curve around her and come back to you like a boomerang—and if you threw it just right, that airplane would continue to circle in orbit around her until it fell to the ground. Her classmates called her the Planetoid, and she hated them all.

"If you so much as touch me, Lourdes—"

Boom!

The final step. Lourdes stood right before Conroy, and the principal's shoulder-length hair was falling forward across her face, reaching toward Lourdes. Her immense belly pinned the principal against the wall, and they looked into each other's eyes. Fear was in the principal's eyes now. Fear and disgust.

"It's not my fault I'm like this," said Lourdes. With that the principal's body began to crush inward, from Lourdes's mere touch, collapsing in upon itself. Barely able to breathe, Conroy snarled out her words.

"You don't belong here," she said, and Lourdes knew she wasn't just talking about school. "Here," for Lourdes, meant this world. She brushed Conroy away as if swatting a fly, and the woman gasped for breath, as if she had just escaped the crushing force of a black hole.

Principal Conroy clutched the railing to keep from collapsing and shouted at Lourdes, but Lourdes didn't listen. She just continued out of the stairwell and onto the first floor.

THE FIRST FLOOR HALLWAY housed mostly English and history classrooms. The nearest exit was to the left, but the school security guard and guidance counselor were standing there, blocking Lourdes's escape route. At the other end of the hall stood the vice principal and a whole legion of teachers. They all began to close in.

Either she could run at them, hoping her momentum would take them out like bowling pins, or she could duck into an empty classroom. Since there were too many of them to bowl over, she chose the classroom. Once inside, she would be cornered, but at least she'd have an arsenal of things to throw at them as they tried to come at her. If it had to be her against the whole world, then the whole world would be made to suffer for what it was doing to Lourdes Hidalgo.

She pushed into the classroom, and instantly caught sight of Miss Benson—the new English teacher—and Michael Lipranski in the front of the classroom.

Lourdes was not prepared for what she saw. Her eyes went wide and her jaw dropped open.

Because Michael Lipranski was kissing his English teacher.

The very sight of it distracted Lourdes a moment too long, and she was caught off guard when everyone burst into the room. With so many people trying to wrestle her under control, not even her crushing gravity could save her. In the end, she had to give up. Her only consolation was that Michael Lipranski was also caught, and he would be in as much trouble as she was. Maybe more.

MICHAEL LIPRANSKI WAS AN unlikely make-out king. Sure, he was attractive, but there was something about him that was unnerving, unclean, and a bit slimy. He was a bit too thin, his dark hair was a bit too long—and always damp. When he would look at you, you could swear that he was reading your most secret thoughts and thinking great mischief.

He wasn't your typical stud—had no great muscles to speak of, and there was always a constellation of bruises over much of his body. Some of these came courtesy of his father, who was known to use his fists, but most were from fights around school. Michael wasn't much of a fighter, but he had learned to defend himself in a world that turned out to be far more cruel and vicious than he ever thought it could be.

Physically, the only thing truly special about Michael Lipranski was his eyes. He had these impossibly intense turquoise-hazel eyes, layered with rich coronas of color that made them seem as deep, warm, and inviting as a Caribbean sea. The girls in school could lose themselves in Michael's eyes, and often did. It happened last year in Baltimore, and it happened here in the Hamptons. Maybe that's why all the guys hated him.

And maybe that's why no teacher wanted him in their classroom. For several years Michael could never figure out why this was so. He was friendly, funny, and personable. He made an effort to do the work. Still, he seemed to be an epicenter for all sorts of disturbances. Since seventh grade, Michael's classrooms had always been remarkably unruly. He always assumed that this was normal. Kids hit puberty and turned into monsters, right? That's what everyone said . . . but the way his classmates acted wasn't exactly normal.

When Michael was in a room, a clamminess filled the air that pulled at the edge of everyone's senses like a smell so faint it was impossible to identify. Whatever it was, it usually attacked girls and guys differently. It made girls' hearts race and made them suddenly feel like there was something that they desperately wanted. They would begin to sweat, and their eyes would constantly seek out Michael's—for if they could look into Michael's eyes, they would begin to feel just a bit better. And if they could move closer to him, they could feel relief. Close enough to smell his breath. Closer still, to taste it.

Of course, guys didn't generally feel that way. Instead they felt like beating Michael up.

So when the posse chasing Lourdes Hidalgo burst into Miss Benson's classroom, word got around at the speed of light squared that Michael "Lips" Lipranski had taken his smooth moves to new heights. Everyone acted surprised, but no one really was.

WHILE LOURDES SAT IN the principal's office under tight guard, Michael had a pressing appointment with Mr. Fleiderman, the guidance counselor, who was everyone's friend—or at least tried to be.

The appointment wasn't held in Fleiderman's office, because when it wasn't too cold, Fleiderman liked to hold his sessions out in the quad—the courtyard in the center of the large school. More relaxed, less threatening, Fleiderman thought. It had never occurred to him that most kids didn't want to talk to the guidance counselor in view of the entire school.

When Michael crossed through the wall of steamy fog, it seemed that the rest of the world slipped off the edge of the earth into gray nothingness. It's how Michael felt inside too— lost, alone, and confused—generally fogged in, but he didn't plan on letting Fleiderman see that. *Let him think I'm calm and in control,* thought Michael as he approached the over-eager counselor.

Fleiderman shook Michael's hand and invited him to sit with him in the moist grass. Michael refused to sit.

"Why not?" asked Fleiderman, pleasantly. "I won't bite."

Michael smiled his winning smile. "Standing is better, strategically speaking," he said. "If you attack me and try to strangle me, I can run. And yes, you might bite, too."

Fleiderman laughed at the suggestion and decided to stand. "All right, we'll do it your way."

They both waited, Michael leaned against a yellowing sycamore tree with his arms folded.

"So talk to me," Fleiderman finally said.

"So talk to you about what?"

"You know what. Miss Benson."

"What about her?"

"You tell me."

Michael shrugged and looked away. "She kissed me. So?"

"Don't you mean *you* kissed *her*?"

Michael smiled slyly. "What makes you so sure?"

Fleiderman grunted slightly. Michael could see irritation building in the mild-mannered man.

"I want to understand where you're coming from, Michael."

"Baltimore."

"No, inside. I want to understand you."

That made Michael laugh out loud. "Good luck."

"I know you keep yourself pretty busy with girls in school. I know you're . . . shall we say . . . 'active.'"

"Active?" said Michael. "Like a volcano?"

"Sexually active."

"Oh," said Michael. "That." He looked away again and paced around to the other side of the sycamore. Fleiderman followed, and Michael noted how the guidance counselor's irritation had already built into frustration.

"I make out a lot," explained Michael. "I don't go much past that. Second base, maybe. You know."

"Am I supposed to believe that?"

"Believe what you want," said Michael. And then Michael smiled again. "But to tell you the truth, sex scares me."

"Why?" asked Fleiderman. "Afraid you might explode?"

Michael shrugged. "Yeah. Or that the girl might."

Fleiderman laughed uncomfortably, but Michael didn't. He became dead serious and noticed that Fleiderman's hands had involuntarily tightened into fists.

"Let's get back to Miss Benson," said Fleiderman. He reached up to wipe steam from his glasses.

"What happened wasn't all my fault, okay?" said Michael, beginning to say more than he had really wanted to. "She didn't *have* to keep me after class to talk about my book report. She didn't *have* to come up to me and touch my shoulder like that—and she didn't *have* to kiss me back when I kissed her."

Fleiderman gritted his teeth. Michael could see his anger heading toward meltdown. There was no logical reason for it; Michael wasn't antagonizing him—Michael was, in fact, being honest and spilling his guts, just like Fleiderman wanted. Still the guidance counselor seethed with anger. "Miss Benson will be dealt with," Fleiderman said. "But now we're talking about you and your problem of self-control."

"How the hell am I supposed to control myself when all the girls in school are after me, and all the guys want to beat the crap out of me?"

Fleiderman's whole face seemed clenched as he spat his words out. "Oh, I see. Everyone either loves you or hates you. You're the center of the universe and everyone's actions revolve around you."

"Yeah," said Michael. "That's it!"

"Delusions!" shouted Fleiderman. He was furious, and Fleiderman *never* got furious at anything. Staying calm was his job. "It's all in your head!" he shouted.

"Oh yeah?" Michael took a step closer to Fleiderman. Michael was five-seven, Fleiderman closer to six feet. "What do you feel now, Mr. Fleiderman? Do you feel really pissed off? Do you want to grab me and rip my head off? It's like you're turning into a werewolf inside, isn't it? An animal. Everyone who hangs around me long enough starts acting like an animal out of control. They either want to kill me or kiss me. Actually I'm glad that you'd rather kill me."

Meltdown! Fleiderman lost it, and he lunged at Michael, grabbing him by the throat. Michael pushed him away, but Fleiderman lunged again, growling—baring his teeth like a mad dog. Fleiderman smashed the boy with the back of his hand, then threw Michael to the ground; Michael tried to scramble away, but Fleiderman was too fast. He was on Michael, pinning him to the ground; he raised his heavy fist, ready to bring it across Michael's jaw with a blow that would surely break it.

"Stop!" said Michael. "They're watching!"

Fleiderman's wild uneven breath gave way to a whine as he looked up to see that the fog had lifted just enough for the school windows to be seen all around them. Faces peered out from classrooms on all sides, as if this was a Roman circus and Michael was fodder for the lion.

"Kill him, Fleiderman," shouted some kid from the third floor. "Kill the creep!"

Fleiderman could have—it was in his power, and it was certainly in his eyes; instead, the guidance counselor bit his own lip and continued biting it until it bled. Then he fell off of Michael and crouched in a humiliated heap, trying to find himself once more.

"My God!" muttered Fleiderman. "What am I doing? What's wrong with me?"

"It's not you," said Michael, refusing to let his own tears out. "It's me. I turn people crazy. I'm like . . . a full moon, only worse."

Fleiderman wiped blood from his lips as he crouched low, still unable to look up at Michael.

"You won't be going to this school anymore," he told Michael, finally getting to the bottom line.

"I'm being expelled?"

"Transferred." Which to Michael was the same thing.

Fleiderman began to breathe hard, fighting back words of anger. Michael could tell because his face was turning red, and although Michael felt like kicking Fleiderman in the gut, he didn't. Instead he dug deep within himself, to find a feeling that was decent, and when he found it, Michael took his hand and gently rested it on Fleiderman's hunched shoulder.

"It's all right," said Michael. "You can say it if it makes you feel better—it doesn't bother me."

"I hate you!" said Fleiderman.

"Say it again."

"I hate you . . ." Just saying the words seemed to release some of Fleiderman's steam. He quivered the tiniest bit.

Although those words hurt, they also gave Michael a sense of control. He could bring people down to their knees in love or hate, altering their very nature. He could turn a bright, sunny disposition into a storming fury. He could turn the heart of an ice-queen into hot steam. Such awesome power must be worth something.

Michael patted Fleiderman's shoulder and turned to leave. As Michael crossed the quad, his thoughts became a bit clearer and what fog was left in his own mind began to lift, along with the fog in the quad. Now that the worst was over, he felt relieved as he went back into school to clear out his locker.

As Michael left the quad, Fleiderman began to feel his fury fading. In a moment, Fleiderman's humanity came crawling back to him, and he began to condemn himself and obsess over this awful thing he had just done—for no reason he could figure out. He felt ashamed and terrified.

Love and hate being two sides of the same coin, Fleiderman began to wonder if the unfortunate Miss Benson also felt this way once Michael Lipranski had been removed from her company.

THAT NIGHT, WHILE THE rest of the Eastern seaboard was densely padded with storm systems, a patch of clear sky stalled over eastern Long Island, making it a perfect night for the annual star-watch. After sunset, four dozen kids gathered to spend an evening on Montauk Point with their science teacher, peering through his telescope, drawing star maps by flashlight, and calculating the speed of the earth's rotation.

Both Michael and Lourdes were advised not to come, which was more certain to assure their attendance than giving them a printed invitation. Michael, who had been sporting a fake license for almost a year now, drove up in his father's van, and no one was quite sure how or when Lourdes got there; at times she was amazingly stealthy for a girl of her size.

Montauk Point was a state park surrounded by cold, rough ocean on three sides, and the bluff beyond the lighthouse was the farthest east one could get in the state of New York. It was the tip of Long Island and simply as far as you could go. Unless, of course, you chose to take one step further east—off the cliff and into the sea.

It was around eleven that night that Michael Lipranski stood at the tip of the lighthouse bluff, contemplating that final step east that would send him plunging to his death in the cold breakers.

For Michael, the evening hadn't begun with such thoughts, but it had begun desperately. The star-watch was a great make-out opportunity—and on his last day at this school, Michael felt compelled to take advantage of that.

Upon arrival, Michael had set his charms on Melissa Brickle, who was, by nature, the school's wallflower. One smile from Michael changed her nature considerably. He took her to the high bluff behind the lighthouse—the most easterly place— and there, to the sound of waves and the pulse of the spinning light arcing over their heads, Michael got down to business.

Michael's kisses were more frantic than passionate, more compulsive than romantic, but Melissa did not notice, for, as Michael knew, no one had ever kissed Melissa Brickle this way before, and her own new and overwhelming feelings blocked out everything else. Michael could feel himself trespassing in the dark places of her mind, releasing those feelings like wild beasts from a cage. A thin ground fog carpeted the grass around them, slipping off the cliff in a slow vapor fall. The mist seemed to be flowing from the two of them.

Through it all, Michael's mind and body were exploding with emotions. Frustration, anger, confusion all fought for control—but what he felt more than anything tonight was futility. No matter what he did, no matter how many girls he lured into secret corners—even if he took them all the way and absolutely gave in to all of his urges—he still would not be satisfied. Instead his urges would only increase—they would grow and drive him insane. Michael's grip on Melissa grew stronger as they kissed—so strong that it must have been hurting her, but she didn't notice. She wouldn't notice even if Michael really did hurt her.

"Tighter," she said. "Hold me tighter."

And as he tightened his grip, Michael came to understand that this frenzied necking was a violation of the girl. He had, in some way, entered this girl's mind—he *made* her want all the things that he could do to her, and this was a violation as real as any other. Michael was terrified of what he was turning into, and what awful things he might be capable of.

Before it went too far, Michael pushed Melissa away.

"What's the matter?" she asked. "Did I do something wrong?"

She moved toward him again, then this shy, sweet girl slipped her hand into his jacket, and shirt, shamelessly rubbing his chest.

Michael gently grabbed her hand and placed it back down in her lap. "Better stop," he said.

"Better not," she whispered. She tried to snuggle up to him, but Michael stood up.

"Just go!" screamed Michael. "Get out of here!" But she did not move—so he reached down, picked up a clump of dirt and hurled it at her shoes.

Confused and humiliated, Melissa ran off in tears.

Good, thought Michael. Because there were worse things she could feel than humiliation.

Soon the sound of her footfalls faded, and Michael was left alone with his bloated, malignant urges. But those urges could be killed, couldn't they? The sound of the crashing ocean made him think of that. Those soul-searing urges that ate him alive could be destroyed by one single step east. Right now anything seemed better than having to feel That Way anymore.

And so, before he knew what he was doing, Michael found himself leaning into the wind at the edge of the cliff, daring his balance to fail him, and gravity to pull him down to his end.

"Do you really think anyone cares if you jump?"

The voice came as such a shock, Michael almost did lose his balance. He stumbled backward, away from the cliff, into the grass. His life did not so much flash before his eyes, as slap him in the face.

"If you jump, people might freak, but they'll forget soon enough," said a voice that was dense and wet, like liquid rubber. Lourdes Hidalgo lumbered out from behind a bush like a buffalo, and Michael wondered how long she had been watching.

In truth, Lourdes had been watching from the moment Michael had brought Melissa to the bluff. Lourdes enjoyed watching the other kids make out—and wasn't ashamed of it either. She had enough things to feel ashamed of—peeping was low on her shame list.

"I don't care if everyone forgets me," said Michael. "I'm just sick of feeling This Way, okay?"

"What way?"

"You wouldn't understand."

"How do you know?"

Michael looked down at the bulge in his pants. They were too tight down there, as always, and in this warped little moment, he didn't care who he told or how dumb it sounded.

"Do you know what it's like to feel totally crazed all of the time? To wake up That Way, and go to class That Way, and not be able to sleep at night because of Those Thoughts going through your head, and then when you do sleep, to be invaded by Those Kind of dreams? They say we got hormones, right? Well, I don't have hormones, I *am* a hormone—one big mutated hormone with a thousand hands and a million eyes. It's like that hormone has eaten me alive, and there's nothing left of *me*. Do you know how that feels?

Lourdes, to her credit, took the question very seriously. "No," she said. "But I do know what it's like to be fat. So fat that I can't sit down in a movie theater. So fat that I have to ride in elevators alone. So fat that when I take a bath, there's no room for any water in the tub. If anyone should jump into the sea, it should be me."

Michael shrugged, feeling embarrassed. "Naah. You'd probably bounce."

Lourdes considered this. "Or splat like a water balloon."

"Gross!" Michael looked at Lourdes. She was truly hideous to behold, even in this dim light.

Lourdes smiled at him and Michael backed off. Was this a trick? Was she just after him like all the other girls? After all, she could not be immune to his full-moon effect, could she?

"Nice try," said Michael. "I'm not going to kiss you, so get lost." He turned toward the edge of the cliff again, contemplating it.

"Kiss you? I don't want to kiss you, your breath smells like onions."

This got Michael's interest. "What do you mean you don't want to? Don't you find me irresistible?"

"I can resist you just fine," said Lourdes. "I mean, you don't use enough deodorant, your clothes are ugly, your hair is stringy—"

Michael grinned, unable to believe his ears. "Go on! Tell me more!"

"Let's see. You've got a crooked lower tooth, your eyebrows are like caterpillars, you got no butt at all . . ."

Michael practically jumped for joy. "That's great," he said. "Do you know how long it's been since I've been able to talk to someone without them either wanting to beat the crap out of me, or make out with me? Do you know how long it's been since *I* could talk to a girl without feeling you-know-how? This is great!" Michael could have gone on for hours contemplating the deep ramifications of their mutual lack of attraction, but hearing about how unattractive Michael found her didn't seem to make Lourdes too happy. He looked at her swollen form and wondered how a girl could get this way.

"You know, you'd probably lose weight if you ate less," offered Michael.

"I'll tell you a secret," said Lourdes. Her head rolled forward on her neckless body, and she whispered in her cotton-padded voice: "I haven't eaten in months."

"No way!"

"It's true—not a bite, and still I get fatter. Almost a pound every day."

"That's wild!"

Lourdes smiled. "As wild as your man-eating hormone, maybe?"

They looked at each other, both beginning to realize that their similarities ran far deeper that they could have imagined—and then, without warning, the sky exploded.

A burst of green, and then a strange pink light lit up the heavens; it shook Michael and Lourdes to the core of their very souls.

"A supernova!" exclaimed Mr. Knapp, the science teacher. "My God! I think it's a supernova!" He frantically cranked his telescope toward the constellation of Scorpius, then flipped through his astronomy book to identify the star.

In a matter of minutes, a star in the tail of the scorpion flared to a fourth the size of the moon. Michael and Lourdes stepped out from behind the lighthouse to see everyone crowding around Knapp, who compared his star chart to the heavens above him.

"Mentarsus-H!" he announced. "It says here that it's sixteen light-years away—that means it blew up before most of you were born!"

Knapp immediately started to explain, "It took all those years for the light of the explosion to reach the earth. Like when you're in the bleachers at the ball park, you see the player swing, but don't hear the crack of the bat until a second later. Space is so vast that light takes years to get from star to star. That star blew up over sixteen years ago, but we're just finding out about it now."

While everyone else marveled at this grand cosmic display, Michael and Lourdes lingered beyond the fringe of the crowd—touched by the nova with an intensity none of the others felt. It was as if the light illuminated some part of themselves that had always been hidden in shadows.

"I have to go!" Michael suddenly exclaimed. "I have to go now!" He was already fumbling in his pockets for the keys to his van.

"I have to go with you," said Lourdes, her eyes filling with tears she could not explain.

Yes! thought Michael. *It had to be the two of them.* They were both being drawn away—drawn west. They had to travel west because . . .

. . . *Because there were others! Others who were like them.*

The truth came to him as if he had known it all along.

Michael could imagine them now—all of them looking up at the supernova at this same instant, in places far away.

"I have room in the van for you," said Michael.

"I have a credit card," said Lourdes, "if we need money."

They hurried toward Michael's van, as if they could afford no lost time.

Now those people standing around the telescope and all the other people in their lives seemed meaningless and unimportant.

Michael turned the key in the ignition with such force the starter screamed as the engine came to life.

"Where do we go?" asked Lourdes. "How will we know when we get there?"

But both of them knew there were no answers to such questions. In a moment they were gone, driving west, while their former classmates looked heavenward through a round patch of clear sky that was fixed over Montauk like an eye, staring unblinking into infinity.

Part II
Free Fall

4. THE SHADOW OF DESTRUCTION

THE SPLINTERING OF STONE.

A deafening rumble as a mountainside pounced upon an unsuspecting neighborhood below. Five homes were destroyed by the massive boulders, and Dillon Cole, his wrecking-hunger now fed, gripped Deanna Chang and collapsed in her arms.

In the dim light they sat on the mountainside, hearing the shouts from below as neighbors came out to help one another. Through it all, Deanna held Dillon tightly.

"Please let no one be hurt," Dillon whispered desperately.

Deanna had watched in horror as the row of homes on this hill above Lake Tahoe was obliterated. She watched in horror . . . but not in fear. Even now, as she held Dillon, she wasn't frightened. Her fears, which had been building for hours, vanished the moment Dillon satisfied his wrecking-hunger—and it had been that way every time.

In the four days since they had run from the hospital in San Francisco, Deanna had stood by as Dillon sent a driverless semi down a ravine; sunk an empty barge on the Sacramento River; and shorted out a switching station, plunging the entire community of Placerville into darkness. She knew she should have felt terror and revulsion at each of these catastrophes, yet, against all reason, a sudden peace always filled her in the aftermath.

All that destruction didn't feel real to her in those moments after—it seemed little more than a painted canvas before her.

But Dillon was real, and she always turned her newfound calm to him, comforting him and his conscience, which had a strong case for feeling guilty. She thought she was beginning to understand that strange calm: she was in the shadow of Dillon's destruction now—and that was far less terrifying than being in its path—for if those horrible things were happening to someone else, it meant that they weren't happening to her.

What remained in that swollen calm was a single question in Deanna's mind.

How?

How does he accomplish these things?

She looked to the night sky—to the supernova that still shone in the heavens, as if it could answer her.

"Is it winking at you?" asked Dillon, turning to look at it as well. "Is it telling you all the secrets of the universe?"

Deanna shook her head. "It's just telling me to go east."

Dillon nodded. "I know."

It was true. From the moment its light appeared in the sky, she and Dillon were falling east; carried by an irresistible current, like driftwood pulled toward a raging waterfall. Suddenly Deanna's aching wrist and aching body didn't matter. Her family didn't matter—they seemed like people from a different lifetime and, aside from a single postcard to tell them she was all right, they had been shuffled far back in Deanna's mind. All that mattered was moving east with Dillon—and all because of that star.

Maybe the others know more, thought Deanna. Oh, yes, she knew about The Others—they both did. Although they spoke of them only once, they knew that it was The Others who were drawing them east. It was Dillon who didn't want to discuss them—as if this knowledge of The Others was too important a thing to say out loud.

Deanna could swear she could sometimes hear their voices in the rustling of leaves—see their faces in dreams she couldn't quite remember. She thought to tell Dillon, but thought better of it.

Far below, at the bottom of the hillside, an ambulance could be heard arriving at the scene of the rock slide.

"No one was supposed to get hurt . . . ," said Dillon, squeezing his eyes tightly shut.

Deanna pushed the sound of the ambulance out of her mind. Instead she focused on Dillon—how he needed her and how she needed him to keep her fears away. How strong they were together.

A trickle of pebbles fell past them on the dark hillside, settling in the aftermath of Dillon's rock slide.

"I don't understand how you did it," she asked him. "All you did was throw a stone . . ."

"It wasn't just a stone," he told her. "It was the *right* stone."

But it was still beyond Deanna to understand just what he meant by that. He had thrown a stone, and that stone had begun an inconceivable chain of events—his stone hit another, which then rolled against a large boulder, and in a few moments the whole mountainside beneath them was falling away before their eyes. It would have been wonderful, if it wasn't so horrible.

"Do you hate me, Deanna?" Dillon asked. "Do you hate me for the things that I do?"

Did she hate him? She probably ought to hate him, but how could she when he was the only one who didn't run from her? How could she hate him when he treasured every ounce of comfort she gave him? The more he needed her, the more she loved him—she couldn't help it. *Whatever you do, I'll forgive you, Dillon,* she said to herself, *because I know the goodness inside you—even if no one else can see.*

But to him, she only said, "No, I don't hate you."

When Dillon heard her words, he relaxed—as if her feelings for him were all that mattered—as if Deanna was his only lifeline to the world.

Now that the wrecking-hunger had been fed, he looked stronger in the dim nova light. He looked *noble*, and when he stood from her arms he somehow seemed larger than life. Now it was her turn to take comfort in him.

"Let's go," Dillon said. "I know a way to get money."

She glanced toward the immense lake, where Tahoe's casinos glittered just over the Nevada border.

"Casino gambling?" she asked.

"We don't need a casino," he answered. "All we need is a bar." He reached out his hand and smiled. He was his old, tender self again. "Come on. I'll show you something incredible . . . I'll show you something magical!"

She reached out and gently took his hand, and he escorted her off the ruined mountainside.

A GUST OF WIND blew through the door of the roadside bar as they stepped in, sending a flurry of cocktail napkins to the sawdust-covered floor.

With the wrecking-hunger deeply satisfied, Dillon felt himself in control of his thoughts and actions. Deanna had seen him at his worst tonight, and now she would see him at his best. He would show her something special.

Dillon was tall, but his boyish features and the style of his conspicuous red hair made it clear he was underage. Still, no one seemed to care, and he had no intention of ordering drinks.

Most of the talk around the bar was about the rock slide.

"Did you hear?" the regulars were saying to one another. "Five homes got flattened. Summer homes mostly, so no one was in 'em . . . except of course for the Barnes' place, where a boulder the size of a Buick tried to come down the chimney like friggin' Santy Claus."

"Sadie Barnes got a concussion," told one old-timer, with wide eyes as if he were telling a ghost story. "Jack Barnes, well, he might lose a leg. Still too early to tell."

Dillon grimaced and tried not to think about it. He caught himself glancing at Deanna's bruised wrist, silently tallying all the injuries he had caused and cursing himself for it.

In the many quiet hours alone with Deanna, he had told her every last thing he had done since the wrecking-hunger had come two years ago. He had told her how it started—not so much a hunger, but an itch; a tiny little urge to break things, which grew with each thing he broke. He had told her how his parents eventually died of "broken minds," before Dillon understood what his touch did to people, and how he had wandered for a whole year alone. Deanna took great pains to listen and not judge. Dillon had no words to tell her how special she was.

He led Deanna to the back of the bar, where an old, worn pool table sat in an alcove. Two guys were finishing a game of eight-ball. They were cowboy types—early twenties, talking about fortunes won and lost in the Tahoe casinos that day. One of them was bursting with energy, because his wallet was bursting with cash. He would be Dillon's target.

"Watch this," Dillon whispered to Deanna. Dillon had only played pool once, years ago. Even then he had found it about as challenging as sorting mail into six different slots. He approached the cowboy with the stuffed wallet.

"I'll play you a game," offered Dillon, sounding naive and inexperienced. "I'll play you for five dollars." Dillon slapped five dollars down on the edge of the table. Cowboy and his friend laughed.

"Sure, buddy," Cowboy said, treating Dillon like a child who had just asked for a quarter for a video game. "You break."

Cowboy racked up the balls, and Dillon broke, while Deanna watched from a peeling red vinyl chair.

The game took five minutes. It was less than magical; Dillon lost miserably. He glanced at Deanna, who was beginning to look nervous.

"One more game!" insisted Dillon. "Double or nothing."

Cowboy agreed, and easily beat Dillon a second time. The smile slipped from Dillon's face now. Deanna came up to him and whispered, "Don't be dumb—we're almost out of money."

"Don't worry about it," he said loudly enough for the others to hear. "I feel lucky, okay?"

Deanna rolled her eyes and stepped away, leaning against the wall.

Cowboy won the third match and was all full of himself. Dillon, on the other hand, looked pathetic and desperate. He took out his wallet and angrily slapped it down in front of the cowboy.

"All of it," said Dillon. "I'll play you for all that's in my wallet for all that's in yours."

Cowboy grinned out of the corner of his mouth.

"Dillon, let's get out of here," said Deanna. "It's not worth it."

"I don't leave a loser," said Dillon.

Cowboy smiled even wider. The picture here was clear; a young kid trying to impress his girlfriend—willing to go to ridiculous extremes to avoid being completely humiliated.

And that was exactly how Cowboy intended on leaving him; completely humiliated, not to mention broke.

Cowboy put his wallet next to Dillon's and racked up the balls. "You break," he said.

Dillon took a deep breath and made sure Deanna was watching. Then he took his cue ball, and stared intently at the wedge of colored balls before him. Dillon stared until he stopped seeing balls, and instead saw angles, vectors, and forces of impact. He examined the lines of motion and rebounds— each one bearing a complex mathematical equation that his mind solved instantaneously. And then, once he saw every pattern of possibility on that pool table, Dillon struck the cue ball . . . sending two solid-colored balls into two different pockets.

His second shot sunk two more balls, his third shot sent his remaining three balls home, and his fourth shot sent the eight ball rebounding off three sides before disappearing into a corner pocket.

Four shots. Like sorting mail.

Cowboy just stared at the table, which was still full of his own seven striped balls. "Beginner's luck," said Dillon. He took his and Cowboy's wallets from the edge of the table, leaving Cowboy completely humiliated, not to mention broke. From behind the bar, the bartender laughed.

Cowboy was furious. He threw his cue down and grabbed Dillon. "Just who do you think you—"

But he never finished. The moment he grabbed Dillon, his pupils dilated, his jaw dropped, and his face paled. In an instant Cowboy's thoughts had become so scrambled, he couldn't even speak. Dillon slipped free from his grip.

"Good game," said Dillon.

"Duh . . . ," said Cowboy.

Dillon and Deanna left him there, his senses just beginning to come back. They breezed out the door, dragging a flurry of cocktail napkins in their wake.

"I DON'T SEE THINGS the way other people see things," Dillon told Deanna that night as they dined like kings in their hotel room above Lake Tahoe. "You want to know how I started the rock slide, and how I won that pool game. I don't know how—all I can tell you is how I see the world—and it's different than other people do."

Deanna just looked at him quizzically, so Dillon tried to explain. "Other people, they just see 'things'—but I see *patterns*—cause and effect. I can see whole chains of events that other people can't see. It's like the way a good chess player can plan ten moves in advance? Well, when I play chess, I can see the entire game the moment the first move is made, not just all my moves—*but every possible move*—all at the same time. It's the same thing with pool; all I had to do was look at the positioning of the balls, and I knew exactly how to hit them to make the balls go into the pockets."

Deanna nodded. "Sort of the way a computer can solve a really hard math equation in half a second."

"Yeah, sort of like that. It was harder for me to make myself lose than it was to win."

Deanna was amazed. "You must be a genius."

Dillon shrugged modestly. "Naah, it's just something I can do. Some people can sing or dance; I can see patterns. A while back, before things got bad, I did this trick with a Rubik's Cube. My friends would get it all completely mixed up, then hand it to me. They would give me five seconds to look at it and then blindfold me. I would remember where the colors had been and solve the cube blindfolded." Dillon began to smile as he thought about it. "There was this one time they took the cube apart and put it back together so it was impossible to solve, but I managed to solve it anyway!"

Deanna looked down and nervously began to scratch at her healing wrist, as something occurred to her. "So then . . . if you can see how things are going to happen—then you *meant* to hurt those people in the avalanche. You meant to hurt *me*."

Dillon cringed and stood up. "Boulders aren't billiard balls. A mountain's not a chessboard," he said. "And it's not like I can predict the future—I just see patterns of the way things *ought* to happen—but things don't always happen the way they're supposed to . . ."

Dillon began to pace. "There was a tree further down the mountain," he said. "The way I saw it, the tree was going to get smashed, and in the end four homes would get hit—the four that were empty. No one would get hurt, and the wrecking-hunger would be fed, right? So I threw the stone that I knew would start the whole avalanche. The pebbles started moving, the rocks started slipping, the boulders began to go, but when that tree got hit—it didn't fall! It deflected the boulder toward that fifth house."

The more Dillon thought about it, the angrier he got. "I don't want to hurt people, but people get hurt, okay? That's just the way it is, and I can't do anything about it!"

Suddenly he took his fist and punched it as hard as he could against the window. It vibrated with a loud thud.

"I don't want to talk about it anymore," he mumbled.

DEANNA WATCHED HIM CLOSELY as he sat there stewing in his own conflicted emotions. Deanna could hear that frightened voice in her head that sounded so much like her mother, telling her to run away from his crazy boy. But if he were crazy, he was no crazier than Deanna.

She sat next to him and gently touched his hand. It was hot from his anger. Hers was cold, as it always was.

"With all that money you won playing pool," suggested Deanna, "we could fly east."

"Fly where?" asked Dillon. "When you get on a plane, you need a destination, you can't just buy a ticket 'east.'"

Deanna sighed. It was true: the eastbound gravity that gripped them could deposit them anywhere between Reno and New York.

"Anyway," said Dillon with a smirk, "you're afraid of flying . . . because if you're in a plane, the plane'll do everything it can to crash."

"Are you making fun of me?"

"No," said Dillon very seriously. "I believe you. All the things you're afraid of—all those awful things you imagine happening to you—your fear is so strong that it makes them come true. It's like your fear is a virus or something running through your veins . . . only it's mutated. Now it's this thing wrapped around your neck, strangling you."

Deanna shivered. "Gee, thanks, Dillon," she said. "You know just what to say to make me feel better."

"But you *should* feel better," insisted Dillon, "because, I can *see* the pattern—and as long as you're with me, none of those bad things can happen to you. I'll push you out of the way of a speeding car, even before it comes around the bend. I'll get you off a train before it derails. I won't let you get on a plane that will crash. I'll be like a good luck charm you wear around your neck! I promise."

Deanna knew there was truth in what Dillon said.

"We're meant to do great things, Deanna—don't you feel it?" he said, gripping her hand tightly. "And every day, we're closer to knowing what those things are!"

"All of us, you mean?" asked Deanna. "Us and the others?" Deanna watched to see how Dillon would react to her bringing up The Others.

Dillon shrugged uncomfortably. "Yeah, sure," he said. "But you and me especially."

Deanna felt her eyelids getting heavy, and so she leaned back, letting Dillon put his arm around her. He did nothing more—just held her with a wonderful innocence as if they were two small children. He asked no more from her than her presence, and it made her feel safe.

In the silence she listened as Dillon's breathing slowed, and he fell asleep. She took comfort in the sound of his breathing, and soon matched the pace of her own breath to his. She imagined their hearts beating in time with each other as well, and wished that they could somehow be part of each other . . .

Then she realized that in some strange and immeasurable way, they already were.

5. GHOST OF THE RAINBOW

AT A CAMPSITE IN THE WOODS WHERE THE MISSISSIPPI AND Ohio Rivers meet, Tory Smythe tended to her aching face. She gently cleaned her cheeks, chin, and forehead with astringent alcohol, and three types of soaps—a ritual performed four times a day. It stung as if she had just wiped her face with battery acid, and although all these cleansers promised results, none of them helped. She put on some perfume, which didn't do much either, then dabbed her scaling face with Clearasil, hoping beyond hope that someday it would work.

"I want to head toward Nebraska," she shouted to Winston, who was standing by the edge of the water. "Last year I read about this astronomer . . . in Omaha, I think. Anyway, he predicted a star was about to go supernova—and since that star seems to have something to do with us, maybe he knows something we don't."

She turned to see that Winston wasn't even listening. He was just looking out over the river.

"What are you doing, praying again?"

"I'm not praying," said Winston. "I'm taking a whiz."

But Tory knew he was just using that as an excuse. Even this far away, she could tell that he was looking at that weird blue cloth again.

WINSTON PELL STOOD BY the water's edge so Tory couldn't see, fiddling with the torn piece of turquoise-blue satin that he had pulled from a trash can three days before. He felt troubled, unsure of his next move, and for some reason fiddling with that torn piece of cloth made him feel better, as if it were a tiny security blanket. He had one of those when he was little. It was just a quilt, but when he wrapped it around himself, he felt safe and secure. Now, as he stood by the edge of the water, he did say a little prayer; he wished for things to be like they once were, before his ma got paralyzed . . . before his dad died. . . . He wished for the days when an old blanket was the only protection he needed. *Please, God, make it like it was,* he prayed, as he often did. *Make everything go back.* . . .

Maybe his old life hadn't been the best in the world, but it was better than it had become in these past few years and much better than what he had to face these past few days. On that first night, suddenly roaring with crickets, he knew his legs were moving him away from home, but it was like sleepwalking. Only after dawn broke did he begin to comprehend that he was running away with this hideous, crater-faced girl.

At first they traveled west: on foot and in the beds of pickup trucks, "borrowing" clothes from clotheslines along the way, and food from unharvested fields. Once they hit the Mississippi River, they followed it north. Winston could feel himself being drawn upriver, the way salmon were drawn against a powerful current.

Winston knew they were moving toward Others like themselves—it was something he had sensed from the beginning—but where would they find them and how long would it take?

And where to go now?

As he stood at the edge of western Kentucky's woods, he looked out across the swirling waters where the Ohio and the Mississippi met—a delta that divided three different states. Where to go from here? Kentucky, Illinois, or Missouri. Decisions were getting harder and harder for Winston these days. The very thought of having to make one made him want to put his thumb deep in his mouth and suck on it to make all his problems go away. He'd been getting that thumb-sucking urge a lot lately—like he used to the first time he was little. But he reminded himself that he was fifteen and forced the urge away. Instead he focused his attention on that piece of turquoise cloth in his other hand, studying the soothing richness of its color. There was something *important* about that color—he was certain of it.

In a few minutes he returned to their campsite and slipped into his sleeping bag, which was just an old comforter he had found in a Memphis Dumpster.

"Did you hear what I said about Omaha?" Tory asked. "About that astronomer? He's supposed to be a kook, but then maybe only a kook will talk to us."

Winston rolled over, away from her. "Sure," he said. "Whatever."

Tory sighed. "It would help," she said, "if you did *some* of the thinking around here."

Winston slid deeper into his sleeping bag. "Thinkin' just makes me angry. I got no use for it anymore."

"You know," said Tory, "you're not an easy person to run away with."

Winston rolled over to face her. "Just because we ran away at the same time, in the same direction, doesn't mean I ran away *with* you." But even as he said it, Winston knew he was wrong. They were stuck with each other—and even if they were to go their separate ways, he knew they'd end up bumping right back into each other—pulled together like two magnets.

Winston began to think of his family. The faces of his mother and brother were getting harder to remember.

"My mama's probably turnin' the country upside down lookin' for me."

"I thought you called her and told her you were all right."

"I did," said Winston. "But she had more questions than I could answer, so I hung right up."

Tory sighed and slipped deeper into her makeshift sleeping bag. "You're lucky you got a mama who cares enough to ask questions. My mama's gone."

"She's dead?"

"No, just gone," said Tory. "Up and left last year. I got stuck with my aunt."

"I'm sorry."

"Just as well. My mama and I never got along anyway. She used to say 'Tory, your bulb is so dim, you'll never amount to anything.' Truth is, I get straight A's in school. But that didn't matter. I coulda been a national scholar, she still would have figured me dumber than a doorpost. Anyway, when I started getting this skin problem, my mother just gave up. She said it was my fault all her boyfriends ran away—and I hoped she was right; I would have been ugly just to spite her. When she got drunk, she would tell me things like how because of my face, I'd spend my whole life alone and unhappy."

"Like her?"

"Like her."

"Sounds like she got on the inside what you got on the outside," said Winston. "I'd rather be you than her."

"I'd rather be neither of us," said Tory. "I'd rather be a prom queen from the right family instead of a . . . a gargoyle."

"You ain't no gargoyle," said Winston. "Gargoyles got big red eyes and ugly teeth, and skin like snakes."

"I am so a gargoyle. I smell like one—my skin peels like one. One of these days my face'll probably start turning green too." Winston looked at her battle-scarred face, and she looked away, not wanting him to look at it anymore.

"You Baptists got a prayer for ugly people?" she asked.

"We got a prayer for everything," said Winston. But try as he might, he couldn't think of a prayer for the ugly.

TWO HUNDRED MILES WAY, Indianapolis was pelted by heavy rain—but the rain that was falling inside Michael "Lips" Lipranski's soul seemed even worse than the rain outside. The storm raging inside him was full of acid rain, and it burned, filling him with the familiar feeling he could never make go away. He couldn't talk about that, could he? *There are some things you don't talk about,* he thought, as he lay uncomfortably in the van, which was parked in a back alley. *There are some things that are just too secret, too personal, so you just never talk about them. Ever.*

The trip from Montauk had been torture. The drenched roads all seemed the same—back roads mostly, because they knew they'd be harder to find if they traveled the back roads. Right now, Michael couldn't bear the thought of another road.

Beside him, Lourdes babbled on about a dream she had the night before, about a gray rainbow—whatever that meant. She was cramped and uncomfortable—none of the van's seats were wide enough for her. When she finally realized that Michael wasn't listening, she turned to him and asked, "How do you feel?"

"You know how I feel," said Michael, adjusting his uncomfortably tight pants. "I feel like I always feel."

"You know, you're not the only guy to feel horny all the time," Lourdes said.

Michael shifted uneasily. "Yes I am," he answered. "I'm the

only one who feels it this bad. The only one in the world."

"Maybe not."

"Yeah, sure. And maybe you're not really fat—you just wear the wrong clothes."

Michael regarded the ceiling of the van above him, listening to the clattering of the rain.

"I got a brother," said Lourdes, "who always had girls on the brain, too."

Michael let out a bitter laugh. If girls on the brain were his problem, then there were thousands of them in there, all with jackhammers.

"Whenever he got the girl crazies," continued Lourdes, "he'd go off into the bathroom. When he came out a few minutes later, he didn't feel that way no more. He thought we didn't know what he was up to, but we did. We just didn't say."

Michael cleared his throat. He just kept looking up at the spots in the roof-lining.

"I do that, too," said Michael. "I do it a lot." Hearing the words come out of his mouth made tears come to his eyes—but Lourdes didn't laugh at him. She just listened.

"My brother—I'll bet he thought he was the only person in the world to do that. I'll bet he hated himself for it."

Michael felt his whole body react to his tears. His throat closed up, his feet felt even colder, his fingers felt weak. Above him, the clattering sound of the rain grew stronger.

"Sometimes . . . ," said Michael. "Sometimes I think . . . what if all my dead relatives are watching me? What if their ghosts can see the things I do?"

"Dead people don't care," said Lourdes. "Because if they really do hang around after they die, I'll bet they've seen so many secret things, nothing bothers them anymore."

"You think so?"

"At the very worst, they think it's funny."

"I don't think it's funny!"

"That's because you're not dead."

Above, the rain began to ease up. *Some things you can't talk about,* thought Michael. He never thought it would be so easy to talk about those things with Lourdes.

"We should go soon," said Lourdes, who, for obvious reasons, preferred to travel by night rather than by day. "Maybe when the rain stops we'll see the rainbow."

Michael rolled his eyes. She always brought up the thing about the rainbow.

"It's night," reminded Michael. "Whoever heard of a rainbow at night?"

"Maybe night's the only time you can find a gray rainbow."

"Maybe there's no such thing as a gray rainbow, and that dream you're having doesn't mean a thing."

Lourdes shook her head. "Dreams always mean something," she said. "Especially dreams you have more than once."

Michael cracked the window and took a deep breath. He could smell the end of the storm, the same way he could smell when it began. He could always smell the weather. An autumn storm always began with the smell of damp concrete and ended with the aroma of yellow leaves trampled along the sidewalk. A winter blizzard began clean, like the air itself had been polished to perfection, and ended with a faint aroma of ash.

As Michael sat there, breathing in the end of the storm, he had to admit that talking to Lourdes had made him feel a little bit better.

"Lourdes," said Michael, "tell me something about you

now. Tell me something about yourself you swore you'd never tell a living soul. It's only fair."

Lourdes shifted and the seat creaked, threatening to give way. Michael waited.

"I don't have secrets," she said in her deepest, most thickly padded voice.

Michael waited.

Lourdes sighed, and Michael leaned closer to listen.

"My parents . . . they love me very much," said Lourdes. "I know this because I heard them talking one night. They said that they loved me so much, they wished that I would die, so I would be put out of my misery." Lourdes spoke matter-of-factly, refusing to shed a single tear. "The truth is, I never felt misery until I heard them say that."

Outside the air began to take on a new flavor—a rich, earthy smell that Michael recognized as fog rolling in, matching the cloudy, numb feeling in his brain.

"Lourdes," said Michael, "I don't care what anyone says, I think you're beautiful."

MICHAEL AND LOURDES ARRIVED in St. Louis the next morning, their van riding the crest of the storm. The black rain clouds followed behind them like a wave rolling in from the distant Atlantic Ocean, baffling the weatherman, who always looked west for weather.

Michael, starved, stopped at the first cheap-looking fast-food place he found, but all they sold were fried brain sandwiches, a local specialty. When Michael returned to the car with his questionable sandwich and a drink for Lourdes, he looked behind him to see a sheet of rain moving across the surface of the Mississippi River, until it finally reached them, letting loose over St. Louis. Michael hopped into the van and managed not to get drenched.

He handed Lourdes her Diet Coke. "What do you know about St. Louis?" she asked.

"I know I'd rather be just about anywhere else in the world," he said, looking miserably down at the brain-burger in his hand.

"Besides that, what do you know?"

Michael shrugged. "The Cardinals," he said. "That's about it. . . ." And then he stopped dead—and started to breathe rapidly. Michael turned to Lourdes and grabbed her heavy arm, trying to speak but unable to catch his breath.

"What's wrong?" she asked.

"Lourdes . . . there's one more thing I know about St. Louis . . . something that never occurred to me until now!"

"So, tell me."

"I think maybe you should look for yourself."

Lourdes followed Michael's gaze to the south. Lourdes wiped the fog from the windshield, and her eyes traced the path of the riverbank, until she saw it, too. It was about a mile away, curving hundreds of feet into the sky—thousands of tons of gray steel, shaped and curved into the magnificent arch that graced the city of St. Louis. The sleek steel wonder stretched deep into the clouds, and back down to earth again, and the very sight of it gave Michael and Lourdes the eerie shivers—because more than anything else, the arch looked like a ghostly gray rainbow.

TORY AND WINSTON HAD already been at the arch for twenty minutes. They had stood with die-hard tourists in a line that wound through the underground museum, waiting to board the tiny car that would take them to the peak of the arch.

The logic made perfect sense. If you were supposed to meet someone in St. Louis, but didn't know where, there were certain places one ought to try: airports, bus stations, train stations, landmarks—and they knew St. Louis had to be the place. They could sense something here they felt nowhere else they had been—the westward current suddenly seemed caught in a swirling eddy.

They had been to all the other places, and now they searched the city's best-known landmark—their last hope—before continuing west. To Omaha, if Tory got her way.

Once at the top of the arch, the view was spectacular, for the very tip of the arch pierced the dense, low-hanging storm clouds. It was like a view from heaven.

Tory wore her scarf over most of her face like an Arabian veil. "I've never been this high," she said. "I guess this is what it must look like from a plane." The clouds beneath the observation window were slow-moving billows; huge cotton snails sliding over one another.

The car brought them back down to the underground museum, and still there was no sign of anyone on the lookout for them. It was worse than the old needle in a haystack. At least then you knew it was a needle you were looking for.

"There's nothing here," Tory finally had to admit. Then Tory and Winston heard a voice deep in the crowd.

"This is a waste of time," the voice said. Tory and Winston quickly turned and saw a boy through the crowds. He had a thin, scraggly body and thin, scraggly hair. He seemed flushed and sweaty. Next to him stood a girl so immense there was no way she'd fit in the tiny car that rode to the top of the arch.

But it was the scraggly boy that caught Winston's attention—not his face, but his eyes. Even from a distance, Winston could see the color of his eyes.

"I know him!" said Winston. "Don't I know him?"

Winston and Tory pushed through the crowd, and as they

did, the sounds around them seemed to become distant. The people milling about and waiting in line seemed like mere shadows of people. The guard mouthed the words "Move along," but his voice sounded as if it were coming from miles away. The only sights clear and in focus were the fat girl and scraggly boy, who were now staring at them with the same troubled wonder.

Winston approached the scraggly boy, pulling his torn satin cloth out of his pocket. One glance at the cloth, and then at the boy's eyes proved to Winston what he already knew. The cloth was the exact same color as the scraggly boy's eyes. Impossibly deep—impossibly blue! This was the connection!

Michael grabbed the cloth and looked at Winston, suddenly overwhelmed with emotion. Michael felt the urge to say *It's good to see you again,* even though he knew he had never met this small black kid before.

Tory approached, staring at Lourdes, and rather than being repulsed, she felt somehow comforted by her large presence. It made Tory want to peel back her scarf, to reveal her own awful face, suddenly not ashamed of it in front of the present company.

"My God!" said Lourdes, as Tory revealed her face, and Lourdes smiled with a look of wonder instead of disgust. Still holding onto Michael, Lourdes reached out to touch Tory, who still had a hand on Winston's shoulder; Winston had put his small palm up against Michael's large one, closing a circuit of the four of them . . . and the instant the circuit was closed, something happened.

Their skin felt on fire, their bones felt like ice. They could not move.

Then an image exploded through their minds with such power and intensity, it seemed to burn the world around them away. It was a vision before sight, a tale before words. It was a memory—for it was so terrifyingly familiar to all of them it could only be a memory—not of something seen or heard but of something felt:

Bright Light! Sharp Pain! One screaming voice becoming six screaming voices. Six! There are six of us!

As the vision filled them, the clouds above began to boil and separate, as a powerful wind blew through the ghostly steel rainbow and the wet earth was finally drenched by blinding rays of sun.

6. THE UNRAVELING

At that same moment, about four hundred miles away, Dillon Cole doubled over in a pain even more intense than the wrecking-hunger. He burst into a men's room in the small bus depot in Big Springs, Nebraska, stumbled into a stall, and collapsed to the tile floor. At first he thought this must have been God striking him down for the sheer magnitude of his sins—but then as the world around him seemed to burn away, he knew it was something else. The vision—the *memory* then burst upon his mind. It was both glorious and awful at once, and so intense that he thought it would kill him.

Awful Awful Awful
Blinding fire
Tearing
Shattering
Unbearable pain
Shard of light
Piercing
Screaming through the void
Then silence . . .
And a beat.
And silence . . .
A heartbeat.
And warmth
And comfort
And the soft safety
Of flesh and blood.

It was the vision of a cataclysmic death . . . followed by life. His own life. Something died . . . and he was born . . . but not just him. Others. *The* Others.

The convulsions that racked his body subsided as the vision faded, and he felt the grip of reality once more. He picked himself up and staggered back into the waiting area.

"Deanna?" He found her still doubled over on a bench. Her head was in her hands and she was quietly crying. She had shared this earth-shattering vision as well.

"You okay?" asked Dillon, still shaking from the experience.

"What was it?" Deanna got her tears under control. "I was so scared . . . what's happening to us?"

"The Others are together," said Dillon, just realizing it himself. The fact struck him in the face, leaving him stunned—and unsure of how to feel about it.

It was all beginning to make sense to him now. There were six of them in the vision, all screaming discordant notes.

They were all here, together, for fifteen years. Maybe thousands of miles apart by human standards, but from the perspective of an immense universe, they were right beside one another . . . and moving closer. The thought of it began to make Dillon get angry, and he didn't know why . . . and then he realized why. It was the wrecking-hunger, suddenly brought to a full boil, as if the vision triggered it to attack.

"I think we somehow know each other—even though we've never met," said Deanna. "There *are* six of us, aren't there?"

"Four of *them*," said Dillon. "And two of *us*."

Dillon could see Deanna struggling to understand—but she couldn't grasp the entire truth yet. She couldn't see the pattern the way he did.

"We need to find them," insisted Deanna. "We have to join them . . ."

"We don't *have* to do anything."

"Yes we do! We have to meet The Others and find out who we really are!"

"I know who I am! I'm Dillon Cole, and that's all I need to know!"

"What's wrong with you?" she shouted. "Isn't that why we've been moving east? To find them?"

Dillon knew she was right. The thought of finding The Others had been like a carrot dangling before them. But now that carrot was quickly growing rotten in Dillon's mind. What would joining the others prove? What would it do beyond making Dillon just one of six? Yes, the wrecking-hunger was awful—but it was something familiar. Joining The Others, however, was a great dark unknown.

They're going to hurt you, the wrecking-hunger whispered to him. *They'll ruin everything. They'll take Deanna away.* He didn't know what to believe anymore.

The hunger was clawing at him now, tearing up his gut as it had done so many times before . . . and from outside came the drone of a bus and black smoke pouring through the open door.

"Oh no!" cried Deanna in a panic. They both raced to the door in time to see their bus—which had only stopped in Big Springs for a few minutes—drive off. Along with that bus went what few things they had: a bag with maps, a change of clothes, and most importantly, Dillon's wallet.

Fine, thought Dillon. *Let the bus go. Who cares, anyway?* Dillon stormed out the door and headed in the other direction. The hunger kept swelling inside of him, and he knew he would have to feed it soon.

"Where are you going?" shouted Deanna.

"Looks like I'm going to Hell," he said, then turned from her and stormed away.

DILLON COLE'S PILGRIMAGE TO Hell began moments later, in a schoolyard across the street, where a tall kid, maybe a year older than he, was playing basketball alone.

Dillon was consumed by the wrecking-hunger now—and his mind was set on seek and destroy. He didn't know how or what he would destroy—but this guy on the basketball court was directly in his path and was therefore a target.

The target bounced his ball without much skill, trying to weave it through his legs. When he saw Dillon coming, he stopped his dribbling antics, and the two of them began to shoot around.

The guy introduced himself as Dwight Astor, and, as they took shots, Dillon tried to hide the wrecking-hunger like a vampire hiding his fangs.

"How about a game of one-on-one?" asked Dillon.

"Okay, winners out," said Dwight. And the game began.

Dwight played fairly well, and although Dillon knew he could beat him—for Dillon never lost any game he played—Dillon didn't try. He let Dwight drive around him for lay ups. He guarded poorly, making sure there were never any fouls—no body contact.

. . . And while they played, Dillon did something he had never done before: he studied the patterns of his human subject.

Until now, Dillon had kept away from people, never making eye contact, thinking only of ways to avoid them. He was always much more comfortable with the simple, predictable patterns of crashing cars, shattering glass, stones, and billiard balls. But today Dillon dared to peer into the workings of a human being, and he discovered something remarkable:

Human beings have patterns too. Patterns of action and behavior that can trace their histories and futures.

Dillon bristled with excitement as he watched Dwight move around the court—and in about ten seconds of basketball, Dillon was able to predict every move Dwight could make on the court—but Dillon could do better than that! He could look beyond the court, right into every aspect of Dwight's life.

It amazed Dillon just how much he was able to figure out; facts impossible for the most observant of people to uncover came to Dillon with the slightest effort.

The hesitation that made Dwight miss his shots told Dillon how long and how often his parents had punished him as a child. The way Dwight's eyes darted back and forth told Dillon of friendships lost and trusts broken. The thrill in Dwight's eyes each time he drove toward the basket told Dillon exactly how high his ambitions were and how successful he was going to be in life. Every move, every word, every breath betrayed a secret about Dwight's days and nights, hopes and dreams, fears and failures.

Dillon had heard it said that every second we live bears the pattern of our entire life, the way a single cell bears the DNA pattern of our whole body. Now Dillon knew it to be true, because what might have taken years for a psychiatrist to uncover, Dillon instinctively knew in just a few minutes on a basketball court.

The blueprint of Dwight Astor's life!

And to think that all along Dillon had this talent—this *power* to peer into the human clockwork. It was the single most thrilling moment of Dillon's life.

Dwight missed a shot, and the ball went bouncing out of bounds.

"Your ball," said Dwight. Dillon took the ball and began dribbling it around the court, thinking about the many things he discovered by watching his opponent:

Dwight Astor. He was a B-plus student. His parents fought. He had at least two brothers and at least one sister. His father was a recovering alcoholic. This was Dwight's past and present, but Dillon could also see the pattern of his future, as if the basketball were a crystal ball. If nothing changed, Dwight would go to college, would major in business, or maybe economics, and would go on to run a small company. It was all there—Dillon saw the complex tapestry of Dwight's past, present and future as if he were simply reading a road map—and in that future, Dillon could see shades of wealth, success, and some level of happiness.

Dillon now had control of the ball. At last he worked his way around Dwight as if he were standing still. Then Dillon went for the lay up and released the ball onto the rim, where it hung, perfectly balanced—not on the back of the rim, but on the front of the rim. The ball just sat there, not going into the basket, and not falling out.

"Wow!" said Dwight. "How'd you do that? That's impossible."

As Dwight innocently stared at the balanced ball, Dillon Cole moved in for the kill.

"Listen to me, Dwight." Dwight turned and was caught in Dillon's gaze. "Your father says he doesn't drink anymore, but he does. He keeps his bottles of booze hidden somewhere in the house. If you look hard enough, you can find them."

Then Dillon whispered into Dwight's ear, clearly and slowly.

"Your father would never notice," said Dillon, *"if you drank some of it."*

The words Dillon spoke were like bullets that pierced deep into Dwight's brain. There was no blood, but the damage was the same—and the only one who could see the damage was Dillon. After all, he had done something anyone could have done . . . he had tossed Dwight a simple suggestion . . . but like the stone Dillon had tossed down the mountain in Tahoe, this was exactly the *right* suggestion to begin an avalanche in Dwight Astor's life. Dillon could already see the road map of Dwight's future changing. Dillon's simple suggestion had paved Dwight a brand-new future filled with addiction. Alcohol first, and then other things. Dwight would drop out of high school. He would run far away from home. He would make the wrong friends, make the wrong choices. He would die young and alone.

Dillon had destroyed him.

There were no crashes, no carnage, no evidence. And yet the wrecking-hunger was gone—it had been more satisfied than ever before; it dawned on Dillon that destroying a hillside, or crashing cars and breaking glass were nothing compared to destroying a human mind. . . . And it had been so easy to do. Finding the weakness in Dwight's pattern was like finding the loose thread of a sweater. All Dillon had to do was to pull on the thread to make the entire fabric unravel.

Now, with the wrecking-hunger quieted, he could only beam with satisfaction, his wonder overcoming any self-loathing he might have felt.

That vague sense of destiny that had begun with the supernova was focused by what happened today. For too long, Dillon had fled from his catastrophes, racked with guilt—begging for forgiveness. But he was stronger than that now. Much stronger.

"I . . . I have to go now," said Dwight. "Good game." Bewildered, Dwight turned and left, forgetting his ball.

Dillon could sense a pattern now unfolding in his own life. A destiny. A purpose—and although he wasn't quite certain what that purpose was, he knew it would soon make itself clear. He could hardly contain the excitement that came with this new reason to be. Its very power filled him with something he thought might be joy.

I could choose this destiny, thought Dillon. . . . *Or I could fight it; I could let the wrecking-hunger make me strong . . . or I could let it kill me.*

The way Dillon felt right now, the decision was as easy as it had been to whisper in Dwight Astor's ear.

As he watched Dwight shuffle off, Dillon made a pact with himself. No more fighting the hunger. He would feed it, he would live it, he would *be* the hunger . . . and if his destination was Hell, then he would learn to accept that. But he would not be alone. There would be others he'd be taking with him. Many, many others.

INSIDE THE DEPOT, DEANNA tried to find out when the next bus came through town, but the fear of being alone overcame her, and she had to get out.

Dillon had never acted this way toward her before. He had always been thoughtful and treated her kindly. She didn't know what this change meant, but they had promised to protect each other, and she would protect him, no matter what he said or did. She drew some comfort from the strength of her own resolve.

She found Dillon playing basketball across the street, alone.

"We need to get going," said Deanna, watching him cautiously, waiting to see how he would react.

"Yes, we do," he answered. "But we're not going east anymore. . . . We're going west."

Deanna studied him, thinking that it might be a joke—but then she realized that Dillon did not joke that way. "But . . . but The Others—"

"We don't need The Others." His voice was calm, his body relaxed. Deanne could tell that he had fed the wrecking-hunger, but she saw no evidence of it . . . and something was different this time. He wasn't racked by guilt. He wasn't cursing himself. She wanted to question him, to take a step away and think about all this, before his infectious peace-of-mind drowned her panic completely.

That's when Dillon grabbed her and did something he had never done before. He kissed her. The kiss felt so perfect, so natural, that she would have agreed with anything he said. She didn't know whether to feel angry because of it, or to feel relieved.

"Listen to me, Deanna," he told her. "Forget The Others; they're nothing compared to us—you and I are the strongest, the most powerful!"

It was true—Deanna had sensed that much in the vision. How loud they were—how *bright* they were compared to The Others as they screamed in the darkness. Her fears and Dillon's hunger for destruction were certainly far more powerful than anything the other four had to deal with.

Until now she had thought the strange gravity that had been drawing all of them together was impossible to resist. But if Dillon could resist it, then she could, too. They were the strong ones. This time she leaned forward to kiss him.

"Where will we go now?" she whispered.

Dillon struggled with his answer. "Deanna, I think I was meant to do some really big things. . . . I have to find out what those things are, and I can't be afraid to do them . . . but I'm afraid to do them alone."

Her mind told her that this was wrong, but her heart was too close to Dillon's now. Traveling to The Others might solve her troubles, but she was terrified of making that journey alone. And the thought of losing Dillon was unbearable.

"These things that you have to do," asked Deanna, "are they terrible things?"

Dillon bit his lip. She knew he wouldn't lie to her. "They might be," he said.

Deanna nodded, knowing she would have given him the same answer, no matter what he said. "Then I'll go with you . . . so you don't have to face those things alone."

As she said the words, she felt something changing around her like a great river suddenly shifting course. Perhaps this was what Dillon felt when he saw a pattern change, and she wondered how large this shift must have been if she could feel it too.

It was too huge a thing to think about, so she decided not to. She ignored it, pretending it didn't matter, and after a moment, it all felt okay. In a few minutes they were hitchhiking west on the interstate.

Meanwhile, in a house not too far away, Dwight Astor poured himself a glass of scotch, downed it, and then poured himself another.

Part III
Scorpion Shards

7. THE SUM OF THE PARTS

I want to forget who I am.
I never want to leave here.
I want to stay in this tight circle of four forever.

SOMEWHERE BETWEEN DUSK AND DAWN, BETWEEN HERE AND there, Tory, Winston, Lourdes, and Michael lay close, touching each other in some way—hand to hand, toe to toe, head to chest, huddling like a litter of mice. This closed circuit of four felt more joyous, more peaceful than anything any of them had ever felt before. Their hearts beat in unison, their breath came and went in a single tide. It felt wonderful to finally be whole.

Almost whole.

The place was as solitary and secluded as a place could be; a corn silo on the edge of town, part of an abandoned farm. The dome of the silo had long since turned to rubble, the victim of storms and neglect, leaving a round hole high above them filled with stars, like a portal to another universe. The storm had been washed away when the four of them had come together, and now the air was so tranquil and calm it didn't even feel cold.

They were silent for a long time as they rested, and when they finally began to talk, the words that came out were things they never dared to speak out loud.

"I shared a room with my sisters until my parents fixed up the attic for me," said Lourdes, her voice so heavy and thick that her very words seemed to sink to the ground. "They said it was to give me more room, but I knew it was to hide me away. That first night in the attic, I dreamed I was floating down Broadway in the Thanksgiving Day parade, so bloated with helium I could burst. A hundred people held me with strings, and all I could do was hang there bouncing back and forth between the skyscrapers, while thousands of people stared and laughed. When I woke up, I could feel myself growing . . . I could feel my body drawing energy right out of the air—maybe even pulling it from other people's bodies. I had stopped eating, but I still grew. That's when I knew the problem wasn't just food."

Then Lourdes gently squeezed Michael's hand, which rested so calmly in hers; Michael focused his eyes on the distant stars. "When I was thirteen," he said, "my friends dared me to talk to this high school girl who I had a crush on. She was three years older, and a head taller than me, but the crush I had on her was out of control, so I just had to talk to her. I went up to her, but before I could open my mouth to say anything, she looked at me and WHAM! I felt there was some sort of weird connection, like I was draining something out of her, right through her eyes—and I knew right then I should have stopped and walked away, but I didn't, because I liked the way it felt. It was cold out, but suddenly the whole street began to feel hot like it was summer. I asked her out, and she said 'yes.' Ever since then no girl has ever said 'no' to me, and no guy has wanted to be my friend."

Winston moved his Nike against Tory's shoe and shifted his head against the comfortable pillow of Lourdes's sleeve, making sure not to break the circle.

"My mother used to get these swollen feet 'cause she stood all day long working at the bank," Winston began. "It was always my job to massage her feet when she got home. We already knew I had stopped growing, but that's all we knew. Then one day, I'm massaging her feet, and she tells me how good it feels, 'cause she can't feel the pain no more, so I keep on massaging. And then, when she tries to get up, she can't. She tries to feel her legs, but she can't feel nothin'. Doctors said it was some kind of freak virus, but we all know the truth, even if Mama won't say it. I paralyzed her legs. A few weeks later, we knew for sure that I was growing backward, too."

Winston wiped a tear from his eye, and Tory began to speak. "There was this blind boy in my neighborhood, with allergy problems so bad a skunk could have walked into the room, and he wouldn't have smelled it. Once I started breaking out, he was the only boy who liked me. Then one day he brushed his fingertips across my face. He pulled his hand away and turned white as a ghost, then he ran off to wash his hands over and over again, trying to wash the feel of my face off his fingers. He came down with pneumonia a few days later and was in the hospital for weeks. He was the first one to get sick from touching me. And that's how I knew it wasn't just zits."

No one spoke for a while. They rested their voices and minds, listening to the singular *whoosh* of their breaths, feeling each other's parallel heartbeats, and it seemed to make everything okay. They needed no more words to express how they felt.

I want to forget who I am.

I never want to leave here.

I want to stay in this tight circle of four forever.

But they couldn't stay like this, could they? They would freeze to death. They would starve to death. And they would never solve the mystery of who they were, and why they were dying these miserable deaths.

Yes, they were dying. Although they never dared to say it out loud, they all knew the truth. Tory's disease would eat away at her until there was nothing left. Michael's passion would consume him like a fire, Lourdes would become so heavy her bones would no longer be able to hold her, and Winston would wither until he became an infant in search of a womb to return to, but there would be none.

Better not to think about that.

I want to forget who I am . . .

While the others seemed content to shut their minds down, Tory could not. Mysteries did not sit well with her and she despised riddles of any sort. From the moment they had come together, she, more than the others, had struggled to understand the truth behind their shared vision, and their shared journey, but all she had were half-truths.

She knew they belonged together, but why?

The vision told them that two were missing, but who?

They must have known each other from somewhere, but how?

The vision had been so contorted, confusing, and overwhelming that it only left more questions in its wake. Questions—and this collective state of blissful shock.

"The truth is bigger than any of us want to know," Lourdes had proclaimed.

"The truth is something we're not supposed to know," Winston had declared.

"What we don't know can't hurt us," Michael had decreed.

But those were all just excuses. Cop-outs. Tory could not accept that.

Up above, a crescent moon was coming into view within

the circle of stars . . . but something was missing, thought Tory. What was it? Of course! It was the nova on the edge of the horizon. She could not see it, but she knew it was there. The dying star.

The dying star?

It began as a single thought, that suddenly grew until it became the key to the vision . . . but not just the vision . . . the key to everything! It was so simple, yet so staggering, she didn't know whether to believe it or just crawl up into a ball and disappear.

She broke the circle of four, and the moment the connection was broken, the world around them became cold and hostile once more. The ruined silo was no longer a haven, it was just a lonely, forgotten place where they could all die and no one would ever find them.

As they all sat up, they began to shiver. It was like coming out of a dream. "What's wrong?" Winston asked Tory. Now that they were apart, they moved away from one another, withdrawing to the walls of the silo, as if, now that their senses had returned, they were ashamed of the words they had spoken and the heartbeat they had shared.

"You sick or something?" he asked.

Tory just shook her head, still reeling from the thoughts playing in her mind.

"You figured something out, didn't you?" asked Lourdes. "Tell us."

Tory began to shake and tried to control it. "I'm afraid to tell you," she said, "'cause what I'm thinking is crazy."

"We won't think you're crazy," said Lourdes.

"I'm not afraid of that. . . . I'm afraid you'll think I'm right."

Winston looked at Lourdes, and Michael just looked down. A wind now breathed across the open silo above them, and the heavy stone ruin began to resonate with a deep moan, like someone blowing across the lip of a bottle.

"Tell us," said Lourdes.

Tory took a deep breath and clenched her fists until her knuckles were white. She forced her thoughts into words. "We know that all of this started when that Scorpion Star blew up last week, right?"

The others nodded in agreement.

"But . . . that star didn't *just* blow up, did it?" continued Tory. "We're just seeing it now, because of the speed of light, and stuff, but it really blew up sixteen years ago."

Winston shifted uncomfortably. "What are you getting at?"

"Winston, you believe we have a soul, don't you?" asked Tory.

"Yeah, so?"

"So does every living thing have a soul?"

He took a moment to weigh the question. "I don't know—maybe."

"How about a star?"

"What the hell are you talking about?" said Michael. "A star's not a living thing!"

Tory looked him right in the eye. "How do you know?"

"Because it's just a ball of gas."

"So? When it comes right down to it, we're all just piles of dirt, aren't we? Dirt and a whole lot of water."

Michael zipped his jacket as high as it would go, but it wasn't just the cold he was trying to keep out. "Speak for yourself," he said.

"Let her talk!" demanded Lourdes.

"I know this sounds wild," said Tory, "but the more I think about that vision we had, the more it makes sense . . . because it wasn't a vision at all. It was a memory."

Tory took a deep breath and finally spat out what she was thinking. "What if the Scorpion Star was alive? What if it had a soul, or a spirit, or whatever you want to call it . . . and when it blew up all those years ago, its soul blew up, too . . . into six pieces that flew through space a zillion times faster than light, and ended up right here on earth. What if it became *our* souls? What if it became us?"

Lourdes heaved herself closer to Tory. "And sixteen years later," added Lourdes, "when we saw the light of the explosion, it reminded us . . . and we started to move toward one another like it was an instinct."

"No!" Winston shook his head furiously. "No, you're crazy." He put his hands over his ears and pulled his knees up. "And anyway," he said, "if it's true, we'd all have been born on the same day, wouldn't we? The same day the star exploded."

Tory hesitated for a moment. She hadn't thought it through that far yet.

"When's your birthday?" Winston asked her.

"May twenty-third?" she offered.

"Ha!" shouted Winston. "My birthday's June fifteenth! You're wrong!"

"Maybe not," said Michael, and all eyes turned to him. "I was born on April twentieth, *but* I was six weeks premature. I was *supposed* to be born at the beginning of June." He turned to Tory. "Were you early or late?"

Tory shrugged. "Don't know. My mother and me . . . we didn't talk much."

"I was right on time," chimed in Lourdes. "June second."

Everyone turned to Winston.

"June fifteenth, huh?" said Michael. "I'll bet you were two weeks late, weren't you?"

Winston wouldn't look him in the eye. He pulled his knees up to his chest again.

"Well, Winston?" said Tory.

Winston picked the ground with a twig and finally said, "My mom always said I was too stubborn to come into this world when I was expected. I came in my own time . . . two weeks late."

Tory gasped. "Then we were all *supposed* to be born on the same day!"

Michael nodded. "Not just the same day . . . but the same second, I'll bet." He looked down, and found in the debris of the silo the shattered remains of an ancient Coke bottle—he picked it up and pieced the shards of the bottle together. "Check this out—sixteen years ago, our parents conceived each of us at the same instant in time . . . and at that same moment . . . BOOM!" He dropped the bottle, and the shards scattered as they hit the hard earth. ". . . The star died . . . and we got ready to be born."

Winston stared at the broken glass, looking a little bit sick. He didn't say anything—just closed his eyes and held his knees tightly to his chest. Tory could tell that he was trying desperately to make this information go away. The way he looked at things—it's like he wanted all of creation to fit nice and neatly in a little box, and whatever didn't fit he just ignored. Well, this time Tory knew he couldn't ignore it—he'd have to stretch that little box.

"C'mon, Winston, you can deal with it," said Tory. "Make the stretch."

"I ain't no bungee cord, okay? I don't stretch that way." Winston shut his eyes even tighter, and Tory could hear him grinding the last nubs of his teeth in frustration.

The soul of a star, thought Tory. *How big—how powerful was the soul of a star?* Even one sixth of it must have been brighter than any other on Earth. "We must be the most powerful human beings in the world!" she told her friends.

"Then why are we dying?" Winston looked at her coldly and left the silo. Since no one had an answer, they silently followed him out.

Why were they dying? thought Tory. *Not just dying—but suffering hideous afflictions. Why would the brightest lights on earth be so consumed by darkness?* This answer she had found was only half an answer, and it made her furious.

Outside the silo, the ground was covered by a thick fog that swirled around their ankles, and the air smelled rich with the decaying remains of an early harvest. A hint of blue on the eastern horizon told of the coming dawn, and although they had not slept, they were too tightly wound to sleep now.

"Yesterday when I closed my eyes," said Michael, "I could almost see the faces of the others . . . but now they feel further away." And then he dared to voice something they were all too afraid to admit might be true. "I don't think they're coming," he said. "Something's gone wrong."

"We have to go to Nebraska," said Tory. "To Omaha. I'm telling you some astronomer at some school there predicted the explosion of the star; he has to know something that can help us."

They *did* have a sense that they had to move northwest, and although Omaha didn't leap out at them as a must-see town, it wasn't out of their way, either—and it was the closest thing to a lead that they had, so Tory got her way. Omaha it was.

By now Lourdes had squeezed her way out of the stone entrance to the silo and joined them. Winston, however, was standing by himself, pondering the glow of the nova, which was quickly being overcome by the light of dawn. Tory reached out to touch Winston gently on the shoulder, but Winston quickly pulled away.

"Don't!" His sleeves fell over his hands, and he had to fight to stick his arms through them again. The jacket seemed much larger on him than it had yesterday, and his boyish voice seemed a little bit higher. "Just don't touch me, okay?"

"Winston . . ."

"I like being one person, okay? I don't want to be one sixth of something, or even one fourth of something."

"But, Winston, if what I've said is right, it could mean so many things—look at the possibilities!"

Winston's face hardened into the expression of a stubborn old man or a very small boy. "I don't care to," he said. Winston's hand began to twitch at his side, and he turned away from Tory, but Tory still watched. He brought his hand up a little, then forced it back down, as if fighting some inner battle—but it was a battle he lost. Tory could only stare in growing dread as Winston Pell, the incredible shrinking boy, brought up his hand, slipped his thumb into his mouth, and kept it there for a long, long time.

THAT AFTERNOON, AT ANOTHER farm hundreds of miles away in Torrington, Wyoming, Dillon Cole tore through a wheat field, putting distance between himself and the farmhouse behind him. He would not look back; he would not *think* back, and what he left behind in that house would be put completely out of his mind.

He felt the wrecking-hunger curl up and go to sleep well fed, and when the hunger was fed, Dillon felt strong—stronger than anyone alive. *What would I be without the wrecking-hunger?* he thought. The hunger answered like a rumbling from his stomach: he would be nothing. Sometimes he felt as if the hunger were a living thing; a weed that had coiled around his soul and he couldn't tell where it ended and where he began. He didn't know whether that was a good thing or a bad thing.

But whatever it was, those four Others wanted to take it away, didn't they? Even now they were drawn toward him, across the miles, and if they found him, they would weaken him; maybe even destroy him. They would drive a wedge between him and Deanna, and Dillon could not allow that. So they had to keep moving until . . .

Until what?

Until the hunger no longer needed to be fed.

He raced across the wheat field to the place where he had left Deanna, but when he got there, she was gone.

DILLON HAD LEFT DEANNA in the wheat field with little warning. They had just left a farmhouse where a family had been kind enough to give them lunch—they were crossing a field, when suddenly Dillon had told her to wait, and then doubled back over the hill toward the house again.

He had gone to feed the hunger—Deanna knew that—she could see in his face how he had been suffering—strangling—but why did he have to leave her alone? He knew what happened to her when she was alone.

A wind swept across the rolling hills of wheat. The ground beneath her seemed to move, and fear gripped her. She felt one of her waking nightmares coming on again, and although she knew it could not be real, it terrified her all the same. Was there something there under the ground? Something coming for her? Yes! She could see it burrowing beneath the wheat. Why had Dillon left her here?

She began to run, but the fear ran with her. Finally she

stumbled into a field that had already been harvested, where thick black mud swallowed her to her ankles. Something was reaching for her. She could feel it. She screamed in terror.

She fell to the mud, and the ground seemed to swallow her. Was the ground alive? Was it climbing up around her, dragging her down into darkness? She couldn't see now—the mud was in her eyes, in her mouth. She swore she could feel a beast coming out of the mud wrapping around her like a snake, and she screamed again to chase the terror-mare away, but her screaming didn't help.

Then something grabbed her by the wrists. At first she thought it was the ground itself reaching up to pull her even deeper, but then there was a voice. A familiar voice.

"Deanna, it's all right!" She could barely hear Dillon through her own screams. "Look at me," he said. "*See* me. Make it go away."

Deanna, her sight still blurry, fixed on his dark eyes, pushing the foul vision of fear away.

When the terror-mare had ended, it was like coming out of a seizure, which is exactly how Dillon treated it. He held her tightly, as if she had been in the throes of convulsions. Deanna was exhausted and let all her muscles go slack, feeling the steady pressure of Dillon as he held her.

"You left me," she said weakly.

"I'm sorry. I was wrong to—I won't do it again." Dillon picked her up and carried her to a place where the wheat was tall and the ground was dry, then he lay her down, and tenderly wiped away the mud that had caked on her arms. Dillon was calm and relaxed. Deanna knew what that meant.

"What happened at the farmhouse?" she asked. "How bad was it?"

"I didn't touch a thing," said Dillon. "I just sort of planted a seed. That's all."

"What did you do?"

Dillon stared at her, considering her question. "I'll tell you, if you want to know."

But the truth was, she *didn't* want to know, so she didn't press the issue. Instead she just lay there staring up at the sky, feeling her fear curl up inside her and go to sleep as she listened to far-off birds crying somewhere over the hill. Their voices sounded like screams in the distance.

"We need to keep moving," said Dillon, helping Deanna up.

"Do we know where we're going yet?" she asked.

"We're not 'going' anywhere," Dillon answered. "We're getting away from The Others."

Dillon had been saying that since they left Nebraska—but it wasn't entirely true, was it? *Dillon knows where he's going,* thought Deanna. *He just doesn't know he knows.* It was clear to Deanna that he was doing what he did best—tracing a pattern—but this pattern was so complex and intricate not even he could see its end.

Deanna kept her faith in Dillon, knowing that wherever this journey was leading, she and Dillon would be together. She held onto that thought as they headed west out of Torrington, leaving behind the farmhouse and the screaming birds.

8. DR. BRAINLESS AND THE SIX OF SWORDS

IT WAS A SMALL OBSERVATORY IN A SMALL UNIVERSITY, where a man of small recognition worked feverishly to get his telescope up and running.

Winston was doubtful about the entire thing—but then he was doubtful of everything since Tory came up with that crazy stuff about the Scorpion Star. Winston feared he'd never be able to stretch himself around that one—but the others had, and now Tory was in the lead wherever they went.

In the two days the quartet had been together, Winston had felt his disease, or whatever it was, start to accelerate. A day ago he had chewed a sandwich on his seven-year molars. But when he ran his tongue through his mouth today, those molars were gone, receding back into his head. His front teeth were starting to get smaller and smaller. Soon all his adult teeth would be gone, and he would have no teeth at all, because his baby teeth had long since been exchanged for quarters beneath his pillow.

The others were no better off: Lourdes's blouse looked like a patch quilt because they kept having to sew scraps of material into it to make it larger. Tory had begun complaining that her joints ached something fierce, which meant that whatever was devouring her skin was beginning to move deeper into her body, and Michael . . . well, sometimes he looked like a madman on the verge of turning into a werewolf. He complained his girl-crazies were getting worse and that his heart beat so fast, he was afraid it might blow up in his chest.

They had all hoped that coming together would slow down their deterioration, but it hadn't—in fact, things were progressing faster, and they all could be dead in a matter of days. Winston didn't know how an astronomer could help, but he was desperate enough to try anything now.

Finding the man was not very difficult. A simple Web search uncovered several articles on the eccentric astronomer. Dr. Bayless was his name, but his crueler colleagues were more fond of calling him Dr. Brainless.

Winston fought to stay ahead of Michael and Lourdes and right behind Tory as they crossed the small college campus toward the physics building. Tory still shuffled through printouts of the articles they had found, trying to read in the late twilight.

"Listen to this—it says here that Bayless's mother was a carnival psychic, and she gyped rich people out of thousands of dollars!"

"So?" scoffed Winston.

"So, the scientific community thinks Bayless is a quack as well and gives him the cold shoulder."

"But he predicted the explosion of Mentarsus-H," chimed in Lourdes, in her deep whale-belly voice. "So who's quacking now?"

Winston turned to Michael, who seemed distracted and bothered as if the air itself was pricking his whole body with needles as he walked.

"What do *you* think?" asked Winston.

"He probably won't help us unless we bring him the broomstick of the Wicked Witch," said Michael.

BEHIND THE PHYSICS BUILDING stood the observatory—a small domed structure painted a peeling institutional green. It was no more an emerald city than their path had been a yellow-brick road.

As they pushed their way through the squeaky doors of
the observatory, they were met by the smell of old floor var-
nish and a twelve-foot telescope with pieces missing. It was
an unimpressive observatory, consisting of little more than the
crippled telescope, a desk in a far corner, and an arrow on the
floor pointing north—in case anyone couldn't figure that out
by themselves.

Across the room, a thin man, with thinner hair, fought
with workers—trying to keep them working on the telescope,
even though it was way past five o'clock. He was tall, with
a slight roundness to his back from too many years making
calculations at a desk. The four kids approached the ranting
astronomer solemnly like a small minion of misery, and when
he saw them, he waved them off.

"No classes today. Go home." His voice had a hostile,
unfriendly tone that could only come from many years of bitter disappointment.

Tory cleared her throat and stepped forward. "Dr. Bayless,
we've come a long way—we have to talk to you."

Bayless turned to take a better look at them, then, with a
disgust he didn't even try to hide, said, "My God! What happened to you?"

"That's what we're trying to find out," said Winston.

Around them the workers were starting and moving
toward the doors, whispering to each other about the freaks
that had just walked in.

"Go on," Bayless shouted to the workers. "Get out—see if I
care." They were more than happy to oblige. "The cosmic event
of a lifetime, and the telescope had to break down this month."

He took a moment to look at the four of them again, shook
his head—shuddering with revulsion—and let loose a bitter
laugh. "Life's misfortunes just fall at my doorstep, don't they?

If it's not a ruined telescope, it's the wretched of the earth. Well, how can I help you?"

"What can you tell us about supernovas?" asked Tory.

"What *can't* I tell you?" he replied, slipping into professor-speak. "Supernovas are the reason we're all here. Oxygen, carbon, silicon—all the heavier elements are created in the explosions. Without novas, the whole universe would be little more than hydrogen gas . . ." He paused and looked at them again, shuddering, but this time not laughing. "But you didn't come here for an astronomy lecture, did you?"

"You predicted the explosion of Mentarsus-H," said Tory. "We think our condition's got something to do with that."

Now Bayless's look turned from revulsion to suspicious interest. He studied them intensely and began to pick at his ragged yellow fingernails.

"My prediction was luck," he said. "At least that's what my colleagues say."

"Don't go playing games with us, all right?" said Winston, pulling his thumb from his mouth. "If you know something, tell us."

"You got a big mouth for a little kid," said Bayless.

"I'm fifteen," growled Winston.

Bayless sighed and nodded reluctantly. "All right, come on and sit down."

Bayless led them to a corner of the observatory that had been set up as his office. Winston noticed that Michael kept his distance, breathing in gasps, like someone suffering from asthma, and shifting his weight from one foot to another like a caged animal. *He's got it bad today,* thought Winston.

"The Scorpion Star," said Lourdes to Bayless. "Tell us how you knew."

Bayless leaned back in his desk chair, took a sip of cold

coffee, and focused on his uneven fingernails, picking at them with an unpleasant click-click-click. Finally he spoke.

"It's a curious talent," said Bayless, "to look at the universe and know what it's thinking. To sense that countless galaxies would be discovered in dark space. To feel that the universe is even older than most scientists think it is. To glance at a star chart and see one star missing in the tail of the Scorpion, only to see it reappear when you blink."

"Intuition?" suggested Tory.

"My mother had it," said Bayless. "She chose to use it to separate fools from their money and turned herself into a sideshow freak. I chose to use it for more noble purposes. Biology . . . astrophysics." Then he angrily flicked a fingernail in an arc over their heads. It landed on the dark floor, where it lay like a crescent moon. "Unfortunately science has no room for intuition. Scientists find a million ways to spell 'coincidence,' and so I've become a sideshow freak after all." Then he smiled grimly, and added, ". . . like the four of you."

His smile made them all squirm. Everyone but Tory.

"The star blew up sixteen years ago," said Tory. "We've figured out the exact date."

"Students of astrophysics, are you?" said Bayless, beginning on a new fingernail.

"No," said Tory. "That was the day each of us was conceived."

Bayless raised his attention from his marred fingertips to the four of them. "Remarkable," he said, studying their faces, and movements. "Remarkable. Perhaps these exploding stars have more to do with us than I've dared to imagine." He pulled out a digital recorder from his desk and hit the record button. "Do you mind if I record all this?"

"We'd rather you didn't," said Lourdes.

He put his recorder in his desk, but Winston couldn't tell if he turned it off.

"Tell me everything," he said. "Everything to the last detail . . ."

THEY TOOK A GOOD hour to go through their stories, and Bayless listened, attentive to every word. When they were done, the astronomer was practically drooling with excitement.

"Shards!" he exclaimed, laughing with glee. "Shards of a shattered star!" He peered at them as if they were subjects he planned to study. The slight hunch of his back made him resemble a vulture.

"I've written about this sort of thing," he said, pacing a short, sharp path, "but never dared to publish it—but now I can present you as proof!" He looked at them with such awe, it made Winston roll his eyes. "Do you have any idea how special—how *luminous* you are? Why, the rest of us are mere smithereens compared to you!"

"Yeah?" said Michael. "So if we got these fantastic kick-ass souls, how come we're so screwed up?"

His words stopped Bayless in mid-pace. "I don't know," he said. "By my estimation you should be living lives like no others— glorious lives with—"

"Shut up," shouted Winston. Hearing what his life *should* have been made it all seem even worse. He started to stomp around like a small child, and Tory put her hand on his head to calm him down. It only made him angrier.

"We don't need ought-a-be's," said Tory. "We need some why-not's."

Bayless looked at them and sighed. The answers they needed were clearly not easy to come by. Bayless pondered his inoperable telescope for a moment, then turned back to them decisively.

"Science can't help you," said Bayless. "Not unless you want to wait and see what they find in your autopsies."

The thought made Winston shiver, and he swore he could feel himself shrink a fraction of an inch.

"Then what do you suggest?" said Michael, his breathing heavier, his voice even more impatient than it had been an hour ago.

Bayless thought about it, sighed in resignation, and reached into his bottom drawer, pulling out an old deck of cards that looked like they hadn't been used in ages.

"When I was young, my mother made me read cards for rich old women. I once told a woman she was going to die before the sun went down. She stormed out of the tent in a huff and was promptly trampled by the fair's elephant."

Michael stood engulfed in his own growing frustration. "We need *real* help and *real* answers, can't you see that? We didn't come all this way to read dumb old tarot cards!"

"And I didn't get degrees in biology and astrophysics to read dumb old tarot cards, but here we are, aren't we?"

Michael, his breathing helplessly heavy, his body uncontrollably tense, his pants unrelentingly tight, looked to the others. "Are you going to sit here for this garbage?" Clearly his frustration had little to do with tarot cards—so Lourdes gently took his hand.

"Just relax," she told him. "Take deep breaths. What you're feeling will go away."

"No it won't," he said. "You know it won't."

He shook off Lourdes's hand and stormed along the arrow on the floor, until he crashed out of the observatory, into the night.

"Don't mind him," Winston told Bayless. "He's just pointing north."

Tory was about to go after him, but Lourdes stopped her. "He just needs some air," she said. "He'll be all right."

When the echo of Michael's exit had faded, Bayless returned to shuffling the cards.

"Does it have to be tarot cards?" asked Winston. "Where I come from only ignorant folk use 'em. They're hard to believe in."

Bayless continued to shuffle. "It's not the cards you need to believe in, it's the skill of the dealer," he said. He pulled out a card and handed it to Winston. "It's like playing poker. Any idiot can deal cards—but how many people can deal a straight-flush every time?"

Winston looked at his card. A small boy on a golden ram, racing out of control through the sky. In one hand the boy held a torch that fought to survive a brutal wind. To Winston the boy seemed terrified.

"The Page of Wands," noted Bayless. "Unless I've lost my touch, that card is you."

Winston studied the card. He didn't quite know what it meant, but he did have a sense of identification—as if he truly could be this boy clinging helplessly to the back of the wild wooly ram.

"If I wanted to," said Bayless, "I could tell your fortune with baseball cards and the result would be exactly the same."

Winston cast his eyes down.

"All right, then," said Tory. "Deal us a fortune."

Bayless smiled. "Yes—let's desecrate the halls of science, shall we?" And with that, he dealt seven cards, face down— six formed a triangle, and the seventh he placed in the triangle's center.

He reached toward the two cards at the bottom. "If I remember correctly, these cards will show us the present." He flipped the first one, revealing a cloaked figure in a small boat, navigating a troubled sea.

"Death?" asked Lourdes.

"No, *the Six of Swords*," Bayless replied. Winston looked more closely at the card to see a cargo of six swords resting in the keep of the ship. "Six souls on a restless journey."

"Then there *are* six of us!" said Tory. "Now we have proof!"

"If you can call this proof," mumbled Winston.

Bayless flipped the second card. A chariot being torn apart by a black horse and a white horse. Bayless looked at the card, and began to sweat just a bit.

"Death?" asked Lourdes.

"*The Charioteer*," said Bayless. "It's making me uncomfortable, but I don't know why. . . . See, the horses that pull this chariot are very powerful. They have to be stopped or the chariot will be destroyed."

"So what does that mean?" asked Winston.

"Not sure yet."

Bayless went to the next two cards. "These cards will show where your journey must take you."

He anxiously flipped the first to reveal an image of a tower being destroyed by lightning.

"*The Tower*. Does the tower mean anything to you?"

The three kids shook their heads.

Bayless nodded. "It will soon."

He flipped the next card. It showed a dark figure covered in shrouds, in the midst of desolation.

"Death?" asked Lourdes.

"No—*the Hermit*." Bayless's voice was becoming shaky, filled with both fear and wonder. "This is someone you must face . . . if you get that far."

"What's wrong?" asked Lourdes, as Bayless began to wring his fingers.

"He frightens me." Bayless said, confused. "*The Hermit* shouldn't frighten me . . ."

His eyes darted between the three kids, and he returned to the cards. "Well, we've begun, we have to finish it," he said. Now Winston was beginning to feel as if he didn't want to see the rest.

"This is what you will find at journey's end," Bayless said. "These two cards are your destiny."

He reached for the first card, hesitated for a moment, then flipped both cards simultaneously.

Winston looked at the first, and his heart missed a beat. Lourdes didn't have to say it this time. The masked figure of darkness was unmistakable.

"*Death,*" said Bayless. "And *the Five of Wands.*" The second card showed a man and woman with five glowing torches doing battle with a dragon. "Death will surround you. And those who survive will face a greater challenge."

"What sort of challenge?" whispered Winston.

"If I knew, I would tell you." Bayless quickly flipped the cards back over so he didn't have to see them. "I forgot how much I hated telling fortunes."

"What about the last card?" asked Tory.

Bayless cleared his throat.

"The central card. It binds your past, present and future. History and destiny." He didn't even reach for it. "Maybe you don't want to see this card."

"Turn it," demanded Tory, and so the astronomer-turned-fortune-teller reached for the central card with a shaky hand, grabbed it by the corner, and pulled on it.

The card ripped in half.

It had caught on a splinter of wood in his old desk. Bayless gasped in horror, as he looked at the torn half of the card in his hand.

Winston took the card from him and pulled the torn half from the table, holding the two halves together. The card showed a golden circle, containing a creature: half-man, half-woman. In the four corners were a torch, a star, a sword, and a grail.

"What is this card?" demanded Winston, but Bayless only shook his head and stammered like a crazy man.

"Tell us!"

"Everything." He said. "This card is *the World*."

And their fortune tore it in half.

Bayless stood up, his eyes darting around the observatory. He gasped, a revelation coming to him, and he began to rummage through his papers. "I understand," said Bayless. He was terrified, but at the same time overcome by some excitement that the others were yet to understand.

And there was something else . . . a strange hum that was growing in the room. A vibration that made everything shake.

"What do you understand?" shouted Tory. "Tell us!"

"I'm ready for this," said Bayless. "Everything I've done—everything I've written, everything I've learned—my whole life has been for this." He began piling up books on his desk, pulling them from shelves and talking as if he made perfect sense, which he didn't. "I'll come with you—I'll document every single moment and no one will laugh at me again."

By now the gears and casing of the telescope had begun to rattle and groan with the strange vibration. The three kids stood up, and looked around in terror. Something was very wrong here.

"Listen to me!" shouted Bayless, ripping open the drawers

of his filing cabinet and pulling out piles of papers. "There are things I can tell you; things I've never published because until now they've never made sense. Things you have to know!"

The roar in the observatory was deafening now, an ear-splitting shrieking that sounded almost like voices. But Bayless was too excited to care.

"I know what's happening to you!" proclaimed Bayless.

But before he could get any further, there was a blast of light, and they all began to scream.

Because the room was suddenly filled with monsters.

MICHAEL DID NOT HEAR their screams—he was far away, bolting aimlessly over the fields, cursing the stars that looked down on him, cursing the earth that supported him, until his wanderings brought him in a circle back to the buildings of the university.

A class was letting out, and he hunched in the shadows, watching every pretty girl that passed—and they were all pretty in one way or another to Michael. As the crowd thinned out, one girl was left by a bicycle rack.

Michael stepped out of the shadows. He thought he would just watch her as she rode away. That's all. Just watch.

For days Michael had looked away from girls—he had fought that burning feeling by standing in the cold rain, by screaming into empty fields—but now his resistance was low. He was tired . . . and before he even knew it, he had turned on his peculiar magnetism like a tractor beam.

When the girl heard his footsteps stalking closer, she didn't think anything of it at first. "Did you enjoy the class?" she asked.

Michael just stared at her, enjoying her every move. "I'm not a student," he answered.

She began to get a bit apprehensive, glancing around to see

if any of her friends were still there, but everyone was gone. They were alone.

"You're very pretty." Michael took a step closer, she glanced at him, and in an instant she was caught.

Before Michael could pause for a moment's thought, he was kissing her and she didn't resist for a moment.

Michael broke away.

"No," he said, fighting it, "that's not what I meant to do. . . . What I really need . . . I mean what I really want to do is just . . . talk. That's all."

But she didn't hear him; she was staring into his eyes the way they always did. She spoke, almost giggling, as if this were all part of a dream. "My name's Rebecca," she said. "What's yours?"

"Michael."

She smiled and leaned forward to kiss him again. "Why am I doing this?" she said.

"Full moon," said Michael, although it wasn't. He was burning inside now, the sweat beading on his face.

Rebecca glanced over her shoulder, to make sure that everyone was gone, then took his hand and led him off down a dim, tree-lined path.

As they ran, Rebecca looked to the right and left. Michael knew she was searching for some hidden place where they could get back to what they had started—a place to match that dark hidden place in Rebecca's mind that Michael had already found. She was already falling into that darkness with the thrill of a sky-diver.

They came to a windowless building—the school's physical plant. Steam billowed from the roof, air whistled through vents, and inside a pump rang out a dull toll sending water, gas, and electricity to the many buildings of the campus.

Rebecca pushed Michael up against the door, kissed him, then giggled. "You kiss good," she said.

It was getting out of hand. He knew that he should never have looked at her, but now his worries were drowning in a stormy sea of Rebecca's kisses. Going around the bases was not a good thing for Michael. He had only done it once—in Baltimore, and after what happened there, he swore not to let it happen again. Since then, bunting his way to first had been the name of the game—but suddenly he realized that he was about to swing away.

"You really don't want to do this," said Michael feebly, but even as he said it, he gripped her tighter and felt his own sense of control slipping away.

They leaned into the door, and it squealed open into a cavern smelling brackish and damp, where a water pump pounded and rattled them from head to toe.

Maybe it will be different, thought Michael, *maybe it will be all right,* and he clung to that thought like a parachute, as he slipped into the darkness, like a man leaping from a plane.

MONSTERS!

The shadows Tory Smythe saw leaping around the observatory became permanently carved into her mind. Although it all happened in just a few seconds, she knew exactly what she had seen.

Shadow-black tentacles wrapped around the cradle of the telescope. A clouded face that swarmed with a million hideous insects descended upon the astronomer's desk, and something with cold dark fur brushed past Tory, its breath sickly sweet.

In an instant the telescope was torn from its moorings and came crashing down. The primary focus lens broke free and spun on the ground like a coin, casting patterns of refracted light around the circular room. Bayless was screaming—everyone was screaming—then the creatures let out their own unearthly wail and a blinding explosion knocked them all to the ground. Something leapt at Tory. She opened her mouth to scream . . . and it was gone. The beasts were all gone. The light faded, and she just sat there, hands pressed against her ears, eyes shut tight, and her face contorted in a silent scream. She heard the others screaming, though—Winston and Lourdes—she heard them burst out of the observatory and race down the hill.

But Tory couldn't move. She had heard old stories of how looking at some monsters could turn you to stone, and she wondered if that had happened to her. She cursed herself for having come here.

I don't believe in monsters, she told herself, but that didn't make a bit of difference, because she knew what she had seen.

At last she was able to force her eyes open. The ruined observatory was silent and still. The only light in the room came from the fading fragments of the telescope lens, which had exploded and sent glass splintering in all directions.

As she finally got to her feet, Tory realized that whatever Dr. Bayless was going to tell them was going to remain his secret. He would be viewing no more stars. He would be telling no more fortunes. Whatever these beasts were, they had not wanted Bayless to tell what he knew. They had caused the explosion—they had come to silence him.

She couldn't help but feel responsible for what had happened to the astronomer. She felt pity for the man, but even more she felt fury that she was again left with more questions and riddles. It was that fury that overcame her fear, and she decided she wouldn't run just yet—there were still things she had to do.

She grabbed whatever was left of the books and papers Bayless had pulled out and shoved them in her pack. She found the seven tarot cards scattered on the floor and took them as well, and then found a canvas tarp in the corner and brought it over to Bayless.

Around the room, the light was getting dimmer as the glowing splinters of the lens faded. The lens had shattered into half a dozen pieces. Five of those pieces were embedded in the walls like glass lightning bolts. The sixth had found a much more specific destination.

As Tory covered Bayless's body, she knew what she had to do—she owed at least that much to the poor man, And so before drawing the canvas over his face, she reached toward the silent astronomer, then took a firm hold of that last shard of crystal and, biting back her terror, pulled it from between Dr. Bayless's eyes.

THEY FOUND MICHAEL AT the edge of the campus, retching his guts out in the middle of the street—and had to rush him out of the way of a speeding fire engine.

He knelt there by the curb, heaving and gripping his stomach.

"What the hell is wrong with you?" demanded Winston.

Tory and Lourdes knelt beside him and helped him stand up.

His face was wet from tears and pale—almost green.

"What happened?" asked Lourdes.

Michael didn't answer. Instead he just held his stomach and forced his breathing back under control. Finally he said, "I got lost . . . that's all." And no one dared to question him further.

They turned and headed off in a direction their internal compass told them was west, while behind them, way down the road, the fire truck stopped in front of a physical plant that was billowing black smoke.

9. LIGHT AND SHADOWS

THAT NIGHT THE STORM RETURNED WITH A VENGEANCE EVEN before the streets had a chance to dry. The night that had seemed so steamy quickly turned cold, and the sky let loose an unrelenting assault of sleet. It battered the windshield of the van with such fury that they had to pull off to the side of the road and wait.

Tory studied the map; they were somewhere west of Omaha now, in the middle of nowhere, and it occurred to Tory with an awful shiver that they were always in the middle of nowhere. It seemed from the moment her journey had begun, Tory had slipped into the dark festering world that existed between the walls and beneath the floors of the rest of the world. A rat-ridden place filled with the torn, ruined things that nobody wanted. They were all now residents of this waste-world, and the eerie capriciousness of the weather—never deciding on hot or cold, wet or dry—made the rest of humanity seem further and further away. It seemed to Tory that their lives had slipped into a place so dismal that souls perished and only weeds could take their place.

As the sleet pummeled the van, Winston sat in the back with Lourdes, sewing pieces of fabric onto her clothes so that they would still fit.

"Maybe The Others are dead," Winston dared to whisper at one point. "Maybe they were killed by those monster-things that tried to get us."

Lourdes shook her head and said, "If they were dead, then why do we still feel pulled to the west?"

And Lourdes was right—the pull was still there and still strong. Tory, who always rode shotgun, was the official navigator, and when she looked at the map, certain roads and cities seemed to jump off the page at her. Interstate 80, Big Springs, Nebraska, Torrington, Wyoming. They had to go to these places, in hopes of finding traces of the other two who were still missing from their little band. It wasn't much, but it was all they had to go on. *The whole is greater than the sum of the parts,* Tory kept telling herself. *When we're all together, we'll be stronger—and it will all make sense.* She clung to that belief as if it were a lifeline.

Michael had little to say on the matter. Since they had left Omaha, he had become completely withdrawn. He sat silently in the driver's seat in an icy daze. His demeanor had become as hard and bitter as the torrents of ice that brutalized the van.

The moment they got to the van, Tory had begun leafing through the things she had scavenged from the observatory. First she puzzled over the cards: *the Six of Swords* and *the Charioteer*; *the Tower* and *the Hermit*; *Death,* and *the Five of Wands*. And the torn world. Then she began to look through the books. Astronomy mostly—textbooks that Bayless had written himself. Page after page yielded nothing relevant to Tory, and now as they sat in the ice storm, she seemed no closer to a solution.

"Something that he said keeps going over and over in my mind," Tory told the others. "He said that his whole life was just preparing him for this . . . for *us.*"

"Then why don't you look at his whole life?"

It was Michael who spoke, and everyone was startled to hear him speak after being silent for so long. "He was a biologist before he was an astronomer," said Michael. "And you've been looking at the wrong books."

Michael then held up the book he had been looking at.

It was a book on parasites.

"Bayless wrote this years before he became an astronomer," said Michael. "It says here in the introduction that when he was a kid his pet dog was just about eaten from the inside out by worms. Since then he was fascinated by parasites—creatures that live off of other creatures."

Then Michael began to read from Bayless's book: *"There are whole universes of life hiding in the dark places where no one dares to explore. They thrive in the hidden expanses we take for granted . . . between the very cells of our body . . . between the walls we call our world."*

Tory gasped. "He said that?"

Michael nodded, and Tory shivered. It was like hearing a man echoing her thoughts from beyond the grave.

Michael passed around the book, and they leafed through it. It was a bizarre collection of diagrams, photos, and case studies, and Bayless seemed to have had a morbid fascination with it all. There was a picture of a tapeworm the size of a garden hose found in the gut of an elephant. There was a barnacle the size of a trash barrel on the back of a whale. There were leeches from the Amazon the size of running shoes.

"This was his specialty before he took up astronomy," said Michael. "The study of parasitic organisms."

A gust of wind rocked the van and a sheet of ice assaulted the windshield like a cascade of ball bearings. Winston asked the question that no one else dared to voice.

"What's it got to do with us?"

Michael couldn't look at him in the face. He turned to look out of the window, but all the windows were fogged with the steam of their breath.

Between the walls of the world, thought Tory. Right now it seemed no world existed beyond the small capsule of the van.

"Something happened to me while you were all still in the observatory," said Michael. "I didn't want to talk about it . . . but I think I'd better . . ."

Everyone leaned closer as Michael began his story.

"I did get lost for a while, just like I said," began Michael. "But then I ended up outside of a lecture hall. There was this girl unchaining her bike. I went up to her, just to talk, you know . . . but before I knew it we were kissing.

"After a while she pulls me into this doorway. The door opens, and we go in—and I know we shouldn't, but by now I don't care, 'cause I'm feeling like nothing else in the world matters.

"But then I think about what happened with that girl, back when I lived in Baltimore—the only time things ever went too far. Thinking about it makes me scared, so I push myself away from this girl. I run clear across the room, and I think it's over . . . but then I look back at her from across the room and that's when I see the most horrible thing I've ever seen in my life. She's surrounded by fire—an unnatural blue-green fire—and it's all over her, but she's not burning . . . and the fire—it has a dozen arms and legs—but worst of all it has eyes. *It's alive!* But all I can do is sit there and watch, too horrified to even scream, as this thing wraps itself around her like a cocoon . . . and she doesn't even know. It's like she's hypnotized.

"Finally the girl goes limp, and the monster turns to me. I try to run, but my feet slip and when I look back, it's moving toward me through the air—and then in a second it's on me and I swear I can feel this monster oozing back inside me, right through the pores of my skin . . . and for the first time I realize that the feeling inside that always drives me crazy . . .

isn't me—it's this thing that's been living here inside me, like a leech, stealing away all my strength.

"When I look up, I see the girl walking toward me. It looks like there's nothing wrong with her—but the room is on fire all around her, real fire, orange and hot, just like what happened with that girl in Baltimore—only that time I never saw the creature, because I didn't rip myself away from it . . . and that time I didn't get the girl out of the fire in time.

"So now, with the fire all around, I pick her up, carry her out before the fire gets us, and as soon as we're outside, she turns to me and smiles, not even noticing anything strange is going on.

"And that's when I realize that she's dead.

"Yeah, she's alive, but she's also dead! That thing . . . it ate her soul and left her body alive!

"She smiles at me and says 'Hi,' like everything's blue skies and sunshine, and I think, *She doesn't even know! Something has just devoured her soul, and she doesn't even know!*

"I couldn't stand it, so I ran from her as fast as I could . . . but only got to the next street before I started puking my guts out. That's when you found me."

ONLY AN ANGRY CHORUS of sleet responded to Michael's terrible tale. No one had anything they could say. No words of consolation. No advice. Everyone's eyes began to sting with cold tears.

Michael bit his tongue to stop his teeth from chattering and wiped the tears from his eyes. "So now I know why we're dying. Those horrible beasts in the observatory didn't just come out of nowhere. They were there all along. They're here now. All four of them."

Someone let out a wail of agony—it must have been

Lourdes—and then tears of anger, terror, but most of all help-lessness, burst out around the van. It was simply too much to take alone, and in an instant all eight of their hands were reaching for the others, longing to make connection once more—even Winston. They clasped hands, the circle of four was closed, and their breath and their heartbeats began to match—panicked and fast. The truth was indeed terrible, but easier to grasp and accept when the circle was closed.

"We're possessed . . . ," said Winston.

"Not possessed, infected," said Tory.

"Infested," offered Michael. "The way people get lice . . . the way dogs get worms. Each of us is infested by some . . . *thing.* They must have found their way inside us years ago, when all the bad stuff started . . . and ever since then, they've been growing."

They looked at each other's faces, for the first time seeing the ravages of the infestation for what they really were. The creature that hid within Lourdes crushed life out of others and turned it into fat. The one clinging to Tory could turn flesh rancid from disease. The one in Winston paralyzed anything it touched and was stealing Winston's life away years at a time. And everyone knew what Michael's did.

"Why us?" said Winston, shaking his head, still not want-ing to believe.

"Because we're star-shards," answered Tory. "It's like that elephant and the giant tapeworm; these monsters can only live and grow inside of *us*." Tory tried to feel the creature within her, but all she could feel was the pain in her face and her joints. "We might have the world's biggest souls . . . but they've become infested by the blackest parasites that ever existed."

"Could be that everyone's got them," suggested Lourdes. ". . . It's just that ours have grown a few million times bigger than normal."

Winston shivered. "Cosmic Killer Leeches," he said. "I wish my father were alive—he could have pulled a cure right out of his pharmacy."

"Yeah," said Michael. "Shampoo twice a day, and drink lots of sulfuric acid." They all laughed at that, and found it strange that they could laugh at all. Perhaps they weren't as hopeless and helpless as they thought.

"We gotta figure out a way to destroy them," said Tory, "before they destroy us."

"Or worse," said Lourdes.

Tory looked at Lourdes, wondering what could possibly be worse than having an invisible parasite rout your soul . . . and then she looked at the central card that Bayless had dealt to them, and shivered. *The torn world . . .*

How powerful were these creatures? How many people in this world could they destroy if they had the chance—and what if the kids lost complete control and gave themselves over to the will of these dark beasts, choosing to feed them by visiting their horrors upon others? To paralyze them. To disease them. To crush them. To devour their souls.

If any one of them chose that path rather than bear the suffering, the devastation left behind would be unimaginable. It would be like tearing the world in half.

They looked at each other, four souls, thinking a single thought.

"My God!" said Tory. *"We have to find the other two!"*

10. THE FALL OF BLACKBURN STREET

DILLON DREAMED HE WAS RIDING ON THE BACK OF A PANTHER— a great, dark beast bounding into a wild unknown. The power he felt in the dream made the rest of humanity seem small and unimportant, and as he rode he saw the weak, guilt-ridden boy he was before trampled beneath the beast's pounding feet. Dillon awoke from the dream exhilarated, out of breath, and knowing that it was not entirely a dream. He wondered why he had resisted for so long.

His wrecking-hunger had evolved. Now it felt like a creature, burning with primal fury, yet acutely intelligent . . . and Dillon had learned that riding this beast was far better than letting it ride him.

He imagined Deanna there beside him, riding her own creature—a powerful pale horse—a terror-mare. Together he and Deanna would charge their beasts into the wind, and no one would stop them as they sped down paths of greater and greater destruction.

Where are you taking me? Dillon would silently ask it, and although it never answered, Dillon knew that it had a glorious purpose that he would soon understand.

Deanna, on the other hand, was no longer so entranced by her situation.

She had watched Dillon change from a teary-eyed boy, crushed by the weight of his own terrible actions, to a young man who was getting far too sure of himself.

Yet in spite of that, Deanna knew that he still needed her.

Who else but Deanna could look deep into his eyes and find something inside that, even now, was still good and worthy of love? And if her capacity for love were greater than her capacity for fear, perhaps it would save her in spite of the destruction. Perhaps it would save them both.

Dillon gratefully accepted her love, and, in turn, she accepted his wisdom.

"Forget about the 'Other' ones," he had told her. "They'll only bring us trouble." If Deanna didn't accept this, she would have to face the alternative, and so Deanna pushed The Others out of her mind as they raced headlong into the great northwest.

"We're the strong ones," Dillon had said. "Those Others are nothing compared to us." And it was true. She and Dillon were stronger than all The Others combined.

Then why did she feel so weak?

Dillon had said he was like her good luck charm, but she wasn't exactly wearing him around her neck; it was more like she had climbed into his pocket and hidden there.

Was her soul so frail that all she could do was follow him, borrowing his will for her own? She had been a hostage of her fears, and Dillon had freed her. . . . Did that make her *his* hostage now? She didn't know—but she did know that she would follow him to the ends of the earth . . . which was exactly where she suspected they were headed as they crossed from Wyoming into Idaho.

THE STREETS OF IDAHO Falls were gilded with a million orange leaves. The tall oaks of Blackburn Street had begun to shed summer, day by day, but still kept a dense cloak of yellowing foliage.

Dillon and Deanna arrived late in the afternoon, his arms

around her waist, and her hand wedged in his back pocket, holding each other the way people in love often do. They stood there, in the middle of the quaint residential street, staring at the old homes on either side. Dillon looked at the homes one by one, then turned his head, as if sniffing the air.

"What are you doing?" asked Deanna.

"Getting to know the neighborhood," he answered. "Looking for a place to eat."

Deanna didn't like the sound of that. "Promise me you won't do anything bad here."

Dillon turned to her blinking, as if he didn't know what she meant. "I promise that I won't do anything that isn't absolutely necessary," he said.

A young boy breezed past them on his bike, stopping at the second house on the right. A small license plate on the back of the bike said "Joey." Dillon slipped his hand from Deanna's waist, and he approached the boy, with Deanna following in his wake.

The boy hopped off his bike and strolled toward his front door.

"Hey, Joey," shouted Dillon. "Your brother around?"

Joey turned to look at Dillon, studied him for a moment, then said. "Naah, Jason's still at practice. He'll be home soon, though. . . . You friends of his?"

"Yeah," said Dillon. "I was on the team with him last year."

The boy looked at Dillon doubtfully.

"Jason tells me you're almost as fast as him now," said Dillon. "Hell, you even walk like him!"

Joey beamed at that, but tried to hide it. Any hesitation the boy had was now gone. "You can wait inside if you like."

Deanna turned to Dillon as they neared the porch. "How'd you know he had a brother?" she whispered.

"It was obvious," Dillon whispered back. "He walks like he's copying someone, but not someone who's grown up. . . . He wears hand-me-downs, even though he can afford those brand-new running shoes. . . . He rode up to the house like he's competing in a race. . . . It's all part of a pattern that says he's some jock's kid brother."

Deanna stared at Dillon in amazement, and he just smiled. "C'mon," he said, almost blushing behind his boyish freckles. "You know me pretty well—this stuff shouldn't impress you anymore."

Joey led them into the house. Dillon noted how the boy used keys instead of knocking, how he glanced up the stairs, and how quietly he closed the front door. Dillon took a sniff of the air, and said, "How's your grandfather doing?"

Joey shrugged. "Okay, I guess. Better, now that he's back from the hospital."

Dillon turned to Deanna and winked. Deanna just shook her head. What a show-off!

"Jason'll be back soon, you can wait for him here." Joey left them alone in the kitchen and went back out to fiddle with the chain on his bike. Once Joey was gone, Dillon got down to work. He began to search through drawers and cabinets—he didn't take anything, he just let his eyes pore over everything he saw, observing . . . cataloguing . . . filing the information away.

Deanna had seen him do this the day before, at the farmhouse they had stopped at. Dillon had secretly rifled through the drawers, closets—even under sofa cushions. Deanna had asked what he was searching for. "Clues," he said softly.

Now his hands were moving quickly through the kitchen, his mind working with such force that Deanna could swear that she could feel it pulsating like a high-tension wire. He was fascinating to watch.

"Tell me what you're thinking," said Deanna. "I want to know what you know—I want to see what you see."

"Okay," said Dillon. "Five people live here. Parents, two sons, and a grandfather. Mother smokes, father quit. Kids do okay in school." He pointed to a picture on the refrigerator. "This is the older brother and his girlfriend, right? But something's not right there—look at his smile; he's not smiling *for* the picture—he's smiling *at* the person taking the picture."

"So who took the picture?"

"Isn't it obvious?" said Dillon. "The angle, the background, the way the girl's gloating to have snagged the track star? Her *sister* took the picture, and good ol' Jason would rather be dating *her*!"

Deanna just shook her head, marveling.

"Let's check out the parents," said Dillon. He glanced around, until setting his sights on a high knickknack shelf. Then he pulled down a small bronze Statue of Liberty pencil sharpener and held it out for Deanna to examine.

"The parents honeymooned in New York—but look—there's no dust on it, even though there's dust on the rest of the shelf . . . that means someone's taken Miss Liberty down recently, and has been thinking about it. Smells like dishwashing soap. The mother took it down—either she's nostalgic, or she's worried about the marriage for some reason. Let's see what the doorknobs have to say."

"Doorknobs?"

Dillon opened the back door and touched the outside and inside doorknobs, then smelled his hands.

"Men's cologne going out, women's perfume coming in—not his wife's, because I can smell that everywhere else. The husband is seeing another woman. Good chance his wife knows, and divorce is in the air. Will they break up? Let's find out!"

Dillon opened the refrigerator. "He keeps his beer on the same shelf as the milk and the soda—not in the door all by itself." Dillon opened the hallway closet. "Everything in this house is neatly arranged—these people love order and tranquility, right down to giving their sons sound-alike names. *But* Dad's coats are mixed in with Mom's, instead of on their own side: their order is tightly intertwined." Dillon turned and glanced at the back door again. "And his dirty work boots—" he said. "They're inside the house, on a mat; he's considerate enough not to leave them on the wood floor, and she's accepting enough not to make him put them outside."

"So?"

"So if we leave this little family-stew to cook, I can tell that dear old Dad gives up the other woman, and the marriage is saved. Ninety-six percent probability."

"You're incredible!" said Deanna. "Sherlock Holmes couldn't be that exact!"

Dillon shrugged. "It's like looking at a work of art," explained Dillon. "It's just a bunch of paint, but when you look at it, you see the Mona Lisa, right? Well, when I look at all of these things, I see a picture, too. I see who these people were, who they are, and who they're probably going to be."

"What do you see when you look at me?" asked Deanna.

Dillon didn't even try—he just shook his head. "You're like me," he said. "Too complex to figure out."

She smiled at him, and he took her hand. "C'mon," he said, "I know all I need to know about this family . . . let's move on."

As they left, Deanna noticed the way he rolled his neck, and the way sweat was beginning to bead on his forehead.

"The wrecking-hunger . . . it's back again, isn't it?"

"I try not to think about it," he said, and tugged on her arm a little more urgently. "C'mon."

Out back, they saw a man in the next yard patching up a hole in a boat.

"Hi! We're Joey and Jason's cousins," said Dillon to the man.

"Josh and Jennifer," added Deanna with a smirk.

The neighbor nodded a quiet hello. Dillon noticed the circles beneath his eyes, and the ghost of a missing wedding ring on his tan left hand. Dillon listened to the way in which a dog inside the house yowled.

"Sorry to hear about your wife's passing," said Dillon . . .

On they went, weaving in and out of homes and yards, pretending to be people they weren't—and no one doubted them because Dillon was so very good at the game. He knew the exact things to say that would make people open up their homes, and their hearts, telling him things they would never usually tell a stranger. It was as if they were hypnotized and didn't know it.

All the while Dillon's sweats had gotten worse, his breath had gotten shorter, and his face was becoming flushed.

In the last home, a woman had offered them iced tea and looked at Dillon with worry in her eyes.

"You sure you don't want me to call a doctor?" she asked, but Dillon shook his head and stumbled into the street.

"He'll be okay," said Deanna, covering. "Asthma—his medicine's back in our cousin's house." Deanna left the house and hurried after Dillon, feeling her own worry explode into fear. More than just fear . . . terror. Her own familiar brand of terror.

At the edge of the street, Dillon leaned against a tree, gritting his teeth and clenching his fists. His breath came in short labored gasps. *Not yet,* he told the hunger that gnawed on the ragged fringe of his soul. It was so powerful now, he knew if he didn't feed it soon, it would turn on him and devour him in an instant. *You have to wait! You have to wait until everything's ready,* he told the hunger. Dillon kept telling himself that he was its master, but all beasts turn on their masters if they're not fed.

By now the sun was low in the sky, casting hazy patterns of light through the trees. Patterns of light, patterns of life— sights, sounds, and an impossible puzzle of relationships between the people on this peaceful street.

Not so impossible. Dillon looked from house to house, jumbling all the patterns in his mind, looking for a common thread . . . and at last he found it. He marveled at the power of the solution he had found. It was like a key to open a great Pandora's box. But it was so *big*—many times bigger than what he had done the day before. Did he dare do it? The wrecking-hunger answered by twisting his gut and bringing him to his knees.

Deanna ran toward him pale and frightened, and held him to keep him from falling to the pavement.

"Tell me what you need," she said. "I can help you if I know."

"You already know," he answered.

Deanna looked away. Yes, she knew. He said he had come here looking for a place to eat. But deep down Deanna knew that he really meant a place to *feed.*

The look on Dillon's face had become so helpless and desperate—so consumed by the hunger, she would have destroyed something herself to save him now.

"Will you let me do it?" asked Dillon. "Will you promise not to hate me?"

"Do it," said Deanna. "Feed it any way you can."

Deanna was shaking now; her eyes darting back and forth

as if death would come swooping at both of them from the sky. His hunger and her fear were so tightly connected, she knew that when the hunger was fed and he was strong once more, she would be strong as well.

Dillon found the strength he needed to get to his feet and stumble off into the road toward the second house on the right, where Jason, Joey's older brother, had just arrived home with his girlfriend.

Deanna watched him go, then turned away as she felt something begin to rise in her own gut—and it wasn't just fear.

Will you let me do it? he had asked. He had never asked so bluntly before, but the question was there every time. He needed her permission. He needed her approval for every monstrous act he committed, and she always gave it—as if in some way she was in control. As if she was the one setting him loose to create chaos.

There were many things she could make herself deny. She could deny the sounds of disaster they left behind, she could convince herself that, beyond all reason, something good would come from all this destruction. But now she could not deny that it was all happening because of her—because she gave Dillon permission. She bit her hand to hold back her own scream.

Across the street, Dillon approached Jason's girlfriend, who was waiting for Jason on the porch. By now anything human had drained out of Dillon's voice, and he spoke in a rough snarl that came deep from his gut. It was the voice of the hunger itself.

"You!" growled Dillon as he approached her.

The girl gasped at the sight of him hobbling closer on his weak legs.

Dillon came right up to her, looked into her eyes, read her soul, and said, *"Ask Jason to tell you the truth."*

One of the girl's wide black pupils suddenly constricted down into a pinpoint in a huge blue eye. "Okay," she said dreamily, "I'll ask him." She turned and headed into the house.

Dillon stumbled across the street, already beginning to feel the tiniest bit better. He found Deanna standing just where he had left her.

"Let's get out of here," said Dillon, but she wasn't budging. Her hands were clenched by her side in tight, anxious fists.

"Tell me what you did to her."

"I thought you didn't want to know," said Dillon.

"I want to know now!"

Dillon turned on her with a vengeance. "I'm trying to protect you!" he shouted. "That's what you want, isn't it? That's what you've always wanted!"

Deanna drew a deep breath and said slowly, forcefully, *"Tell me what you did!"*

Dillon kicked the ground hard. "I planted a seed, like I did at the farmhouse. I just made a suggestion, that's all." Dillon told Deanna what he had said to the girl, and Deanna listened to his words, thinking that there must be more . . . but that was all Dillon said. A suggestion? A mere suggestion was going to satisfy the wrecking-hunger? How could that be?

But it wasn't just any suggestion, was it? It was the *right* suggestion. Dillon had sized things up and knew the exact words that would set powerful forces in motion that would grind these people up.

"I found the girl's button," said Dillon. "Everyone has a button, you just have to find it . . . and then push it."

Deanna shook her head, her hands trembling so violently she felt her fingers might shake themselves off.

"We have to leave now," said Dillon. "I don't want to see it happen."

"But I do!" insisted Deanna. "If I'm a part of this, then I want to know what we've done!"

Dillon tried to pull her away, but she wouldn't go. They would weather this one out, whether he liked it or not. "All right," he said, "but just remember, I tried to keep you from seeing." Since Dillon knew it wasn't safe where they were standing, he climbed a tree and helped Deanna up. From there, they had a bird's-eye view of the entire block.

"It'll start over there," said Dillon, pointing to Joey's house. Sure enough, inside the house two people were arguing. The argument got louder and louder, until the girl burst out the front door in tears . . . just as Jason and Joey's mother came home, holding a bag of groceries.

"You're just like your father!" the girlfriend shouted back at Jason. "Everyone knows the way he sneaks around!"

The mother heard this, and the shock of this news made her drop a bag of groceries. Inside, a furious Jason took out his frustration on his kid brother. In a moment Joey came running out of the house crying, not seeing the groceries spilled on the front walk. He slipped on a can of peas, went flying, and hit his head on the ground. Hard.

His mother screamed.

Dillon turned to Deanna. "Once it starts, it's like a boulder rolling down a hill," he said. "Watch!"

Deanna watched with sick fascination as a delivery boy riding by on a moped turned his head to see why the woman was screaming—and was distracted just long enough to hit a car head-on.

The widowed neighbor man came out to his porch at the sound of the crash, and his neglected dog bolted from the house, ran across the street, freaked at all the noise, and attacked a woman in her garden. The woman's husband, a nervous man, ran inside to get a shotgun to save his wife from the mad dog. But his aim was very bad. And very unlucky.

Then, in a moment, the events began to happen so quickly, the chain of cause and effect was completely lost. One thing led to five things, led to five more things, and in a matter of minutes the twilight was filled with shattering windows, screaming people, and brutal fistfights, until the entire block had disintegrated into a savage frenzy . . . an explosive chain reaction of unlikely, unlucky "coincidences" that had all been started by a single, simple suggestion.

"People are like dominoes," explained Dillon, in the midst of the cataclysm. His voice was eerily calm, as if the people on this street were just numbers he was crunching through an equation. "You can make them all fall down, if you know exactly who to push, and when to push them."

Somewhere a gunshot echoed. There were crashing sounds in many of the homes and, in one of them, somewhere the *whoosh* of igniting flames.

Dillon's hunger was fed with every blast, with every crash and every wail as yet another person fell from sanity. He closed his eyes and felt the life-patterns in the street around him falling like a spiderweb clipped from its branch, until the only pattern that remained was the unrelenting spiral of chaos in every life around him.

Deanna, too, felt her own terror mysteriously fade away into a dizzy numbness.

"I've fed us both, now," said Dillon.

Deanna just looked at him, blankly.

"Haven't you figured it out yet?" he said. "You've got it as bad as I do—only with you it's not a wrecking-hunger; it's a terror-hunger."

Deanna just shook her head, not wanting to hear it, not wanting to think about it.

"It's true, Deanna; you need fear, the same way I need disaster—why do you think you feel better whenever you're around me? It's because you live on the terror I create—and when you can't live on other people's terror, you start feeding on your own."

Deanna closed her eyes and tried to deny it . . . but the more she thought about it, the more true it rang. Didn't she feel her strongest when those around her were in fear? Didn't she draw strength from other people's terror?

"You'll never feel fear again, Deanna," said Dillon, "as long as I can leave people terrified for you."

The streets around them still echoed with the wails of dozens of souls losing their minds to a nightmare.

"Now do you see why we have to be together?" asked Dillon with a tenderness that clashed with the violence on either side of them. "We're like thunder and lightning—you can't have one without the other. Destruction and fear."

He was right. He was right about everything, because every terrified wail seemed to feed something inside her. Was this who they were? Two hideously twisted creatures that lived like vampires, drinking up the misfortune of others? The very thought made her stomach turn.

This is not who I want to be!

She hid her face in shame and disgust.

Heat flashed as a fireball exploded somewhere down the street, and it was over. All that remained were the weak wails and moans, like the moment after a tumbling airplane came to rest. Survivors wandered the streets, some milling about aimlessly, others talking to themselves. The fine lattice of their minds had dissolved like sugar in water. Those who were dead were the lucky ones. The rest were irreconcilably insane.

My God, thought Deanna, *these people had put so much energy into creating their lives* . . . and now all that energy was being released as their lives detonated. That energy had to go somewhere . . . and that was the energy Dillon was feeding on!

She tried to shake the thought away. No! Human beings don't drink that kind of energy . . .

And for the first time, Deanna began to see that there might be something else living inside of Dillon—a creature that was anything but human. *"I have to feed it,"* Dillon often said. He even spoke about his hunger as if it were a living thing.

Was there something like that inside of her as well?

Only now did she begin to realize the dizzying depths of the pit they were falling into. The severity of their actions was beyond comprehension, and it made her wish she could tear off her body and slide into someone else's, just to be away from herself and this hideous destiny.

"You see there?" said Dillon, pointing down the street toward some homes that seemed just beyond the circle of destruction. "Those are the people I saved. I was actually able to save people! The hunger wanted them but I said no." He spoke with the blind innocence of a child and leapt from the tree, bouncing around in the midst of the disaster as if it were a playground. Stronger than ever before, he gazed past the Armageddon to the homes he had "saved."

"See, I kept my promise," he said, helping Deanna from the tree. "I didn't do any more than was absolutely necessary . . . and I did a good thing saving those people, didn't I?"

The thoughts were swimming in Deanna's head now. Nearly fifty people's lives were destroyed, but all Dillon was willing to see were the fifty whose lives weren't. Was this the best they could hope to do—damage control? Was that something to be proud of?

"See how I control it?" he said. "I don't give it any more than it needs—I leave it a little bit hungry—that's how I control it!"

And Deanna could see that Dillon believed this—he believed in his own ability to control this thing like a small child believed no one could see him when he closed his eyes.

Deanna shook her head to drive out Dillon's excuses and rationalizations, but couldn't.

"Deanna, c'mon—you're looking at me like you hate me or something. You don't hate me, do you? You promised you wouldn't."

Did she hate him? Did she find him beyond redemption? She instantly thought back to a python she once saw swallowing a live rabbit. It was awful to watch, but, after all, that's what pythons had to do. If this was how Dillon survived, could she blame him any more than she blamed that python? And wasn't she doing the exact same thing?

Deanna looked into his eyes, trying to find him there. There was intense darkness inside of him now, surrounding him, eating away at him like a vile parasite. So much of him had turned vile, it was hard to find any good left in him, but she continued to search until, through that blackness, she found the glimmer of light hidden deep within. It was that part of Dillon that was decent and kind—still fighting for life inside the blackness, like a star in the void of space. She focused on that shrinking light within Dillon, and to it she said, "I love you."

Dillon smiled, a tear in his eye. "Me too," he said. He touched Deanna's cheek, gently held her around the waist, and set the pace as they strode off of Blackburn Street, even before the first police car arrived. As they walked, Deanna forced her own will deep into Dillon's back pocket, but this time it didn't slip in as easily as it had before.

I LOVE YOU. DILLON let her words echo from one side of his mind to the other. He drew strength from it, and, in a matter of moments, he had successfully forced the evening's unpleasantness out of his mind. These people here—they didn't matter. They weren't real the way he and Deanna were real. The wrecking-hunger told him so.

Dillon's spirits were high as he left town. The night was refreshingly cool, and he felt he could walk all night. He didn't need sleep anymore. Come to think of it, he didn't need food. He had already gorged himself on the fall of Blackburn Street, and it would be at least another day before he felt the hunger again.

He wondered what he would have to do next to satisfy the hunger. Surely it would be an even greater challenge—for each challenge was greater than the one before.

In the back of his mind he idly imagined an endless cascade of dominoes all lined up and ready to fall if the right one were pushed. The thought was enough to make him giggle like a child.

Part IV
Demolition Day
11. BIG BANG

AT 4:30 A.M., MOUNTAIN TIME, LOURDES HIDALGO DECIDED it was time to die.

It had been two days since that night in the ice storm. With little money, and even less time to spare, the four had searched for a trail—any sign of the missing two. Nothing turned up along I-80, and nothing in Big Springs, but in Torrington, Wyoming, they found a newspaper article that led them to a devastated farm. It reeked of something unnatural.

Once they found the farm, they knew they were on the right track, because the presence of the fifth and sixth shards was as strong as a scent on the wind. What they had feared was now confirmed; those other two had lost control and had set off on a mad rampage to feed the parasites that were strangling their souls. Intuition told them that number five was the dangerous one and that number six probably fed on the aftermath of destruction like a vulture fed on a lion's kill.

After that, following their trail was like following the ashen trail of a burning fuse. News reports had led them to the ruined neighborhood in Idaho Falls, which seemed ten times worse than what they found at the farm. They were only a day behind as they headed deeper into Idaho, terrified of what they would find next.

They rested in Boise, finding a cheap hotel for the night. It had been a major effort for Lourdes to haul herself out of the van this time, and each footstep felt like it would be her last.

Like everywhere their journey took them, this hotel was right in the armpit of town, where old decrepit buildings loomed ripe for the wrecking ball.

Lourdes could see one such building from the hotel window, across the expanse of a vacant lot: a concrete warehouse seven stories tall, with slits for windows and a big faded sign painted on the side that said "Dakins Worldwide Storage." The building's few entrances were boarded over, and the abandoned property was fenced in. Apparently Dakins had found better worldwide storage elsewhere.

While the others slept, Lourdes kept a vigil and watched that solitary, lonely building, feeling a strange affinity for it as she pondered the short time remaining to her own life. Few buildings on earth could be as unloved as this one.

In the days since they had banded together, they had witnessed wonders and had watched each other deteriorate. Winston's dignity was the first casualty, for his body had grown so small he couldn't see out of the van's windows when he sat, and he had to eat soft food because all his teeth were receding. Tory, who had been a driving force all along, was slowing down, as her disease turned inward, swelling her joints with painful arthritis . . . and Michael . . . well, rather than allowing his passion to wreak havoc on the soul of every girl he encountered, Michael had turned his mind to a dark lonely place within himself and seldom came out. Brooding and silent, with dark, wan eyes, he looked like he was dying of cancer.

As for Lourdes, there were no mirrors large enough to present her full image. She could feel the weight on her bones growing, building density, like ice on the branches of a tree.

She could feel her heart pounding in her chest, fighting to force blood through clogged arteries. She could feel her bloated self, ready to burst through the shell that contained her, and knew that it could happen at any moment.

So she stayed awake . . . and at 4:30 a.m. one of the many seams on her blouse tore so violently that the blouse itself literally burst in two.

That's when Lourdes decided that it was time to call it quits.

Outside, the rain had let up a bit, and Lourdes could see the warehouse more clearly. There were people milling about the building, and it seemed odd to Lourdes that such a lonely place would be the center of anyone else's attention but hers, so she watched and wondered. In a few moments, things became very clear to her, and she knew exactly what she was going to do.

"MICHAEL, WINSTON, WAKE UP!" Tory shook them both, dragging them out of a deep sleep. "It's Lourdes! She's gone!"

Wearily, the three searched the room and the hallway. Tory looked in the closet. The others looked under the beds—as if Lourdes could possibly fit in any of those places.

That's when Michael happened to glance out the window. Dawn was beginning to break on the distant horizon, and in the faint half-light he could see a huge shape lumbering through a vacant lot toward an old Dakins warehouse a block away.

"Look," he said. "There she is!"

THE FRONT OF THE old warehouse was teeming with activity, but Lourdes approached from the rear and no one saw her. She smiled as she approached. All this time the four of them had been running, unsure of their destination. It was nice, for once, to have a destination.

Her momentum took her through the fence that surrounded the property as if it were paper, and she pushed on through the police line, tearing the ribbon as if it were a finish line. She leaned against the boarded-over door, and her sheer weight forced the door inward, leading her into a dark cavernous space where her labored breathing echoed from distant concrete walls. To the right was a flight of stairs and, without pausing for further thought, she began to heave herself step by step toward the upper floors of the desolate building.

ACTIVITY WAS GROWING AT the front of the warehouse as the three kids followed Lourdes in through the back door.

Once inside they paused to listed and heard the heavy footsteps of Lourdes straining on stairs high above.

"What she gonna do? Climb out on the roof and jump?" said Winston, trying to catch his breath.

The very thought made Michael turn and bound up the stairs as fast as his legs could carry him.

Tory took a moment to look down at her hands. Her knuckles were swollen and they cracked when she bent them. It made her so angry that she squeezed them in a fist, but that only hurt more. She turned to Winston, who was still catching his breath. "Did you ever think you'd be chasing someone through a warehouse at the crack of dawn?" she asked.

"No," said Winston, in a voice that was higher pitched than the day before. "But then I never thought I'd be five years old again either."

It was as they turned to go upstairs that Tory glanced at the great cavern around her. The tiny slits of windows were mostly boarded over, and in the dim half-light, she could see a series of pillars stretching down the empty warehouse, holding up the floors above. There were bulges near the top of a good dozen of those pillars; bulges like tumors growing out of the concrete. And each of those bulges had a tiny, blinking light.

Tory grabbed Winston's arm, and yanked him around. "Winston, tell me you don't see what I see . . ." This time when they looked, not only were the tumors visible on the concrete, but so were the wires. They draped from the dark tumors, snaked across the floor, and all came together in a bundle that made a determined path out the front door.

It didn't take a genius to figure out that the tumors were explosives.

MICHAEL REACHED THE SEVENTH and final floor of the ware-house, before the others had even begun to climb.

"Lourdes?"

She stood at the far end of the vast empty loft. She wobbled a bit and finally collapsed under her own enormous weight. As she hit the ground, the concrete echoed with a boom like the slamming of a heavy vault door, and the dust burst out from beneath her like her very soul dispersing. She didn't move.

Michael, afraid to say anything, for fear that she wouldn't answer, approached with caution, and to his great relief saw that she was still alive.

"You okay?" asked Michael.

"Go away." Lourdes made a mighty effort to turn her head, so Michael could not see her tears. In all the time he had known her, Michael had never seen Lourdes cry like this. She had stoically borne all her hardship with a stiff—if somewhat fat—upper lip, but not now.

Michael sat beside her and wiped the tears away.

"I feel like a beached whale," she said.

"Well," said Michael, "the Pacific Ocean's only three hundred miles away . . ."

Lourdes laughed in spite of herself.

"When I die," she said, "I'm gonna sit on God until he yells uncle." They both laughed again, then a silence fell between them.

"Why did he do this to us, Michael?"

Michael shrugged and thought for a moment. "He didn't *do* it to us, he just didn't stop it."

"That's just as bad," said Lourdes.

Michael lifted her heavy head and began to gently stroke her hair. "Maybe he's a clutch player," said Michael. "And he's just waiting for the right time to make a move."

Winston and Tory finally made it to the top floor.

"We gotta get outta here now!" shouted Winston as he ran with Tory from the stairs. "This building's condemned and it's coming down today. They've already rigged the explosives."

"I know," said Lourdes.

That caught everyone off guard.

Lourdes gritted her teeth and closed her eyes to keep herself from crying. "Maybe the three of you have some time left, but not me. If I have to die today, then I want to go out with a big bang, not a whimper."

"We won't let you do this," said Tory. "Can't you feel how close The Others are? . . . If we just hold on a little longer . . ."

"I don't feel anything anymore," said Lourdes. "All I feel is fat, and I'm tired of feeling it."

Outside there were shouts from the demolition crew.

"That's it!" shouted Winston, the preschooler on the verge of a tantrum. "I don't care how lousy you feel! Get your ass down those stairs!" His voice slipped deeper into his Alabama drawl, which always grew stronger when he got angry.

"I can't," said Lourdes. "I can't move anymore. At all."

They all looked at her there, straining to breathe as she lay on the ground. Winston panicked and rammed into her with what little weight he had. "C'mon, help me!" They all took to pushing against Lourdes, but she wouldn't budge.

"Grab her arms," suggested Tory. They grabbed her arms and legs to pull her, but nothing helped.

"Just go!" shouted Lourdes, through her thick throat. "It's better if you just go!"

They let go of her arms and legs, and just stood there, unable to help her . . . and in that moment of silence Michael made a decision.

"I'm not leaving you," he said, and he sat down next to her.

Winston stared at him incredulously. "You're just gonna sit here and let yourself get blown to smithereens?"

"Face it," said Michael. "None of us has much time left. A day or two at the most . . ."

Tory, grimacing in pain, looked at her swollen knuckles, then at her swollen knees. "Michael's right. We haven't had control over anything for the longest time. . . . Maybe here's something we can control . . ."

Winston turned to her, his eyes filled with terror. "No!"

"If I gotta die," said Tory, "then I want to die with dignity,"

Winston threw up his hands. "I can't believe this! You said it yourself, Tory, The Others are close now—we can find them—we can stop them . . ."

"We lost, Winston," said Michael. "We fought hard, but we lost."

"No!" shouted Winston defiantly. "With our luck, instead of dying proper, our souls'll get blown up again into a thousand cockroaches or something. No! If I gotta die, I ain't going out in flaming glory—I'm going the way I was meant to go!"

Winston grew red in the face as he looked at them. He threw himself on the ground kicking and screaming in a full-fledged tantrum, then finally gave up on his companions. "Fine," he said, tears swelling in his eyes. "We started this together, but if I have to finish it alone, then I will." Then Winston, all three feet of him, stormed across the dusty floor and disappeared down the stairwell.

When he was gone, Michael turned to Tory. "When we die," said Michael, "you think those . . . those awful things will die with us?"

"That's what I'm counting on," said Tory.

Lourdes, without the strength to move her lips anymore, could only rasp her breath in and out.

They held hands, now just a circle of three. "I'm glad," whispered Tory. "I'm glad we all found each other. No matter what, I'll never regret that."

Outside the rain had stopped, the wind had stopped, and the black clouds above waited with guarded anticipation. Far away lightning struck, and every distant rumble echoed within the warehouse, shaking the walls and reminding them of the great thunder that would soon tear out the foundation of their lives. With every rumble, concrete flakes skittered to the ground, like the footfalls of a thousand cockroaches.

WINSTON, WITH THE PHYSIOLOGY of a five-year-old, found his days swinging back and forth between complete exhaustion and uncontrollable energy. Had he been exhausted when they asked him to stay, he might have just curled up, thumb in mouth, and fallen asleep before the big blast came—but Winston was feeling very much alive and did not intend to go quietly. Today was a day to live.

As he leapt down the stairs two at a time, he had to keep reminding himself that he hadn't abandoned the other three. They, in fact, had abandoned him. They had given up. Now he would be alone. He would chase the tail of the other two shards until he could no longer walk, until he could no longer crawl. When his body had withered itself out of existence, he would die knowing he fought to the end. *That* was dying with dignity, not being buried beneath ten tons of shattered concrete.

Winston bounded down the stairs to the first level and was surprised to see, just twenty yards away, a worker in a hard hat, facing away from him. Winston could see he was double-checking the wires, and the realization that there were still a few minutes till the building blew made him reconsider his options.

There was time to save the others! Even if they didn't want to be saved, he could save them. He would run up to the man in the hard hat, he would tell him of the others still upstairs, he would ruin their awful plan.

Winston took a few steps closer, about to shout out, when suddenly a second figure that had been eclipsed from Winston's sight came into view. It was a boy—no older than fifteen, and he was staring straight at the worker. The boy had red hair.

Immediately Winston felt a rush of dizziness that took the wind right out of his lungs. This was wrong. This was very wrong. He ducked behind a pillar and watched.

The worker was frozen, his flashlight at his side, casting a light on the dusty floor. The boy with red hair seemed anxious and sweaty, and very, very intense.

"You've placed the explosives wrong," suggested the boy to the man in the hard hat. *"You should do something about it."*

The worker just stared at him. "Okay," he said dreamily and strolled off into the shadows.

Winston gasped, and the red-haired boy snapped his eyes to Winston.

The second their eyes met, Winston knew *exactly* who this was.

He was the fifth shard.

Winston couldn't break eye contact with the redheaded boy. His gaze riveted Winston to the ground. If there were indeed six shards, then this boy had inherited the largest, most powerful one, and in its shadow had grown the worst parasite. Winston knew he was no match for the force behind those eyes.

The redheaded boy stood stunned by the sight of Winston— but only for a moment. Then he turned and disappeared down a hole in the concrete floor.

Once he was gone, a hundred thoughts flew through Winston's mind fighting for purchase. *Run for your life! No—follow him! No—break the worker out of his trance!* But the one thought that overrode them all was the urge to race back upstairs and tell the others!

He bounded up the stairs, racing past the demolition man, who mindlessly whistled a Beatles tune as he moved a pack of explosives from one end of the building to the other.

ON THE SEVENTH FLOOR, Lourdes, Michael, and Tory waited in silence. They could hear the sounds of morning in full swing. Car horns, diesel engines. The occasional shouts of the demolition workers as they diligently prepared for the morning's spectacle.

Then they heard footsteps racing up the stairs and knew by their lightness that it had to be Winston. He had changed his mind. In the end they would be together. As it was meant to be.

Winston burst through the stairwell.

"We've got to get out of here!" he shouted.

"Winston . . . ," said Michael. "We've made up our minds . . ."

"We're not leaving Lourdes . . . ," said Tory.

"No! You don't understand!" He grabbed Tory by her plagued arms and looked into her eyes. "Tory, you were right! You've been right all along—*The Others are here!*"

Realization slowly dawned in Tory's eyes.

"What?"

But the only answer was a blast louder than thunder that shook the world and sent pulverized concrete dust flying into their faces.

Seven floors below, the foundation of the old Dakins warehouse blew apart, and the building began its freefall journey to the earth.

THE CHINESE TONGS THAT had built the impossible maze of tunnels beneath Boise were long dead, and the opium dens those tunnels once connected were gone and forgotten. Now, more than a hundred years later, Dillon and Deanna traveled those lost passages. Dillon should have found the pattern of twisting, intersecting tunnels easy to figure out, but as he raced wildly to reach Deanna, he found himself lost. He had never been lost before, but what had happened in that old warehouse had thrown him for such a loop, he wasn't thinking straight.

They were here.

The Others.

Somehow they had found him, and he was convinced that they were here to kill him.

At last, down the long dim underground corridor, Dillon saw Deanna, just as the blast went off somewhere above their heads. The explosion was so loud, it sent pain shooting through his ears, and the rumble that followed rattled his teeth. He fell into a puddle of stagnant muck, while behind him concrete dust shot through the tunnel like steam through a pipe.

Then, through the dust blasting into his face, Dillon saw and heard hideous things. Sinewy gray tentacles reaching for him through the dust cloud—blue flaming hands around his neck, sharp claws digging into his chest, fangs, and eyes—so many angry eyes!

It must be my imagination, he thought in a panic. *It can't be real,* yet even so, he felt a tentacle wrap itself around his ankle and dig in. Dillon clawed at the ground to get away, he gripped a stone in the wall, but something stung his hand.

Choking from the concrete dust filling his lungs, Dillon could swear he felt hot breath on his face and heard a sound in his mind louder than the collapsing building.

Knocking.

Many hands knocking on a door—a furious horde demanding to be let in. *Anything!* thought Dillon. *Anything to stop that horrible knocking in his brain.* He opened his mind as easily as opening a door, and the creatures were gone, leaving only the blinding dust in his eyes.

As the dust around him began to settle, Deanna appeared in front of him.

"Dillon! What's happening?" she asked desperately.

Dillon coughed out another lungful of dust. And forced himself not to think about the monster-hallucination. Instead he let himself feel the wrecking-hunger feed on the collapse of the Dakins building. But that was only a first course.

"Listen," said Dillon. "Listen, it's wonderful!" The relief filling him soon grew into joy, and then ecstasy.

The first building had come down far above them, but the

roaring had not stopped. From the right came another rumble, just as loud as the first, and then another, further away, and then another until they couldn't tell where one ended and the next began.

Deanna sank to the ground, shivering as if it were the end of the world. "It's like a war out there," said Deanna.

Dillon beamed a smile far too wide. "Oh, it's much better than that!"

His dim flashlight went out, but that was all right. Dillon didn't want Deanna looking at him right now, because something was beginning to happen to him. He was beginning to change; he could feel it all over.

Dillon closed his eyes, imagining the beast he had learned to ride so well . . . only now when he tried to picture it, he saw a whole team of beasts instead: a wave of dark horses teamed together by a single yoke carrying him along at a breakneck pace.

There in the dark, his flat stomach began to slowly swell, and his many freckles began to bulge into a swarm of angry zits.

IN THE DIM LIGHT of this awful morning, the foreman of the demolition crew could do nothing but watch as his well-orchestrated detonation became a nightmare.

It should not have happened. The way the explosives had been set, the building should have come straight down . . . but it didn't. Instead the entire building keeled over backward and landed on Jefferson Place—an office building across the street that had been evacuated as a precaution. The old office building shifted violently on its foundation, and keeled over to the left . . .

. . . Where stood the Hoff Building—a city landmark.

No one had thought it necessary to evacuate that one.

The Hoff Building took the blow, and for a moment it looked as if it was only going to lose its eastern face. But then it, too, began a slow topple to the left, its domed tower crashing into the Old Boise Post Office.

Dominoes, thought the foreman. *They're going down like dominoes.* It was impossible; it would take a pattern of incredible coincidences for each building to hit the one beside it with just the right force to bring it down as well . . . but the evidence was here before their eyes.

Debris struck the capitol building, which seemed to be all right . . . until the pillars holding up its heavy dome buckled and the dome crashed down and disappeared into the building, hitting bottom with such force that all the windows shattered.

And it was over.

Seven buildings had been demolished.

Beside the foreman, his explosives expert just stood there, rocking back and forth, and happily whistling "Twist and Shout." Another crew member was screaming at the top of his lungs.

They're insane! thought the foreman. *They've completely lost their minds.* And finally, the combination of everything around him was exactly enough to make the foreman snap as well. As he felt his own mind slipping down a well of eternal madness, he realized that the destruction he had just witnessed was somehow not over yet. In fact, it was just beginning. In a moment he started laughing hysterically. And he never stopped.

MICHAEL LIPRANSKI NOW UNDERSTOOD death. It was blind, cold, and dusty. It was filled with a loud ringing in one's ears that didn't go away. Death was oppressive and choking.

These were the thoughts Michael was left with after having died. There were, of course, many questions to come, but the one question that was foremost in his mind was this: Why, if he was dead, did he still feel like coughing?

Michael let out a roaring hacking cough and cleared concrete dust from his lungs. He opened his eyes. They stung, but he forced them open anyway. Around him were three other ghosts . . . or at least they looked like ghosts. They all began to stir, and as they sat up, a heavy layer of white dust fell from them.

"What happened?" asked Winston.

And as they looked around, the answer became clear. They were still on the seventh floor . . . or at least what was left of it. Just a corner really. The rest of the building was gone. So were quite a few other around it. It looked as if downtown Boise had been hit by a small nuclear bomb.

"He did this," said Winston.

"He, who?"

"The Other One . . . the fifth one. I told you I saw him!"

"He saved our lives?" asked Tory.

"I don't think he meant to," said Winston.

They looked out at the devastation once more. Lourdes, her death-wish forgotten, stood and walked to the jagged edge where the seventh floor gave way to open air. The rest of the building had shorn away and had turned to rubble. Had they been anywhere else on that floor, they would have been part of the rubble . . . but they weren't anywhere else, they were right here . . . and Lourdes began to wonder idly what sort of intuition had made her collapse in the north corner rather than the south corner, or was luck so incredibly dumb that it didn't even know an easy target?

Tory looked stunned. "I guess it takes more than a few thousand pounds of explosives to get rid of us."

"Lourdes, you're standing!" Michael approached Lourdes

at the jagged edge of the concrete floor. Indeed, she had found the strength to lift her weight again . . . or was there less weight to lift? "Is it my imagination . . . or do you have one less chin?"

The others came closer. The change was almost imperceptible . . . but the others were able to notice.

Tory looked at her hand and flexed her fingers. Her skin was still as awful as before, but the swelling that had come to her joints was fading. Tears came to her eyes, and the salty tears didn't even sting, for her sores were slowly beginning to close.

They looked at each other, afraid to say what they now knew, for fear that speaking it would somehow jinx it. Finally Tory dared to utter the words.

"They're gone . . . ," she whispered. It took a few moments for it to finally hit home. Then, in the midst of the devastation Tory's voice rang out from the top floor of the ruined Dakins building, a clear note of joy in the midst of sorrow.

"We're free!"

THE JAGGED BROKEN WALL provided them with a treacherous path down to the rubble below.

There was chaos around the scene, but not the chaos one might expect. People screaming, crying, wandering like zombies—it was as if the shock wave of this event had driven everyone around it completely insane.

Winston looked around him and fumed. The redheaded boy had created this wave of destruction. The physical wasn't enough for him—he had to destroy the minds of the survivors. It made Winston furious . . . furious at himself for having seen him and not trying to stop him! Not even the knowledge that his own parasite was gone could calm his fury.

Winston approached a policeman sitting on a fire hydrant.

He was staring into the barrel of his own gun with a blank expression. When he saw Winston, he turned to him, pleading.

"Am I in trouble?" asked the officer. "Am I gonna get a whooping?"

Winston reached out and gently pulled the revolver out of the man's hands. The officer buried his head in his hands and cried.

"How did he do this?" asked Winston, as they stumbled their way through the nightmare of insanity.

"How?" said Tory. "How many thousands of people could you have paralyzed if you wanted to? How many plague epidemics could I have started? The only difference between him and us," she said, "is that *we* didn't want to."

About three blocks away from the wreckage, sanity seemed intact. People gawked and chattered and paced, but not with the same mindless chaos that surrounded the site of destruction.

As they left the insanity circle, it was Lourdes who took a moment to look back. In the midst of the rubble, the only thing left standing was the seven-story sliver that had been the corner of the Dakins storage building.

"Clutch player?" Michael suggested with a grin.

"Maybe," said Lourdes. "I was thinking that it looks like a tower. A tower that was struck by lightning."

As the sound of approaching sirens filled the air, Tory turned to the others. "I don't think those *things* died," she told them. "I mean if we're alive, then they're probably alive, too. I think they bailed because they thought they were going to get blown up. The explosion scared them out . . . but that doesn't mean they're gone for good."

Tory touched her face, to make certain that the pain there

was still slipping away. "We still may have to fight those things," she said. "But maybe when the six of us are together—"

"When the six of us are together," said Winston, feeling the weight of the revolver in his pocket, "I'm gonna send that redheaded son-of-a-bitch where he belongs."

12. SHROUD OF DARKNESS

AT THE EDGE OF THE WRECKAGE, A MAN WITH NO MIND stumbled away from his Range Rover. It was just one of many cars left idling in the middle of the road. Deanna and Dillon used it as their ticket out of Boise, and in a moment they were careening wildly northwest.

Deanna, who had never been behind the wheel of a car before, gripped the wheel and taught herself to drive at ninety miles an hour on the straightaway of I-84.

"How many people died?" she demanded. She would not turn her eyes from the road, but out of the corner of her eye she could see Dillon sitting beside her. He seemed completely absorbed in his map, pretending not to hear her.

"How many?" she demanded again.

"I don't know," said Dillon. "I can't tell things *that* exactly. Anyway, what's done is done," he said, and spoke no more of it.

Things were changing far too quickly for Deanna to keep up. What had begun for both of them as a cleansing journey, filled with the hope of redemption, had become nothing more than a mad rampage with no end in sight. It made her want to get out and run . . . if only she could bear the fear of being on her own. Stepping out of that car and leaving Dillon would have been like stepping out of an airlock into space. She needed him, and she hated that.

She glanced at Dillon as he pored over the Triple-A map. He tossed it behind him and pulled another from the glove compartment.

"I won't keep running like this," said Deanna.

"We're not running, we're going somewhere," he finally admitted.

"Where?"

"I don't know yet . . . ," he snapped; then said a bit more gently, "I'll tell you as soon as I know, I promise."

"We were wrong," said Deanna. "We should find The Others—"

"The Others are dead," he said.

Deanna knew this was a lie. It was the first outright lie he had ever told her.

The road ahead of them was straight and clear, and Deanna dared to take a long look at Dillon. He had changed since she had first seen him in that hospital room. There he had been a tormented but courageous boy who had whisked her from her hospital bed. He had been a valiant, if somewhat disturbed, knight in shining armor. But now his courage had turned rancid. There was no armor, just an aura of darkness flowing around him like a black shroud—as if his body could no longer contain the blackness it held.

It was more than that, though—his body was changing as well. Had he gained weight? Yes, his slender figure had begun to bloat. She could see it in his face and hands—in his fingers, beginning to turn round and porcine. His skin, too, had changed. It began to take on an oily redness marked with whiteheads that were appearing one after another. *He's beginning to look on the outside what he's becoming on the inside,* Deanna thought, and shivered.

"Damn it!" said Dillon, hurling the map behind him. "I need more maps! These don't tell me what I need to know!" He took a deep breath to calm himself, then rubbed his eyes and said, "There's a town—when we get to the Columbia River—a good-sized population."

"Why does the population matter?" Deanna couldn't hide the apprehension in her voice.

"Because it means they'll have a decent library," Dillon answered. "And a decent library will have a decent almanac, and an atlas. A world atlas."

"And?"

Dillon rolled his eyes impatiently as if it were obvious. "And when I see what I have to see, I'll know where we have to go."

She heard him take another deep, relaxing breath, then he gently put his hand on her neck. It felt clammy and uncomfortable. She could feel that aura of darkness. How revolting it felt.

"It's okay," he told her. "Everything's gonna be great."

This too was a lie, but she knew that Dillon believed this one.

"When we get where we're going," Deanna asked, "is this all going to be over? Will it end?"

Dillon nodded. "Yes," he said. "Once we get there . . . everything will end."

BURTON, OREGON. POPULATION 3,255. In the center of town, a harvest festival sent bluegrass music wafting toward Main Street, where all was quiet. The library was empty today, except for Dillon and Deanna.

Dillon piled the large wooden reference table with volume after volume of atlases and almanacs. The librarian was delighted to see a young man so involved in his studies. Deanna, as curious as she was unsettled, helped him pull down heavy volumes describing the people and places of the world. First he stared at the maps—the way roads connected and wound from city to city, state to state, nation to nation. Then he looked at numbers—endless lists of numbers, graphs, and charts. Populations—demographics; people grouped in whatever ways the researchers could find to group them; by race or religion; by economics; by profession; by politics; by every imaginable variable.

"What are you looking for?" Deanna asked. But Dillon was so engrossed in his numbers he didn't even hear her. He was like a computer, taking in thousands of digits, and processing them through some inner program.

Then, one by one Dillon closed the books. The atlas of Europe, and of Asia. The books on Australia and South America. The studies of Africa, the American Almanac... until he was left with the map of the northwestern United States. He stared at the map, drawing his eyes further and further northwest, his finger following the tiny capillaries of country roads until he stopped. Dillon's master equation had finally spit out an answer.

"There."

His finger landed in the southwest corner of Washington state. "This is where we have to go."

"What will we find there?" asked Deanna.

"Someone."

"Someone we know?"

Dillon shook his head. "Someone we *will* know. Someone important."

They left, not bothering to shelve the books.

THEIR COURSE OUT OF town took them right past the harvest festival. They had no intention of stopping, but the Rover needed gas. The gas station was right across the road from the festival, where most everyone in Burton was spending this fine day.

Dillon, who was driving now, got out to pump, while Deanna scrounged around the messy car, finding dollar bills

and loose change to pay for the gas. It was when she looked out
of the window at Dillon that she knew something was wrong.
The old-fashioned mechanical pump clanged out gallons and
racked up dollars, but Dillon wasn't watching that. Instead, he
was looking at the pump just ahead of them, where a tattooed,
beer-bellied man stood pumping up his run-down Trans Am.
His equally unattractive wife stood beside him.

It seemed that Dillon had caught the wife's attention, and she
was staring at him in a trance. Dillon stared right back. Then
this woman in high heels and decade-old tight pants stepped
over the gas hose and began to approach Dillon, but her husband, sensing something out of the ordinary, held her back.

He scowled at Dillon. "Got a problem?"

Dillon looked away, shook it off, and the episode was over
. . . but it lingered in Deanna's mind. There were many strange
twists and turns on the roller coaster the two of them had been
on, but in some way those other turns were consistent. This
seemed to take the coaster wholly off its track. She turned to
Dillon again and noticed the beads of sweat beginning to form
on his forehead. She knew what that meant, and she began to
panic. What happened in Boise should have satisfied his rapa-
cious hunger for a good while. She knew she had to get him out
of town, so she quickly paid the attendant in crumpled bills and
loose change—but when she turned, Dillon had already disappeared into the crowds of the fair.

It was twilight now. The lights had come up on the Ferris
wheel, and the Tilt-a-Whirl spun its merry victims past one
another in flashes of neon blue and red.

Deanna searched everywhere for Dillon, in every dark
corner, in every crowd, but he seemed to have completely dissolved into the mob.

Finally she spotted him on the midway. He was walking . . . no, wandering, down the hay-strewn path with the aimlessness of a zombie. He was drenched in sweat.

Deanna ran toward him, but stopped when she saw him once more lock eyes with another girl, just as he had with the woman at the gas station. This one was sixteen—maybe seventeen. She ate cotton candy and watched her muscle-bound boyfriend launch rubber frogs into the air with a sledgehammer, trying to win her a prize. The boyfriend grunted as he swung the hammer and didn't seem to notice as the girl dropped her cotton candy, crossed the midway to Dillon, and then, for no apparent reason, leaned forward . . . and kissed him.

Deanna just stood there gawking.

Clearly this girl had never met Dillon before . . . and here she was launching herself into his arms with the same passion that her boyfriend launched his rubber frogs.

Deanna watched as Dillon brought up his arms and pulled this girl closer, kissing her in a powerful way—a way in which he had never kissed Deanna. It was not an embrace of love, or even lust—it was passion turned rancid. It was everything that a kiss should not be.

But it wasn't a kiss, was it? It was more like a bite.

The girl's arms turned white from the tightness of Dillon's grip, and she gave in to his embrace completely. Deanna's mind swarmed with powerful, conflicting emotions—jealousy not the least of them.

Although she never wanted him to steal this kind of kiss from her, she didn't want to see him steal it from anyone else, either.

How could a kiss be so evil—and what had possessed the girl to step into it? It couldn't have been Dillon's looks—not anymore. What once had been an attractive face was now puffy and infected. His dark eyes had become an icy, unnatural turquoise.

Here he was kissing another girl—right there in front of her, and he didn't even care! The sense of betrayal was unbearable.

Dillon squeezed the girl against him, and Deanna could see his dark aura stretch around her—then Deanna saw—no—she *felt* something invisible pass from the girl to Dillon.

The boyfriend, who had just won a pink dinosaur, turned and gawked with blinking idiocy at his girlfriend, kissing this sick-looking kid.

"What the hell is this?" he said.

At last Dillon moved his lips away from the girl's, and she looked into his eyes. This time his touch had not scrambled her thoughts.

The boyfriend stepped in and delivered a right hook that sent Dillon's head snapping to the left. Dillon recovered quickly . . . but not the boyfriend. He gasped and looked at his hand, where it had touched Dillon's chin. His knuckles were locked. Not just that, but his whole forearm was locked in a muscle spasm that caused his sinews to bulge like ropes from his elbow to his wrist.

The boyfriend stumbled away, forgetting the girl, staring at his paralyzed arm. As for the girl, she just wandered off wide-eyed, and Deanna sensed that something had been stolen from her—something very important that she would never get back.

Dillon just grinned dumbly.

"Why did you do that?" Deanna demanded, overwhelmed with disgust.

"I don't know . . ."

"You really enjoyed it, didn't you?"

"Yes . . . no . . . I don't know." He put his hand to his temples, as if keeping his head from blowing apart. "Deanna, what's happening to me?"

She had no sympathy for him now as she locked eyes with his, and scrutinized him.

"Deanna, don't look at me like that . . ."

Deanna peered deep into his eyes, searching as she always did . . . seeking the glimmer in the darkness. She looked long and hard, through the rank and fetid decay that encased his body and soul . . . and finally Deanna realized that the light in him was gone. The part of Dillon that had shone so brightly in his darkness all this time had been wrapped in so many shrouds of evil that she could not find him anymore.

The moment she realized that, was the moment she knew she had to run—to get as far away as she possibly could. She instantly turned without pause for another thought and abandoned the shell that had once been Dillon Cole, racing into the crowds—but Dillon desperately pursued.

"Deanna!" he screamed. "Don't go!"

She couldn't stop herself from glancing back as he chased her, and what she saw made her run even faster.

Dillon was pushing through the crowds just as she was, and everyone he touched fell from him with hideous afflictions. Some collapsed in paralysis, others lost their minds, others seemed to deflate as if their chests had been crushed inward, and still others turned red and diseased. "Deanna!" he screamed, not even noticing the people he had destroyed.

She broke free of the crowd and scrambled away from the fair, to the top of the hill.

"Deanna, come back!"

When she reached the top of the hill, she dared to look back once more. Dillon was still standing there at the edge of the crowd. He stared at her a moment more . . . and finally with a scowl on his face, he turned and defiantly grabbed the first girl in sight. She came to him like he was a gift from heaven, and he kissed her, stealing her soul away with his kiss. Then he turned and headed back into the crowd.

From the top of the hill, Deanna watched him go, the living darkness now cloaked around him and trailing behind him. He stalked his way to the center of the crowd around the bluegrass band. He looked left, then right, until he finally found The Right Person—a matronly woman clapping her hands happily to the beat. Then Dillon whispered something into her ear.

And the crowd detonated.

From where Deanna stood, she could see how it happened. It began with people becoming irritated, then irritation built into anger, anger into fury, fury into rage, until the entire crowd thrashed in a chaotic screaming tarantella—a dance of destruction, wild and insane, spreading outward like a shock wave. The music stopped and was replaced by wails of anguish and pain. In five minutes the townsfolk had turned into chaotic, murderous fiends, their sanity wiped from their minds by Dillon the destroyer.

Deanna turned and ran, screaming, into the woods.

WOODS ARE A RIPE place for fears, and Deanna's were thriving on the branches and shadows that surrounded her. She had refused to feed on the terror Dillon had unleashed, so now every shape was a threatening demon, every shadow a portent of pain. She stumbled over and over as she raced through the lonely woods, not knowing where she would go.

At last she came to a road and tumbled to the gravel, skinning her knees through her jeans. She sat up on the empty asphalt, breathless, her voice ruined from all her screaming.

Finally a pickup truck swerved to stop in front of her.

A man got out—a middle-aged, family-looking man. There was a boy in the back of the pickup, all dressed up in an Indian outfit.

It seemed normal, and Deanna just wanted to dissolve into this man and his family, forgetting who she was and what was happening.

"I have to get out here," Deanna rasped. "So do you! You have to get away from this town!"

"Now hold on, there," said the man warmly. "Let's just calm down." He looked her over as he stepped from the cab of his pickup. "You've had some fright," he said. "I know just the thing for you."

"Please," begged Deanna, "you don't understand . . ."

"Now just wait a second," he said, with a calm and soothing voice. "I'll be right back." He reached into the back of his pickup and grabbed something, then turned back toward her, revealing what he held. It was a piece of a white picket fence, broken so that the white wood came to a sharp point.

And then Deanna noticed the man's eyes. One pupil was closed down completely, the other wide and wild. This man had already been to the fair.

"We'll take care of you," said the man. "Fix you up real good."

Deanna could now see that the tip of the picket was already covered with blood.

In the pickup, the boy mindlessly sang a single line from a nursery rhyme over and over like a broken record, lazily rolling his head from side to side, as he watched his father throw Deanna to the ground.

"This won't hurt but a bit," the madman said as he raised the picket above his head and pointed it at Deanna's heart.

Deanna would have screamed if she still had a voice.

13. TURNING NORMAL

TUFTS OF WHITE SPECKLED A RICH BLUE SKY ON THE IDAHO–Oregon border. It was a weak legion of clouds that could not even block out the sun.

Michael could not remember blue sky; there were always clouds and storms tormenting the heavens, and when the storms slept, there was always a rumbling fog keeping the sky an everlasting gray.

But not today.

Michael lay on a brushy hillside staring up at the glorious sky. Beneath them lay Huntington, Oregon. They were barely a hundred miles out of Boise, but to Michael, what they left behind in Boise was a million miles away.

"What do they look like?"

Michael turned to see Tory come up beside him.

"That's what you're doing, isn't it? Looking for shapes in the clouds?"

"I was just looking." Michael sat up and glanced down the hill, where the town spread out before them. Changing leaves glimmered in afternoon sunlight turning the town to gold. The air was neither hot nor cold, but temperate. Nice. Normal.

They had spent an entire day and night in and around Boise, spiraling outward from the epicenter of Chaos, searching for *The Others*, or, more specifically, the redheaded boy who was at the core of the nightmare. But they had also wasted time as they reveled in this new feeling of freedom now that the beasts were gone. It had taken until the next morning for them to feel the slightest pull northwest, and they realized he had left town long ago.

Now they had driven into Oregon and, somewhere in the town below, a tireless Winston was searching for signs of ruin, but he was the only one. Here on the hill, Lourdes lay on her back, asleep, with every exhalation breathing out another ounce of fat, and he and Tory just looked at the clouds.

Michael glanced at Tory and smiled.

"What is it?" she asked.

"Your eyelashes," said Michael. "The way you were before, I could never see them." What he didn't tell her was that he never really looked at her face before. It had been so hideous. He could not bear the sight. But now the sores had closed, and bit by bit the swelling was going down.

Tory gingerly touched her face. "There'll be scars. They're always scars from bad skin conditions, you know?"

"Maybe not," offered Michael, wondering about the scars his own condition might leave behind.

Michael lay back down and turned his eyes on the clouds again, his mind finding their shapes. An angel. A unicorn. A tall sailing ship. He had always played this game as a child. He was very good at it.

"Can I tell you something, Tory?"

"Shoot."

"I don't think I'm as brave as the rest of you."

"How do you figure?"

Michael kept his eyes on the drifting clouds. A wind seemed to fill the sail of the tall ship. "Well, take Winston, for example; he feels this in his gut. He knows he has to go out there and take care of this bad kid. And you—you were the strong one, who pulled the rest of us all this way . . . and if it weren't for Lourdes, I would have given up a long time ago . . ."

"I was ready to call it quits lots of times," said Tory.

"How about now?" He turned to Tory, but Tory didn't answer. "I saw that horror in Boise," said Michael. "I know what that other kid is capable of . . . I know what *I* was capable of too . . . but now I've come out of the nightmare, Tory. Maybe there's some blood-sucking Hell-thing driving him to do what he does—but the one that was inside of me is gone! The problem is, it was living in me for so long, I can't remember being any other way. I don't know how to feel about anyone or anything, you know?"

Michael looked away. "Tory . . . I don't have any of the feelings I used to have. Feelings for girls, I mean."

"You mean . . ."

"I mean I don't know what I mean. I don't know *anything*." Michael took a deep breath. "It's like everything inside me has been locked in a vault since I was eleven, and now that same eleven-year-old kid is coming back out. I've got to learn how to *feel* all over again, because right now I don't feel anything either way."

"Well, I don't think it's something you can figure out in one day. If we make it through this, we'll have our whole lives to deal with the regular stuff, but right now we've got other things to think about," reminded Tory. "Our friendly neighborhood Hell-pets are still out there—they can still come back . . ."

"If they're not back already, then maybe they've found a better place to be," said Michael. "Anyway, I don't want to go looking for them under stones. I just want to go home, figure out who I am, and how I'm supposed to feel . . . and then be normal. I don't even care what shade of normal it happens to be. Any kind of normal would suit me just fine."

Michael turned to see Tory dab a tear from her face.

"I don't think we get to be normal," she said. "We're Scorpion Shards, remember?" Then she took his hand. "Come here, I want to show you something. It's sort of a . . . magic trick."

She led him over the hill to a burned-out campsite—a place with torn mattresses and soggy cardboard. It reeked of urine and rot, and it reminded Michael of the type of world they had traveled through to get this far—to get into the light of this pleasant day.

"Find me something disgusting," said Tory. "The most disgusting thing you can find."

There were plenty of disgusting things around to choose from. Michael settled for a sopping rag, so rank it had turned black. It smelled like death on a bad day. He picked it up with his fingernails—just touching the thing made his body shiver in disgust.

"Now give it to me," requested Tory.

Michael held it in her direction. "What are you going to do?"

"You'll see."

She took the disgusting rag and, to Michael's horror, used it to wipe her hands, then, as if that wasn't bad enough, she brought it to her face and wiped her face with it. Michael had to look away. Finally, when she was done, she held the rag back up to Michael.

"Take it," she said.

Michael reluctantly held out his fingertips and grabbed the corner of the rag. The rag was still wet, but that's all it was. A damp rag, perfectly clean, as if it had just been taken out of the washer. Even the smell was gone.

"Kills germs on contact," said Tory. "I'm better than Listerine."

Michael smelled the rag again, amazed. He wiped his own face with it and felt its cool sterile dampness on his face.

"Everyone's got a hidden talent," said Tory. "I suppose ours are a bit more interesting than most. Our talents are less . . . normal."

Tory glanced up at the puffs of clouds blowing across the sky. "An angel," she said. "A unicorn . . . and that one's a schooner ship."

Michael glanced back at the clouds, wondering how on earth she had seen the exact same things he had seen. The reason became clear in an instant, and Michael couldn't believe his eyes.

The clouds had become like soft, white figurines, hovering in the sky. The wind had carefully sculpted the clouds into exactly what Michael had seen them as!

Tory smiled. "You make nice clouds," she said. "Or at least you do when you're head's screwed on straight."

MICHAEL STARED AT HIS clouds for a good ten minutes, but then they were finally torn apart by powerful crosswinds. He tried to create them again, but found he didn't have the concentration. As he watched them dissolve, Michael began to wonder how many of the storms on their trip had been of his own creation.

Meanwhile, Lourdes had woken up and was staring at a dead squirrel . . . only it wasn't dead.

"I was talking to it gently—coaxing it closer," she told Michael. "And then it just keeled over and fell asleep. What could possibly make it do that?"

Michael looked at the silent squirrel, realizing that this could be the first hint of Lourdes's "hidden talent." Then suddenly the squirrel snapped open its eyes and scampered off.

"Isn't that weird?" said Lourdes.

Michael chuckled as he imagined Lourdes surrounded by animals like Snow White . . . but it wasn't about animals, was it? This was just a trick—like Tory's rag, or Michael's sky sculptures. As with all of them, Lourdes's talent had many layers to be discovered, and it took Michael's breath away to think of the possibilities.

"We need to talk," Michael told Lourdes, and she began to look worried.

"About what?"

Michael smiled and gently touched her arm, which was not quite as massive as it had been that same morning. "Good things," he assured her. "Only good things."

Just then Winston came bounding up the hill, out of breath.

"The redheaded kid didn't stop in this town," he announced. "We gotta keep moving." Michael noticed that Winston's pants, which they had cut down to match his diminishing stature, were already an inch above his ankles. Then Michael caught a glimpse of the revolver Winston had taken from that crazy cop in Boise. He kept it with him in his inside jacket pocket.

Michael imagined the days ahead of them now, and the joy he had felt only moments ago began to dissipate as quickly as his clouds in the windswept sky. He knew what they had to do. Stop the destroyer. Stop him at all costs, before he . . . *before he what*? It was hard to imagine anything worse than what they had seen in Boise.

As they gathered their things, Tory came up to Michael once more. "Still thinking of going home?" she asked.

Michael shook his head. "What would you do without me?" he said.

"Stay dry?" suggested Tory. "Keep warm?"

"I promise," said Michael, "no more storms." But even as they turned to go, Michael could feel a cold wind blowing, as nature itself reacted to the growing chill he felt within.

14. FEAR IS AN ICY WIND

THE DRY BRUSH OF EASTERN OREGON SLOWLY BECAME GREEN, then turned into dense woods as I-84 cut a tireless path west. With Michael behind the wheel, the four kids tried every exit off the interstate, in search of anything that didn't seem right. It was a slow and painstaking task, but it gave them the time they needed to talk.

"So now you two are Rain-man and Mrs. Clean?" said Lourdes to Michael and Tory. "I wonder what that makes me—Squirrel-girl?"

"It might not seem like much," said Tory, "but we'll need every skill we have if we're gonna stop this guy."

Tory looked at Winston, anticipating his usual reaction. "I know it's a big stretch," she said to him, "but these talents are for real—you have to believe us!"

Winston looked at her, insulted. "Why shouldn't I believe you?" he said. "It makes sense—I just wish I knew what mine was."

Michael laughed. "Nice stretch, Winston. Maybe you're a bungee cord after all!" Michael jokingly tugged on Winston's arm, as if it would stretch like plastic-man. It didn't of course, and Winston tumbled out of his seat belt.

"Hey watch it!" said Winston, only half angry. "Before I grow some teeth and bite you!"

BURTON, OREGON, WAS SIX miles off the interstate, in a densely forested valley. About a mile down Old Burton Road, Michael stomped on the brakes, and they all tumbled forward.

An object loomed before them—something so bizarre that they could only stare at it, trying to make their minds accept what they were seeing. It was huge and blue, lying half on the road and half off. It looked like a giant metallic Q-tip that had crashed from the heavens and taken down a dozen trees with it.

"Water tower," said Lourdes.

Tory swallowed hard. "I think we found the town where he stopped."

The word "Burton" was still visible on the toppled water tower. Its bulbous tank had ruptured, sending its full load of water flooding the forest around it, turning it into a swamp.

"If I read the sign right," said Michael, "there's more than three thousand people in this town."

He turned to Tory, but Tory turned her eyes away. They were all thinking the same thing. The demolition of downtown Boise, as bad as it was, had only a quarter-mile radius. . . . But if the redheaded kid had found a way to shatter the people of this town . . . it meant that the range of his ability had grown, and the human wreckage would be unimaginable.

The car itself seemed to shudder.

They slowly navigated the gravelly shoulder of the road down the long, slender cylinder that had once held up the water tank. At its ruined base sat a burned-out eighteen-wheeler with a crushed grill.

Across the road, in the drenched undergrowth, a woman sat knitting, wearing nothing but the strands of clashing yarn that draped over her and into the mud.

Lourdes casually pushed down her door lock. It engaged with a dull *thud*. It was echoed by the thud of the other three doors being locked as well. Michael eased onto the gas pedal, and they pressed cautiously forward.

The first homes came into view—lonely homes set back from the road, about a hundred yards apart. In the first house, a shadow leered from an upstairs window, staggering back and forth. On the porch of another home, a woman in a rocking chair let out a ghostly sound.

"We still have three miles to go till we get to the center of town," reminded Tory.

Winston nodded. "It's going to get worse before it gets better."

And it did. A car was parked through a living-room window. Several homes were smoldering ruins . . . then all at once, Michael slammed on the brakes as a local kid no older than them, screaming and bloody, dashed out in front of them. He was stalked by a band of teenagers, as if the prey of some awful hunt.

They watched as the mob disappeared up the hillside.

"I've had nightmares like that," said Tory; then added, "Whoever he is, I hope he wakes up."

Lourdes mumbled something in Spanish and let out a groan of grief. She grabbed Michael's hand; he held Tory's shoulder; she gripped Winston's leg; he reached back until he found Lourdes's wrist, completing the circle of four. They took a deep breath and tried to force out the grim images that assaulted them from outside.

"Nothing can hurt us," said Tory. "Nothing can hurt us when we're like this." But it wasn't true. Yes, they were stronger, but they weren't invincible—and the sum of the horrors outside their car was far greater than the sum of the four of them.

"We shouldn't look at what happened here," said Lourdes. "You should never look when you're passing through Hell." And with that in mind, Michael gritted his teeth until his face began to turn red.

"What are you doing?" asked Winston.

"Making the sky fall," was his answer.

Up above the dense cloud-cover began to ripple. "If I can make myself feel fog on the inside, it'll happen on the outside."

"How do you feel fog?" asked Winston.

"Fog is confusion," said Michael, through clenched teeth. "Just like anger is a lightning storm, and hopelessness is a rain of sleet."

In a moment the clouds descended into the valley, sinking over their windshield until the entire town of Burton was shrouded in fog. Then an icy wind that could only be Michael's fear hit them from behind, whistling past the car, and blowing the fog before them. The wind left a tunnel through the fog that followed the road to the center of town.

DOWNTOWN BURTON HAD BECOME a ghost town. The mad had long since disappeared into the woods—their anguished cries echoing across the valley like a thousand dispossessed souls. Michael slowly drove the van into the heart of havoc, but the fog could not hide everything. Through the mist, shadows of the dead seemed to stretch in all directions off the side of the road. The town's firetruck lay on its side. Shattered window glass crackled beneath the wheels of the van.

At one point Winston got up on his knees and looked out of the window, toward a gas station, which could barely be seen through the fog. "Stop the car!" he said. Michael did, and they all watched as Winston pressed up against the car window, not daring to open it—as if the very air of this town was poisoned. Finally, Winston said, "He was there . . . then he crossed the street . . ." Winston pointed into the fog. "But where did he go from here?"

"Feels like he went straight on through town," said Tory.

"I feel that, too," concurred Lourdes.

They turned to Michael, but his struggle to maintain the fog didn't leave room for him to feel much of anything else.

IN ANOTHER MILE, MAIN Street faded behind them, and Michael lost control of the fog. The wind shifted the haze away through the woods, revealing a narrow country road ahead. They all breathed a sigh of relief, thinking the worst was over . . . until the road took a blind curve and they almost broadsided a pickup truck that sat diagonally across their lane.

Michael hit the brake, sharply turned the wheel, and the van spun out of control, tires squealing, until they spun to a stop, narrowly missing the pickup.

It was the moment the van stopped that they began to feel a sense of *presence* that was so strong it bristled their neck hairs like static electricity.

"He's still here!" said Tory. "Somewhere nearby!"

They quickly unlocked their doors and got out.

Once outside, the smell of smoke was strong and pungent. From the woods they could still hear the distant wails of the wandering mad, chasing each other through the timberland maze.

In front of them, the pickup truck barred their path; beside the truck lay a man, face-down in the mud, very much dead. In his hand he held a bloody fence picket. A crude arrow had caught him right in the jugular.

Michael turned away and leaned against a tree, gasping for breath. "I think I'm gonna puke," he said.

"Don't," said Tory. "We might get hail."

It was Lourdes who was able to get a sense of direction. She turned to the right and pointed to a house about a hundred yards further down the road.

"There . . . ," she said. "I think he's in there."

They took action instantly. Lourdes stalked forward, ready to rely on her bare hands, but Tory had her own ideas. Grimacing, she grabbed the dead man's picket from his stiff hand.

"Maybe if I stake him through the heart, it'll sanitize his soul," she said.

Michael pulled a crowbar from the pickup truck. "Maybe I can use this as a lightning rod," he said.

Winston, still not knowing his hidden talent, reached into his coat and pulled out the revolver, taking off the safety. "No maybe's about what this'll do to him," he said.

The dwelling seemed very innocent as they approached. Just a two-story country house.

"What if he's armed, too?" said Michael. "What if he shoots us?"

"Then we die," said Winston. The thought of dying in this town did not sit well with any of them. It would be better to die anywhere else but here.

The front door was slightly ajar, and they stood there on the porch for a quick moment, then burst in. Tory held her stake high, Michael gripped his crowbar in both hands, the sky already rumbling with his fury, and Winston aimed his gun at anything—*anything* that moved.

Inside the living room, a figure stood silhouetted against a window, holding something large and heavy in its arms.

Winston, his hands shaking, leveled the gun at the figure's head.

The figure stepped closer, Tory and Michael froze, and Winston hesitated.

"Shoot!" shouted Lourdes. "Shoot now!"

Winston almost did, he pulled his finger back on the trigger halfway . . . but then hesitated . . . because there was something he suddenly remembered.

The figure stepped out of the shadows. It was a girl with long, black hair, and slightly Asian eyes.

There are six of us, thought Winston. *Six! . . . and this one was not the destroyer.*

Winston lowered the gun. Michael dropped the crowbar with a clang.

The girl held a young boy in her arms—about seven or eight years old. He wore a toy Indian headband on his head, and he clung to her as she approached them.

The girl glanced at Winston's gun, but didn't seem intimidated by it at all. In fact, she didn't seem frightened by any of them. "Could one of you go into the kitchen and get a towel?" she asked calmly.

There was a foul smell in the air, and from the smell, they knew that the boy in her arms had soiled his pants. Tory put down the picket and hurried to find the towel.

"I've been waiting for you," said the girl. "Dillon said you were dead, but I knew he was lying."

"Dillon? That's his name?" asked Winston. "The guy with red hair?"

"Yes. I'm Deanna."

They introduced themselves as Tory returned with the towel. Then Deanna put the boy down on the sofa, cleaning him the way a mother would clean a baby—with tender care and patience.

"Who's the kid?" asked Michael.

"Just a boy from town," said Deanna. "He doesn't seem to know his name, so I call him Carter, since that was the label on his shirt."

When the boy looked up, they could see how truly terrible his eyes were. One of his pupils had closed down completely, and the other one was open wide and black.

"They all look like that once Dillon is done," explained Deanna. "There's not much we can do for them."

She told them the story of how she met Dillon—the things they had done together, and how she finally broke free. She explained how the boy's father was going to kill her with the bloody picket, but just before he brought the deadly spike down upon her chest, the man was hit by the arrow.

"I got him!" said the boy. "We were playing cowboys and Indians, and I got him good."

Deanna cleaned the boy, and dressed him in oversized pants she found lying around the house. Tory took the soiled towel from Deanna, held it tightly in her hand, and the stench quickly vanished.

"You thought you were going to die, didn't you?" Tory said as Deanna washed up. "You thought you were dying, so the thing living inside you panicked and ran away—the same thing happened to us—they got scared out of us!"

"I saw it," said Deanna, calmly. "It was like a snake. . . . No . . . more like a giant worm."

Everyone else shuddered, but Deanna didn't seem bothered by the memory at all. She seemed rather fearless about the whole thing. "Anyway it vanished through the woods, heading west."

Carter wandered around the living room and found his bow and arrows. He set to work removing the rubber suction-cup darts, and sharpening the wood with a pocket knife, as he had done with the first one. Lourdes went over to watch.

"Do you have a car?" asked Deanna.

"Just down the road," answered Michael.

"We have to get going. . . . I knew you'd be coming, so I stacked some supplies by the door—I know where Dillon is headed."

"Look!" said Tory, and they all turned to catch sight of Lourdes at the other end of the room with Carter. Lourdes had gained the boy's attention now—he had put down his knife and arrow. Together they seemed to be playing some sort of game—a mirroring game, where the boy would copy whatever Lourdes did.

"Lourdes, this is no time to be fooling around!" said Winston.

"Shh!" said Tory, sharply.

Lourdes kept her eye contact with the boy. She raised one arm; so did he. She raised the other arm; so did he. Only this wasn't a game, and he wasn't simply mimicking her, his actions were too perfect, too exact.

"She's controlling him like a marionette!" said Michael, staring in wide-eyed disbelief. "She's controlling every movement of his body!" Each motion Lourdes made was exactly duplicated. She wiggled her fingers; so did he. She rolled her neck; so did he. Was it just the boy's muscles, or did it go beyond that? Could she control his heartbeat? His breathing? His very metabolism? Until yesterday, she couldn't control her own grotesque physiology, but now the physiology of others seemed within her grasp!

Lourdes looked at the boy, and the boy's ruined eyes began to close. He nodded off to sleep.

Lourdes turned to the others. "Did you see that?" she said, just as surprised as the rest of them. "I think I did that!"

They all just stared at the sleeping boy in wonder, realizing that the title of "Squirrel-girl" for Lourdes didn't quite hit the mark.

"Those creatures turned our strengths into weaknesses!" said Tory. It was becoming clearer to each of them now. Michael's ability to affect nature had been used to wreak havoc in the very nature of people around him; Tory's cleansing touch had been turned into a touch of disease; Lourdes's ability to control the metabolism of others had been used to draw the flesh out of their cells and add it to Lourdes's.

Tory turned to Winston. "We can figure out what your strength is now!"

"I already figured," said Winston uneasily. He looked around, then asked Michael to bring down a potted plant from a shelf Winston couldn't reach. Winston put the plant down on a coffee table, took a deep breath, then grasped the stem in his hand and concentrated. Right before everyone's eyes, the plant grew until it had doubled in size and flowers bloomed. Winston smiled. It was the first time any of them had seen him really smile.

"Looks like we got a flower-child," said Michael, with a grin. "What are you gonna do, beat Dillon with a corsage?"

Winston shrugged. "Ain't *my* problem if *you* can't see the possibilities."

"You'll find a good use for it," said Deanna. "Don't worry."

And indeed it seemed that Deanna was not worried. By anything. Her fearlessness was a powerful strength. It gave them focus; it gave them clarity. She told them how Dillon had changed in the end, making it horribly clear where all their beasts had gone—and it seemed likely that Deanna's beast had found him as well.

"He's stronger than all of us," said Tory. "If he can survive with all six of them inside him."

"You said you knew where he was going?" asked Michael.

Deanna nodded, and picked up sleeping Carter, refusing to leave him alone in this awful town, and they all headed back to the car.

"There's still time to stop him, but it will take all of us to do it," said Deanna.

"Stop him . . . from what?" asked Lourdes.

"Don't you know what he wants to do?" she asked, look-ing at each of them. Only Deanna had the courage to say the words aloud.

"He's going to shatter the world, the same way he shattered this town . . . and once it starts, we won't be able to stop it."

15. RESONANCE

JAGGED SPIRES OF DEAD WOOD STRETCHED THROUGH THE morning mist. Thousands upon thousands of trees had once blanketed the steep hills, stretching toward a distant mountain. . . .

. . . But now every last tree was dead.

Wind, rain, and rot had eaten away their branches, leaving vast acres of wooden monoliths standing in a mulch of peat and heavy gray ash. This forest had died long before Dillon Cole got to it, and the cause of death was still there on the horizon, breathing steam like a fire god asleep.

The sheer power of it, thought Dillon as he drove from life into the miles of death that surrounded the northern face of Mount St. Helens.

The smell of decay within this realm of desolation blended with the rich, dark smell of volcanic ash, creating an aroma that was at once both clean and vile, like the awful smell of a sulfur spring.

As he drove into the volcanic wasteland, fear began to writhe in his gut, but he beat it down. The fear had descended on him shortly after Deanna had left him. Terror had suddenly coiled itself around his gut like a serpent, making him feel paranoid and claustrophobic in the cab of the Range Rover as he left the dying town of Burton. He had fought it down until it wasn't so overpowering, but still the fear kept coming back, urging him to drive faster and more recklessly to his final destination.

The hands that now gripped the steering wheel were not

his hands—at least not the hands that he remembered. These were bloated and swollen—covered with red boils. This body was not his either. His growing gut had burst out of his pants in the middle of the night. He was forced to find a truck stop and confiscate larger clothes from a trucker whose life had come to a sudden and unexpected end. Now Dillon had to roll up the pant legs as well—he swore that he was an inch shorter than the day before. Inside he could feel many, many hungers now, coiled within him, competing for his will, all screaming to be fed.

The wrecking-hunger, however, still screamed the loudest, and its final feeding was all that mattered—a feeding so great that when it was done, there would be nothing left to devour.

Back in the Burton Library, he had studied the maps, the charts, the statistics. He had worked calculations that a super-computer would have shied away from, and he had pulled out an answer, sifting it through a secret sixth sense. The answer he came up with was this: of all the locations in the world from which to set up the ultimate chain reaction, only one rested in North America. The epicenter of destruction was in Washington state, in the shadow of Mount St. Helens. Here, in this secret fulcrum of human existence, Dillon would have to find a human fuse. It would have to be someone with no ties to the outside world and filled with a lonely anger. Someone separate and alone. It would have to be a hermit, whose destiny Dillon could aim with the pinpoint accuracy of a sniper.

Although the calculations that brought him there were complex, the actual plan was simple: Dillon would find his hermit, then find the hermit's weakness and fire him toward a nearby city. In the city, there would be a gathering place—a bar, perhaps—where this man would create a chain of events that would drive everyone there beyond the limit of their sanity. Those who survived would carry the insanity home with them.

At least one would board a plane.

At least ten of the people on that plane would board other planes, and in this way, the seed of destruction would be planted within the minds of thousands of travelers, moving in hundreds of different directions. In a matter of days, people around the world would suddenly be faced by the exact chain of events that would bring them to their breaking points and drive them mad. Millions of patterns collapsing like a house of cards.

In the end, the destruction of mankind would not come as a great nuclear holocaust. It would not come as a meteor splitting the earth in half. It would come from a simple thought whispered in one lonely man's ear. A single thought, which would breed a rage of chaos that would sweep across the globe in a swift chain reaction.

Dillon remembered seeing a film once about a great steel bridge that had violently collapsed, brought down by mere resonance—the simple vibrations of the air around it. Dillon's thought would surely resonate and bring down something far more mighty than a steel bridge. He was the hammer that would fracture every thought mankind had ever had, making civilization crumble to its very foundations.

Dillon pondered how a single thought—the right thought—had always had such power to create. Simple thoughts pushed in the right direction at the right time.

The idea of the wheel; the thought of the written word—simple ideas that had picked up momentum across the globe, swelled like a tidal wave and created civilization. How fitting that a single thought was all it took to bring it crashing down.

The power of such an act could only be surmounted by the

power released when everything fell—power that would feed the wrecking-hunger like it had never before been fed. Just imagining it made Dillon drool, and he longed for the great process to begin.

For an instant the image of his dead parents flitted through his mind.

Are you proud of me now, Mom and Dad?

He didn't wait for an answer. Instead he floored the accelerator, and the engine's powerful roar drowned out the question before it could resonate in his mind.

Part V
Between the Walls

16. THE HERMIT

SLAYTON.

He didn't need a first name.

Most of the time he didn't need a name at all. He'd only drive his rusty pickup down into Cougar every few weeks or so for supplies, paying with ancient, crumpled bills, then he would disappear again down a dirt road that passed from life into death, from green trees into the dead valley in the shadow of the smoking mountain.

He was forty.

His skin was beginning to age, his hair beginning to gray—but inside, his thoughts and ideas, his very perception of the world had never grown beyond age eight or nine.

He was slow.

Not only in the way he thought, but in the way he moved. He had come to accept this as the way of things, and it only bothered him when he was among others, whose thoughts and actions were quicker. For that reason, he didn't care much for people—being around people drained him—made him feel less of a man. So he steered clear of them and made himself the center of his own solitary universe, where things moved at his own speed.

He learned to care for himself at an early age.

He built a shack in the woods, and when the timber company

that owned the land kicked him off, he moved, and built another. And then another. Now, he finally thought he had found a place where no one would bother him—a dead forest gray and bleak that no one wanted. Here they would finally leave him alone.

He drank too much.

A habit he had picked up from his father, years and years ago. When the wind would blow, and the alcohol would swim through his mind, he would swear there were ghosts in the trees, like in stories his ma used to tell. Ghosts and demons were very real to Slayton. And so he was not entirely surprised when the Devil appeared at his door one bleak October evening.

The door creaked open to reveal him standing there. Slayton didn't make a move. He just sat at his table, holding his half-full bottle of whiskey. The other half was already in his head. Slayton knew who it was without him having to say a word.

"You must be Slayton."

"How do you know my name?"

"They told me about you in town."

The Devil did not look quite the way Slayton expected. He was fat and young. A redheaded teenager with an awful complexion.

"I've been looking for you," the Devil said.

"I'll bet you have."

Slayton invited the Devil in, watching him carefully as he moved. Darkness surrounded him like a black hole. Shadow flowed in his wake, rippling like a dark cape. A living fabric of death.

The Devil closed the door behind himself, and suddenly fear and anger began to overtake Slayton—but he bit it back, determined to stand toe to toe with the Devil. Slayton reached up, got a glass and poured some whiskey as the visitor sat down at the table. His darkness ebbed and flowed on the table like waves lapping the shore.

"Drink with me?" asked Slayton.

The Devil-boy shook his head, pushing the glass away.

"What's the matter? Not old enough?" And Slayton let out a rough wheezing laugh at the thought of the Devil being underage. That was a good one!

"No time," said his guest, looking into Slayton's eyes, probing his thoughts. "No time, I'm in a hurry."

Only then did Slayton notice that this Devil-boy across the table was sweating something awful. He was breathing quickly, and shallowly as if he was out of breath—as if he was panicked, but trying to hide it.

"What's yer angle?" asked Slayton.

"Angle?"

"If ya come to take me, how come y'aint done it? Go on—get it over with. I ain't got no patience for the likes a you!"

The Devil-boy smiled a crooked, leprous smile. "You have no idea how very important you are," he said. "I wouldn't touch a hair on your head."

"Then what are ya here fer?"

"Dinner," said the Devil.

Slayton shook his head, and the world spun in circles one way and then the other. He took another swig of whiskey and left to see what there was to eat in the kitchen. *What was the Devil likely to eat?* he wondered. *Beef jerky? Saltines?* When he stumbled back out of the kitchen, he saw his visitor searching through his munitions locker, which had been locked.

"You get your nose outta there!" shouted Slayton, but the fat Devil-boy didn't move.

"You collect weapons?" asked the Devil-boy.

"What business is it of yours?"

The Devil-boy swung the door wide to reveal Slayton's cache—a regular arsenal of all types of weaponry from rifle to pistol, from Bowie knife to crossbow. All shiny and clean.

"Most of 'em never been fired," said Slayton. "All loaded, though. You never know when you might need one."

"It's a fine collection," said the Devil-boy. Then he turned to the many items on Slayton's shelves. Old family pictures. Knickknacks from here and there. He brushed his finger across the dusty shelf, and his eyes darted back and forth, looking at everything—first everything on the shelf, then everything in the room. His eyes moved so quickly, Slayton couldn't keep up with him. Those awful blue-green eyes—they were invading him, weren't they? They were violating all of his personal things. Slayton could not stand for this, so he grabbed one of the many weapons stacked in his closet—a rifle—and aimed it at the Devil.

"I don't got no dinner for you," Slayton said. "You'd better go now."

The Devil-boy ignored Slayton. Instead, he tilted his head slightly, as if listening . . . then he sniffed the air . . . and then it was as if something snapped into place. He turned his eyes to Slayton once more and fixed his gaze.

"You loved your mother very much, didn't you," said the Devil. "It's sad she died so young."

"Wh . . . what do you know about it?"

"I know enough. I know your daddy worked the timberline and was always gone. I know he never gave a rat's ass about you. I know how he and most everyone else called you names . . . but your ma, she defended you against all those cruel people, didn't she?"

Slayton lowered the rifle a bit and nodded slightly.

"She had a special name for you. Something secret—between the two of you. What was it?"

Slayton swallowed hard and lowered the gun to his side. *How does he know this?*

"Little Prince," said Slayton. "Just like the book."

The fat Devil-boy smiled. "When she died, your daddy just left you. How old were you, fifteen?"

"Just turned it," said Slayton. "Then he drunk hisself to death. I was glad, too."

"I know you were." The Devil began to move closer and Slayton couldn't turn his eyes away.

"This is important, Slayton. After your father died, you lived in a city for a year or so, before you moved back into the woods. . . . Tell me the name of the city."

Slayton bit his lower lip to keep it from quivering. *The Devil knows everything, don't he?*

"Come on, Slayton. Tell me the name of the city."

"Tacoma," said Slayton weakly.

"Tacoma!" The Devil smiled in some sort of deep relief. "Listen to me, Slayton," he said. "I'm going to make you the most important man in the world, and all you have to do is listen to me."

"I'm listening," said Slayton, his gaze locked onto the Devil's swimming blue eyes.

Then the Devil got as close as he possibly could to Slayton's ear, without touching him, and whispered in the faintest of voices:

"There's someone in Tacoma . . . who owes you."

It took a moment to register . . . and then the words hit home, ringing as true as a church bell in Slayton's mind. Every fiber of his soul resonated with the thought, until he felt as if his very brain would be rattled apart. *Yes! Someone in Tacoma did owe him.* He didn't know who it was, but whoever it was, Slayton would find him and make him pay!

Even Slayton could sense that this was the start of a grand chain of events that would greatly affect his life and the lives of many, many people.

He was about to turn to his munitions locker.

That's when all hell broke loose.

WINSTON HAD GRASPED THE gun in his pocket for so long, its cold handle had grown warm in his palm. A tip in the nearest town led them to this shack, and now as they kicked in the crooked door, Winston held the revolver out in front of him, afraid to pull the trigger, but also afraid not to. Everything was crucial now. No mistakes could be made.

The room was dim as they burst in, and it was hard to see. The others filed in, creating commotion, getting in the way.

There were two figures in the room, and in a moment he had identified which one was Dillon—but as Winston's eyes adjusted to the dim lamplight, he hesitated. They all hesitated, because they could not believe what they saw.

"Madre de Dios!" cried Lourdes.

Dillon barely looked human—his body had bloated like a balloon, his face was swollen with festering blisters. His eyes were blazing sapphire holes.

Winston could feel the presence of the creature that had laid waste to his own soul in there as well. It was true—all of their monstrosities were now inside of Dillon!

"No!" screamed Dillon. He tried to make a break for it, but the five of them lunged at him, trapping him in a web of ten hands. He twisted free of their grasp and backed into the corner, a terrified, caged animal.

Across the room, the old hermit could only stand there by the open closet door and gawk, while the little boy, Carter, looked in from the cabin's threshold with his awful empty eyes.

"Do it!" Tory shouted to Winston. "Do it now!"

"It's too late!" Dillon screamed. "It doesn't matter now, whatever you do won't matter!"

"Shut up!" shouted Winston.

"It's too late!" cackled Dillon again.

Winston stared at this creature in the dark corner and raised his gun. *The plan, the plan, follow the plan.*

Winston tightened his two-handed grip on the revolver, steadied his shaking hands, then leveled his aim and pulled his trigger.

The roar from the six beasts drowned out any sound the gun could have made.

A flash of light—a flash of darkness—shadowy figures leaping in six different directions—screaming—blue flames—tentacles—horrid fangs! Six dark shadows clinging to the walls screeching and wailing in fury . . .

. . . And in fear.

"They're afraid of us!" shouted Tory. "Look at them!"

The beasts recoiled from the kids in the room, leaping, slithering, flying from wall to wall.

"Don't let them inside you!" shouted Michael. "Fight to keep them out!" Although none of them knew how to do that, they willed themselves to stand firm against the raging, snarling shadows, and the creatures did not dare come near them.

Without a host, the beasts could not survive long in this world. And so they left it.

It was something the kids could not have anticipated. The six hideous leech-things came together in the center of the room, and with a blast that rocked the weak foundations of the tiny cabin, they ripped the world open.

A ragged hole tore in the fabric of space, and the creatures escaped through it, into blind darkness.

The hole! thought Winston, before he even understood what it was. *We're all too close to the—*

Dillon's limp body slipped into the gaping breach—Deanna grabbed him, losing her balance. Winston caught her, and before any of them knew what was happening they had all grabbed hold of one another in a twisted huddle as they lost their footing and slipped into the vortex, from light into darkness.

And for an instant . . . just an instant they felt it:

Wholeness.

The six of them touching.

Complete and invincible.

Perfect and joyous.

An absolute union.

But the feeling ended when the six of them came through the darkness and hit a hard, unearthly ground, crashing apart once more like a fragile pieces of glass.

SLAYTON WATCHED THEM GO.

It had all happened so fast, he wasn't sure what he had seen . . . but then he realized that it didn't matter because

someone owed him in Tacoma.

Nothing mattered but that simple fact. Not the sudden disappearance of the Devil-boy and his devil friends. Not even the hole to Hell that still hung in the middle of the room. Nothing mattered because he had a mission.

Five minutes later, he had loaded most of his weapons into his pickup truck. He hadn't noticed the little boy who stood there watching, until the boy spoke.

"Mister, you playin' a game?" asked the boy, his head lolled to one side like he was half dead.

Slayton didn't have time for questions, or things that got in his way, so he reached into his pickup bed and grabbed a loaded shotgun.

"Are you a cowboy, or an Indian?" asked the boy.

Slayton took aim at the boy. No one would get in his way between here and Tacoma.

17. UNWORLD

DILLON FELT HIS MIND, BODY, AND SOUL RIPPED APART, then a moment later he was torn from the world.

He never heard the gunshot, but the pain was very real. It exploded in the back of his head where the bullet must have left his skull.

All was still now. Silent. He felt his blood pouring from the back of his head, and he moved his hand toward his forehead, certain that this would be the last action of his life. He would touch his own shattered forehead and then die.

But there was no entry wound.

And in the back of his head, there was no exit wound either. There was only a sharp stone upon which he had fallen, and a gash on the back of his scalp that spilled blood onto sands that were already the color of blood.

Everything was spinning in Dillon's head. He felt an unbearable emptiness. A hollowness. He had been crammed tightly with seething, horrid creatures, but now they were gone, and the emptiness they left behind was strange and terrible. He heard the voices of the other kids around him—the ones who had tried to kill him.

"They're getting away," one of them said.

"We can catch them!"

"Don't just sit there, run!"

He heard feet running off, then saw the black kid who had fired the gun standing over him.

"You dead?" asked the black kid.

"Yes," groaned Dillon.

"Good," said the black kid, and he took off with the others.

Dillon closed his eyes again. And tried to feel something . . . anything. He could feel the blood pulsing in his hands and feet, he could feel the pain in the back of his head, but he couldn't feel anything *inside*. The events of the past few weeks were slowly coming back to him, like the details of a nightmare . . . he remembered Boise, and Idaho Falls, and Burton, and the many other people and places he had carefully destroyed, but with those memories came a fog of numbness. No feeling. No remorse. No sorrow or joy. Nothing. He had no feeling inside him at all. No heart. No soul.

"Dillon?"

He opened his eyes, and there beside him knelt Deanna. She helped him to sit up, and as he shifted, he felt something hard against the small of his back. He reached behind his back and pulled out the gun that should have killed him. Deanna gently took it from him and exposed the barrel.

"Four chambers; three bullets. We fired the empty chamber hoping we could scare them out of you. If it hadn't worked, we still had the three full ones."

Dillon felt weak, feverish. He realized he hadn't eaten for days.

"Where are we?"

His eyes had adjusted to the strange harsh light, and he looked around. The sands were vermillion red, the sky an icy frost blue. A much smaller tear, ten feet in the air above him, marked the passage back to their own world.

And all around them was despair.

Downed airplanes and crushed ships littered the sands. Rusted cars with crusty skeletons lay strewn every few hundred yards like a great garden of death. All the people and things that had ever disappeared without explanation were well accounted for in this unnameable place, having fallen through tears in the fabric of time and space. And yet this was not quite another world—it was an unworld—an unloved, unseen, unattended-to place. A place between.

Dillon turned to see a solitary mountain looming behind them; it seemed as out of place as everything else. At the top of this peak stood what appeared to be a castle carved out of the rock itself.

Dillon's beast was climbing this mountain. So was Deanna's. The other four kids had taken off in various directions across the sands after their demons, but Dillon's and Deanna's were getting away.

And still Dillon felt nothing.

He turned to Deanna.

"Deanna . . . I want you to look at me and tell me what you see."

Deanna looked him over, and tried to hide the grimace on her face. "It's not so good . . . but the weight is already going away, and your skin . . ."

"No," said Dillon. "That's not what I mean."

He gripped her tightly and looked into her eyes. "I mean . . . what do you see . . . when you look at me . . ."

Deanna peered into his eyes, as she always did. He could almost feel her probing inside of him . . . searching . . . and then a tear trickled down her face.

"They've killed me, haven't they?" asked Dillon. "Those monsters left my body and my mind, but they killed my soul . . ."

"No . . . ," said Deanna, smiling gently though her tears. Dillon could now see that these were not tears of sadness; they were tears of joy. "The other day," said Deanna, "I thought you were gone forever, so I ran. . . . But I was wrong. . . . You're still alive, Dillon, body *and* soul."

Deanna leaned forward and kissed his blistered, swollen lips. And for a moment Dillon felt a twinge of feeling coming back to him.

He glanced up at the rift in space just out of their reach, remembering the extent of their situation.

"Slayton," he said weakly. "I launched him toward Tacoma . . ."

Deanna calmly helped him to his feet. "First the beasts," she said. "They're too powerful—they have to be destroyed."

Dillon couldn't keep his eyes off of her. After everything he had done, she still cared for him—and after all the terror, she could face this new challenge with fortitude and peace. "How can you be so strong?" he asked. But Deanna only smiled. *What a wondrous gift,* thought Dillon. *To be so strong. To be so brave.*

He stood on wobbly legs like a dead man refusing to give up the ghost and tapped into Deanna's will, borrowing it for his own. Then they set off toward the mountain to face their demons.

TORY HAD BEEN THE first to realize that these beasts could be destroyed. She knew by the way the beasts moved. They didn't zip across these sands like shadows; they ran, they crawled, they slithered, like beings of flesh and blood. Indeed, in this unworld these beasts were creatures of flesh. That meant they would have weaknesses and could be hunted! The creatures raced off in different directions, and the kids took off after the beast each recognized to be their own.

In this world, Tory's beast appeared to be an amorphous gray blob, continually shifting and changing shape—but as she drew closer she realized it was not a blob, but a swarm. Millions of mutated bacteria—a colony of pestilence—buzzing in perfect formation, like a single being with a million minute bodies all following a single will.

Like a swarm of bees.

It was that thought that made her realize how she might kill it.

The swarm, only a dozen yards away now, took off, darting through strange leafless trees and bulky derelict vessels until reaching the wreck of an old propeller plane. When the swarm disappeared into the side of the plane, Tory knew she'd be climbing into a hive.

The wreckage was filled with rotted airplane seats and skeletons of passengers long dead. Toward the front of the cabin, the beast waited; a buzzing horde that had taken on a new formation complete with arms and legs, roughly in the shape of a human body.

Tory stalked closer, and the buzz in her ears grew as the creature advance, then attacked. Hideous ugly bugs surrounded her, crawling over every inch of her body. They stung and bit; they gnawed and drew blood; they burrowed under her skin. The pain was unbearable, and Tory cried out in horror. She was being eaten alive by these things! She would die right here. With her body burning from the stings of the swarm, she reached deeper and deeper into it, hoping beyond hope that she'd be able to carry out her plan before the swarm killed her. Then, in the center of the buzzing mass, she found what she was looking for. There was a creature hovering there, twice the size of her fist, with a grotesque bulging body, tendrils, and insectile eyes. It seemed half mosquito, half jellyfish. The thing's segmented eyes stared at her in fear and fury, while all around her the swarm continued to bite—raising welts, burrowing into her, fighting to make her their hive.

The colony of disease—this *ugliness*—had once found a

place in Tory, but she had no room for such ugliness anymore. Now as she gripped the queen of the swarm, she pumped all of her anger into her clenched fist and drove out her own revulsion, replacing it with determination. This thing had turned Tory's own unique power against her . . . but now the creature was on the *outside*, and it had no defense against Tory's cleansing touch.

The filthy thing writhed in her grasp, the disease draining from it, its flesh fading from sickly gray to jelly-clear. Its swarm fell to the ground one by one, pattering like a fall of rain, until the queen was alone and unprotected. Without her guardians and without her filth, Tory knew this creature in her fist was nothing. . . . So she hurled the thing to the ground and crushed it beneath the heel of her shoe, the way she would crush any bug that became a nuisance.

MICHAEL CHASED THE BLUE-BURNING beast of many hands toward the shore of a violent sea, where black water lapped like oil upon the vermillion sands.

As he dove on the beast, bringing it down, he felt himself overwhelmed by a tempest of emotions so powerful he thought it would tear him apart. Sorrow, slashed by anger, scalded by desire, and each emotion was so extreme, Michael felt the turbulence alone would destroy him. He flipped the creature around to face him—but it had no face; only eyes. Turquoise, hypnotic eyes, and many burning hands, each stronger than his own.

Then the creature did grow a face around those deep, deep eyes. It was the face of a beautiful girl; somehow a mixture of all the girls he had known and wanted—and its many hands no longer clawed him but caressed him. Those soft hands tingled across his chest and his legs. His arms slipped from around the creature's neck to its shoulders. He felt hands on his head pulling him closer into a powerful embrace, and all his battling emotions were flooded by something more powerful than all the rest. It was the old familiar feeling; the brutal passion that ruled his days and nights.

The beautiful creature pulled Michael into a fiery kiss.

You can't imagine the pleasure I could give you, he felt it say. *All the Joys you could imagine . . . if only you stop resisting . . . if only you feed me . . .*

Michael could feel the intensity of its passion mingling with his own.

Take me back, he felt the creature say. *Invite me back in.*

Michael could feel it trying to slide beneath his skin and dissolve into his blood.

Invite you in? thought Michael. Is that how it had happened in the first place? Did it have to be invited in?

He thought of the girl in Baltimore, and then the one in Omaha. This thing had now become so powerful that it could steal a soul with a kiss. Was he going to invite this thing to rule him?

Michael knew he could not let it happen, so he turned everything off—and was amazed to find that he had the power to do it. He shut down the fear, he closed off his anger, he doused his lust. He made himself feel cold, calm, and unaffected by the grip of this sensual creature that clung to him.

The air around them began to chill and fill with flurries of snow, but there was no icy wind of fear.

The creature wailed, its hands becoming claws again, digging into him, its face melting away into those burning blue eyes. It thrashed as if each snowflake were made of acid, and the snow kept falling heavier by the moment.

Only now did Michael realize that he was killing it—but he didn't allow himself to feel excitement.

Cold. Calm. Unaffected.

Michael pulled away, standing above it, feeling the snow grow stronger; feeling himself feel nothing for this creature.

For all the spirits we destroyed, for all the girls whose souls we invaded together, I leave you cold. I will not be your accomplice. I will not be your slave. My body will not be your vessel. And I will walk away feeling nothing for you.

The snow was like a mountain of sand around his wailing creature now. With a hundred flaming blue hands it tried to free itself, but could not. Michael watched as it sunk into the snow and drowned. The snow itself flowed a bright blue for a few moments as the creature dissolved into it, but then the hot, black waters of the unworld sea crashed upon the glowing mound, melting it. In a moment, nothing was left but a thin blue foam shredded by the dark, churning surf.

LOURDES STRUGGLED WITH HER immense, slow-moving beast, but as strong as her muscles had gotten beneath all that fat, this beast was far stronger. It was like an octopus; a great boneless jet-black thing with tentacles as thick as her thighs and a singular, hateful eye.

But the worst was its mouth—a great toothless maw that stretched itself open wide as the tentacles pushed Lourdes toward it. She tried to dig her feet into the sand, but it was no use. It pulled her in and swallowed her whole with a mighty roar.

Lourdes took a last gasp of breath before the mouth closed around her, forcing her into a wet, airless darkness. She pushed her elbows against it, she scraped its gullet with her fingernails, she felt her heart pounding, using up the last of the oxygen in her lungs . . . but she heard the beast's heart beating. She was inside it now, rather than it being inside of her . . . and it dawned on Lourdes that this made all the difference. She fought to stay conscious and concentrated on the sound of the creature's bloated heart, until she saw it in her mind. . . . Then, in the same way she had made Carter and the squirrel sleep, she forced her will into the nervous system of this beast.

And she shut down its heart.

The creature began to thrash as its heart seized into a heavy knot. It violently spat Lourdes out onto the sand, and Lourdes, wet and slimy, but very much alive, gasped for breath, feeling her head spin. She kept the creature under her control, clenching her fists, imagining its heart clenched as tightly, until finally the thing quivered and fell to the ground, its life slipping away with the steamy breath from its swollen mouth. Lourdes watched the hatred in its awful eye vanish into the indifference of death.

WINSTON CHASED HIS BEAST into the looming shadow of a steamer ship that listed dangerously in the sand, its rusted hull wedged between two boulders.

Winston's creature was small—even smaller than he was, and it surprised him. It loped on all fours, with stubbly legs and long arms. Winston could have caught it easily, if his ankle hadn't been twisted in the fall, but now he had to limp after it, grimacing with every step.

In the shadow of the listing steamer, Winston got close enough to grab the beast's furry leg; to Winston's surprise, the creature did not resist. It turned to Winston and gazed into eyes.

This was not the creature Winston imagined. Its eyes were large and friendly; its fur was soft; it's face seemed innocent . . . inquisitive, and it resembled a cross between a monkey and a bear cub.

As Winston looked at it, he felt a sudden urge to hold it

close to him, so he did. It wrapped its furry arms and legs around him.

It felt good. Comfortable. Safe. He felt as if he could take this soft thing beneath his arm, curl up, and fall asleep.

The soft creature did not slide beneath his arm, however. It slid around him, clung to his back, and held him tightly around the neck.

Winston felt its open mouth by his ear. He smelled its breath; it was clean, like a baby's breath.

I can make everything like it was, it whispered to him. *Just like it was before your father died. I can make it all go back, and you can feel the way you used to feel all those years ago.*

The creature's sweet smell and the softness of its fur was enough to comfort his doubt. Enough to paralyze his fear.

Paralyze?

The creature's mouth opened wider and its fangs drove deep into the back of Winston's neck, settling in his spine. He felt his days slipping away again; his life moving backward, his body growing down. Winston roared with anger. He might have once longed for time to take a giant step backward, but not anymore! He grabbed the beast and flung it from him so hard that it hit the side of the rusty old ship with a clang that echoed inside the hollow hull.

The creature was advancing again, long sharp claws on its fingers, fangs in its mouth, but those longing, innocent eyes never changed.

It came at him through the sharp nettles that had grown in the shade of the behemoth boat, moving much faster than Winston.

What am I going to do, beat it with a corsage? The words came slinging back through his mind . . . and then he realized that he could do just that and more! Without an instant to lose, he grabbed the gnarled hardwood stem of the bush before him, painfully gripping the thorns, and pushed life into it.

The ground beneath him began to rumble and undulate. Lines like mole tunnels pushed up the dirt, and shoots of thorn-laden branches sprouted from the ground. The furry creature found its fur caught in a sharp web of growth. It whined and cried and bleated like a lamb, as bright flowers sprung from branches, hiding the sharpness of the thorns.

Winston fought his way through the malevolent shrubs until he found a branch that was close to the creature. He touched that branch, and immediately it sprouted new shoots that wove in and out of the dirt, winding around the creature until it was trapped in a prison of thorns.

The earth around them continued to undulate, as beneath them the roots grew deeper and stronger. The leaning ship creaked on its precarious bed of sand.

The creature bleated and cried, writhing in agony, its fur shredding on the barbs of the new growth.

"Cry all you want," Winston told it. *"But I'm growing up!"*

A heavy root the width of a tree trunk forced up the earth beneath the steamer. The great ship let out a ghastly metallic moan as it was shifted by the massive roots.

Winston began to scramble away, leaving the beast in its thorny prison. He pulled himself across the sand, through the nettles, until he was out from the shadow of the ship.

Another ghastly moan and a heavy rattle.

Winston looked back to see the keel of the steamer finally lose its battle with gravity. The entire ship began to fall to its side and, beneath it, the screaming, bleating beast fought to get free of the thorns, until the mighty ship came down upon it. The ship shook the earth with a colossal rumble, crushing the small, deadly beast under a thousand tons of steel.

. . .

DILLON AND DEANNA HEARD the falling ship, and felt the shock wave shake the mountain beneath them moments later. Stones and pebbles, dislodged by the shaking of the earth, flew down the mountain toward them—but their only concerns now were the creatures climbing thirty yards ahead of them.

From behind, Dillon's appeared half-human, but moved with powerful, otherwordly grace. Its skin was smooth, hairless leaden-gray over bulging muscles; both magnificent and repulsive at the same time—the very sight of it churned Dillon's stomach. Deanna's beast had no grace. It had no arms or legs either; it was a serpentine thing, flat and segmented like a giant worm.

They soon reached a plateau that was too smooth to be natural. It was, in fact, a grand stone court that led to the crumbling palace carved out of the stone, and the creatures disappeared into the dark recesses of this ancient acropolis. This was their home. Their lair.

"Don't be scared," said Deanna. "We'll find them."

Then she disappeared down a corridor that led to the left, and Dillon headed off to the right.

DEANNA KNEW THAT SHE should have been frightened, but she was not. She kept her wits about her as she ascended the stone stairs, passing the crumbling bones of ancient human skeletons as she stepped deeper into darkness. It could have been crouching in any dark corner she passed. It could have been waiting inches above her. She knew that somewhere nearby it was coiled like a cobra, ready to strike.

Her foot touched something. A stone? No—it moved. A rat? Were there rats in this forgotten place? She turned but was faced by more darkness. Webs brushed across her face that were too thick to be made by earth-born spiders.

She smelled it before she saw it—an acrid, dank odor of peat and fungus as it sprang at her from the left. She turned and it struck her shoulder, clamping on with toothless, powerful jaws like a bear trap. She felt its slippery scales coiling around her, its icy body constricting around her chest, cutting off her air and circulation. She lost her balance and rolled down a flight of stone stairs.

At the bottom of the stairs she was able to wrench her hand free, and she grabbed the thing by its neck, tearing its awful jaws from her shoulder. Her eyes had adjusted to the dim light, and she could see it now as she held its flaring head away from her. Its breath was chill and foul, and its face was almost human . . . except that it had no eyes.

Then Deanna realized something. It was in the way it darted left, then right—the way it snapped sightlessly and frantically in the air. Deanna knew that feeling all too well.

You're terrified, aren't you?

The serpent coiled itself tighter around her.

You're terrified that you'll die!

Deanna could sense that although it had a stranglehold on her, it didn't want to kill her. It wanted her to let it inside. To let it come . . . home.

Take me back, it seemed to plead. *Please let me in. . . . I'm sooooo frightened. Don't make me kill you!*

Deanna, on the other hand, felt no fear at all within her. She calmly held its head away so it could not strike. She felt herself growing weak from the lack of air as its body coiled around her chest.

I am not your home, she told it silently. *And I am not afraid of you. So I suppose you'll have to kill me.*

The serpent, more terrified than ever, squeezed her tighter, but Deanna forced herself to her feet and pressed her thumbs firmly against its neck. It, too, began to gasp for air, and as they staggered across the rough stone floor in a lethal dance, it became a simple matter of who was going to strangle who first.

DILLON COLE, STILL FEELING a mere shell of a human being, slowly stalked the halls of the ruined place. Window glass had long since crumbled to sand. Bones of the dead crumbled to dust beneath his feet. He wondered if, perhaps, he would join the minions of the dead in this godforsaken place.

The creature was easy to follow; its large feet left clear footprints on the dusty floor. Dillon followed the steps up, until he came to a great room.

There, between two pillars, sat a regal stone chair, and in that stone chair sat the crumbling remains of a man. His clothes were still intact, but the threads had mildewed and decayed until it was barely recognizable as a tattered royal robe. This palace—this whole mountain—had fallen here from another world, and all that was left of its royal occupants were bones crumbling to dust.

On the other side of the room stood Dillon's beast.

Dark gray flesh, rippling with strong muscles . . . and a familiar face.

Dillon's face.

The creature made no effort to run. Instead it stalked closer, mirroring Dillon's movements, until they stood five feet apart. It made no move to attack, nor did Dillon. Instead, Dillon stared into its eyes, trying to read some pattern there.

As complicated as it was, Dillon could read the pattern of its past. This being had begun as something small and insignificant—a maggot that he had invited into his soul in a moment of weakness. And once there, it had grown, evolved into something larger, then something larger still. Even now it seemed on the verge of a new metamorphosis. Through its translucent skin, Dillon could see a new form taking shape, ready to emerge . . . as soon as it was fed.

Dillon pulled the revolver from his shirt. This time the first three chambers were all full.

A smile appeared on the creature's face. It was a twisted, evil version of Dillon's own smile.

I can destroy you with a single thought. You'll be gone long before the hammer hits the chamber.

Still Dillon tightened his grip on the trigger.

So the creature pushed a single thought into Dillon's mind. *Suffer the weight,* it said to him. *SUFFER THE WEIGHT!*

Dillon's finger froze on the trigger, and from somewhere deep inside he felt all his feelings return to him at once. His crippled soul was called out of hiding, and with it came an eruption from the pit of his stomach that came screaming out of his mouth. All his emotionless memories finally locked in with their meanings, and they surged like bile through his brain.

Remorse!

Sorrow!

Shame, blame, and guilt echoed through his brain like a sonic boom, rattling his mind until he felt himself about to fall into the same chaos that he had created around him. He tried to deny all the things he had done—tried to deny that he had *chosen* this path, but even among shades of gray, the truth was there in black and white: it had been his choice to destroy. It had been his choice to feed the beast.

The sheer weight of his crimes weighed upon him now with such a pressure that he wished that fourth chamber had been full when Winston had pulled the trigger.

But he could right that mistake, couldn't he? The first three chambers were full. He could rid himself of the pain—the horrible guilt.

Suddenly the creature standing before him didn't seem to matter. All that mattered was ending the pain, so he turned the gun around and touched the cold barrel against his own temple.

And then, in front of him, he saw the creature flex its fingers and take a deep breath, waiting to be fed.

To be fed.

Dillon gritted his teeth and with all his might kept his finger from pressing that trigger. Destroying himself would be feeding the creature. It suddenly became clear to Dillon that the only way to deny this creature satisfaction was to bear the pain. And so Dillon did. He accepted the blame for the death and for the insanity. He felt the awful weight on his shoulders . . . and that weight, pressing like a thousand stones, almost killed him right there.

But it didn't.

And instead he was left with just enough strength to turn the gun around again and pull the trigger.

The bullet caught the creature in the shoulder. It wailed in pain and surprise, then grabbed Dillon and hurled him across the room.

Dillon came crashing down on the throne, shattering what was left of its former occupant. Bone fragments splintered into the air and a cloud of dust rose from where Dillon sat.

The creature, bleeding a viscous, dark blood, leapt toward him, and Dillon fired again.

The second blast caught the creature in the stomach.

It doubled over in pain.

Dillon rose from the throne and the creature backed away

toward an open veranda, pulling itself along, limping, leaving a path of its slippery blood.

Dillon stalked after it. Then, at the threshold of the balcony, it turned its eyes to him once more.

Finish it, the beast said, taunting. *Shoot now!*

Something inside Dillon told him to look at the patterns— to check the series of outcomes that firing the bullet could create. But he didn't listen; instead he just leveled the gun and let his anger fly uncontrolled with the firing of the final bullet.

The beast moved its head at the last moment, the bullet barely grazed its ear, and when the beast stepped away, Dillon realized how fully and completely he had been tricked . . . and how much heavier the weight of his soul had suddenly become.

Behind the creature, on the veranda, Deanna was coiled in a death grip with her serpent of fear, when suddenly her arms went limp from the bullet that had grazed the ear of Dillon's beast . . . and then hit her in the chest.

"No!!!!!!!!" Dillon ran to her.

The serpent squealed, uncoiled, and retreated to the corner, quivering, and Dillon caught Deanna's collapsing body.

The dark spirit laughed a healthy, hearty laugh. It flexed its muscles and absorbed this act of destruction. It fed on Deanna's dying breaths.

Deanna gasped for breath in Dillon's arms.

"I'm sorry," he said. "I'm sorry, I'm sorry, I'm sorry." But his words felt impotent and useless. She tried to speak but couldn't. He felt the wound in her chest, which was pouring blood, and saw the light slipping from her eyes.

Deanna gazed at him weakly. "I'm not afraid," she said. "I'm not afraid . . ."

Dillon could see the pattern of death. He could see her mind imploding—feel death beginning to break down her body. He felt her disappearing down that long tunnel.

And then he realized he could stop it.

He concentrated on her wound. He concentrated all his attention. His talent was not only to *see* patterns but to *change* them. Could he close the pattern of a wound the way he could instantly solve a Rubik's Cube? Could he reverse the patterns of chaos and death the same way he could create them?

He put his hand on Deanna's wound, which had stopped pumping blood. He felt the wound ever so slowly beginning to close—

—But then he felt the pattern of her mind collapsing, so he focused on that, keeping her mind from giving in to death—

—But then he felt the pattern of her cells begin to slowly decay, so he turned his attention to keeping her flesh from giving over to the silence of death—

—But her wound had begun to bleed again . . . so he turned his attention to that.

A screaming, tear-filled rage overcame Dillon. This was a task he could not accomplish, no matter how powerful his talent. He did not yet have the skill to prevent Deanna's death. In the end all he could do was hold her in his trembling arms and watch her great light disappear into eternity.

Standing just a few feet away, Dillon's creature fed on Deanna's death and completed its metamorphosis. Its outer skin broke away to reveal a lattice of veins and fine bones that pulled away from its body spreading wide, casting a shadow of a pair of wings, blacker than black, over Dillon and Deanna.

The creature still bled—wounded, but still alive.

Suffer the weight, Dillon, it said to him again. *And every moment you suffer is a moment I grow strong.*

Then it turned from him and leapt off the balcony, soaring

high on its great black wings and leaving a veil of darkness that trailed behind it, followed by Deanna's serpent, which slithered down the rocky slope.

Dillon leaned over Deanna's body and cried, but his tears did no good, and when he had no more tears, he lifted her up and brought her to the throne. He brushed off the dust and fragments of ancient bone, and he gently set her down, wrapping her in the moldering royal robe . . . and as he held the robe, he could see its pattern coming back together in his hands. It was a simple pattern, just a weave of fabric. In a few moments what had been tattered, disintegrating cloth became a rich royal-blue robe of silk.

Order out of chaos.

How could he have been so blind as to let his talent be used to destroy when it could have been used to create?

He held the cloth a moment longer until all its fragments had woven together in his hand and it was as bright and clean as the day it was made. Then he finished wrapping it around Deanna's limp body and closed her unseeing eyes.

He kissed her cold cheek. "I'll come back for you, Deanna," he promised. "I'll bring you back."

Was it possible? Was life out of death something he could ever manage? Could his talent ever be honed to weave back a tapestry of life the way it rewove a tapestry of silk?

He kissed Deanna again and let her go. She seemed to recline regally in the throne, like a queen in repose.

"I love you," he whispered.

He turned and stepped out on the veranda once more, the sorrow almost overtaking him so that he had to hold onto the stone to keep from doubling over. Down below, he could see the others trying to climb back to their world. While way in the distance the winged Spirit of Destruction soared into the icy sky, and the serpentine Spirit of Fear followed in its shadow, like thunder after lightning.

IN THE HEAT OF the red desert, they didn't discuss how they had defeated their foes—instead they focused all their attention on the task at hand. There was a hole fifteen feet off the ground, and it was quickly healing itself closed. They pushed a rusted car beneath the hole, then piled everything from stones to airplane seats to rusted bicycles—anything they could find to get themselves high enough. Then, when their mound was done, Winston laid his hands on a vine, which grew around the mass of loose objects, locking them together in a living mesh.

They only stopped in their task once; the moment they felt one of them die. Then they all took a deep breath and continued stacking, not daring to talk about it.

They had already begun to climb toward the hole when they saw Dillon coming toward them.

"They got away," said Dillon. ". . . And Deanna's dead." The four hesitated, not even wanting to get close to him. It was Tory who finally stepped down.

"We need to know about the hermit on the other side," said Tory. "What can we do to stop him?"

Slayton! He had forgotten about Slayton! He was long gone, somewhere in Tacoma by now, already beginning the great collapse.

"I don't think he can be stopped," said Dillon sadly. "You should have killed me."

But instead, Tory reached her hand out to him. "Hurry, the hole's almost closed."

Up above, Michael and Lourdes had already forced their way through the hole, which was no larger than a basketball now.

"You're gonna let *him* come with us?" Winston shouted down to Tory. "After what he's done? With his leech-freak still out there?"

"He's one of us," was the only answer Tory gave.

Winston threw a bitter gaze at Dillon, and then threw himself into the hole and vanished. When Tory got to the top, she took a moment to look at the desolation here in this infinite "between." Then she pushed her way into the hole, which stretched around her like tight elastic, until she disappeared into darkness.

Dillon hesitated. If the world on the other side of that hole was already starting to fracture, it would soon be more of a Hell than this tormented place they were leaving. But it was *his* world, and *his* responsibility to face what he had done there. So he took a deep breath and grabbed the lip of the hole with both hands, stretching the rend in space as wide as it would go. Then he squeezed his way into a layer of cold, suffocating darkness, and finally he pushed himself through the gap on the other side, into the world of life.

THE WEAPONS LOCKER WAS empty.

This was the first thing Dillon noticed as he fell from the hole to the cold wooden floor of Slayton's shack. The weapons locker was empty, and Slayton was gone.

Dillon squeezed his eyes shut, trying to somehow disappear inside himself, but could not. "You don't know how awful it's going to be," he told the others. "You can't imagine what the world will be like tomorrow . . ."

They all looked at each other, then turned back to Dillon.

"There's something you should see outside," Lourdes said.

It was light now, and the hermit's old pickup was still there, its headlights shining straight at them. Its engine was on—

overheating and billowing steam; radiator fluid soaked the ground.

Two figures were in the light of the headlights: a small boy making rivers in the dirt with the spilled radiator fluid, and Slayton, who was sitting up against the grill. It seemed Tacoma was no longer of any interest to him.

"Was this part of the plan?" Michael asked Dillon.

Clearly it wasn't.

"You were good . . . ," Tory told Dillon. "But I guess there's some things not even you can predict."

Lourdes picked Carter up in her arms, as the five of them stared at Slayton, loaded shotgun still in hand, sitting motionless against the grill of the pickup.

The radiator was leaking because it had been punctured by a steel arrow. The same steel arrow that pinned Slayton's lifeless body to the radiator grill.

"We was playing cowboys and Indians," said Carter, still gripping Slayton's crossbow in his hands. "I won."

Inside the dead hermit's shack a hole in the wall of the world quietly healed itself closed and disappeared with a tiny twinkling of light.

18. THE FIVE OF WANDS

THEY BURIED SLAYTON BESIDE HIS SHACK WITH HIS OWN shovel. He had lived forsaken, but was laid to rest with more tender care than he had known in life. They buried his weapons with him and, with each shovel of dirt, they not only buried the man, but also the nightmare they had lived under for so long.

They finished at dawn, and now the forest that had seemed so desolate revealed its own slow recovery in the growing light. Between the gray, lifeless trees, grass and wildflowers had come back to begin the process of life again.

Winston gathered some of the wildflowers, strewed them across the barren grave, then brushed his fingers across them until the grave sprouted into a colorful garden. Then the four of them built a fire to warm themselves, and stood around it, talking of small, unimportant things, which they never before had had the luxury to do.

Only Dillon stayed away, still an outsider.

He had been the first to begin digging the grave, the first to gather wood for the fire, but when nothing was left for him to do, he placed himself in exile. They all were painfully aware of his presence.

"Someone should say something to him," suggested Tory.

Winston gnawed beef jerky on teeth that were still coming in. "I got nothing to say to him," he declared coldly.

They all stole glances at Dillon, who sat alone by the hermit's grave, aimlessly shuffling a worn deck of cards he had found in the shack. He was thinner now, and his face almost cleared up, but there was a burden in that face, so weighty and oppressive, it was hard to look at him.

"What can we say that will make any difference?" wondered Lourdes, and glanced toward Carter, who now busied himself dropping sugar cubes into a bucket of rainwater, watching them dissolve with the same mindless indifference he must have felt when he fired that crossbow. The boy was a living testament to the people and places Dillon had shattered, and nothing any of them could say would change that.

"Any one of us could have ended up like Dillon," said Michael. "I know I almost did."

Michael left the warmth of the fire and was the first to brave the distance to the boy they knew only as The Destroyer.

"Solitaire?" asked Michael as he approached Dillon.

Dillon didn't break the rhythm of his shuffling. "A trick," he answered.

"Can I see it?"

Dillon looked at Michael apprehensively, then handed Michael the cards. "Shuffle them and lay them face up," he said.

Michael sat down, shuffled the cards, then spread them out, showing a random mix of fifty-two cards.

Dillon picked up the deck again and began to shuffle it himself. "I never liked playing cards," said Dillon, "because no matter how much I shuffled the deck, the first card I always turned over was the ace of spades. The death card."

"That's not the death card," said Tory as she came over and sat beside them. "Believe me, I've *seen* the death card, and it's not the ace of spades."

Lourdes came over as well, leaving Winston the only one refusing to talk to Dillon. They watched as Dillon shuffled the deck over and over, and when he was done he handed the deck to Tory. "Flip the first card," he said.

Tory flipped it. It was the ace of spades.

"Cool trick," said Michael.

It was Lourdes who realized the trick hadn't ended. "Why don't you flip the second card?" she suggested.

Tory flipped it; the deuce of spades.

"So?" said Michael.

Tory flipped another card; the three of spades; then the four of spades; then the five. She looked at Dillon warily, then turned the entire deck over and spread the cards face up.

The cards were in perfect order; ace through king, spades through diamonds! They stared, not sure whether to be aghast or amused.

"Pretty good trick, huh?" said Dillon. His eyes betrayed the truth; this was much more than a mere trick.

"So what's the big deal?" asked Michael as he examined the deck.

"Entropy," said Tory.

"Entro-what?"

"Entropy," she repeated. "Newton came up with it—it's one of the basic laws of the universe, just like gravity."

"What is?!" demanded Michael.

Tory rolled her eyes. "*That things go from a state of order to disorder.* You know—mountains erode, glass breaks, food rots—"

"Cards get shuffled," said Lourdes.

"Right," said Tory, "but Dillon here . . . he's breaking that law."

They all stared at him. "Is that true?" asked Lourdes.

Dillon quivered a bit, and said, "Go directly to jail, do not pass 'Go.'"

While Michael chuckled nervously, and Lourdes just stared at the cards, Tory scoured the area for a way to test her theory. She finally settled on Carter, who had long since drowned all his sugar cubes, and was just staring into the bucket of water. She took it from him, and he hardly seemed to notice it was gone.

"The law of entropy say that sugar dissolves in water," said Tory, brining the bucket over to them. "Right?"

Everyone looked into the bucket. The water was clear; not a granule of sugar left.

"Dillon, put out your hands," asked Tory.

Dillon did, and Tory slowly poured the water through his fingers.

What they saw didn't appear spectacular. . . . At first . . . it just seemed . . . well, weird. As soon as Tory began to pour the water, granules of sugar appeared in Dillon's hands, out of the clear water. The water kept spilling through his fingers, and his palms filled with the white powder . . . but it didn't stop there. The grains seemed to be pulling themselves together as Dillon concentrated, and once the water had poured through his fingers and the bucket was completely empty, Dillon was left with not just a handful of sugar . . . *but a handful of sugar cubes.*

They stared at the cubes, stupefied.

"That's awesome!" said Michael. "It's like reversing time!"

"No it's better," suggested Lourdes. "It's reversing *space.*"

Dillon put his handful of sugar cubes down, and they slowly dissolved into the mud.

"What do you do with a talent like that?" wondered Michael.

"What can't you do with it!" said Tory. "It's better than all of our talents put together. . . . It's like . . . creation."

The very thought made Michael pale. A chill wind blew and somewhere in the distance a small cloud began to darken.

"Don't mind Michael," Tory said to Dillon, "he gets a little bit moody."

But it wasn't just a matter of Michael's being moody. He had something else weighing on his mind.

"So what happens now?" asked Michael.

The question had hung heavily in the air since dawn, but had gone unspoken. *What now?* Any urge they had felt to come together had long since faded away, just as the light of the supernova had dimmed in the night sky. If anything, the urge was to drift apart. They all turned to Dillon for an answer—as if somehow he were the one holding them together like crystals of sugar, and they needed his permission to go their separate ways.

"We do," said Dillon, "whatever we want to do."

It was a quiet declaration of independence, but seemed as profound a moment as when the exploding star first filled the night sky.

"I want to go home."

It was Winston who spoke. They all turned to see him there, a fraction of an inch taller than he was just moments before. "I gotta fix things—*change* things, get my life moving," he said, then he wiped a tear from his eye before it had a chance to fall. "And I miss my mom and brother."

No one could look each other in the eye then. Thoughts of home that had been locked away all this time now flooded them.

"By the time I get home," said Lourdes, "they won't even recognize me.... It's all gonna be new ..."

The shifting wind blew cold again. "What if we don't go home?" whispered Michael.

"You will," said Dillon.

Winston crossed his arms. "How the hell do you know?"

Dillon shrugged. "I can see the pattern," he said. He studied the four of them—the way their eyes moved, the way they breathed, the way they impatiently shifted their weight from one leg to the other.

"You'll leave here not sure of anything; not even the ground beneath your feet," he told them. "But the further you get away from this place, the saner it's all going to feel . . . and every place you stop, there'll be people coming out of the woodwork talking to you—wanting to be near you, and not even knowing why. Waiters will tear up your checks—strangers will open up their homes to you; everyone will think you've gotten your lives together, and you'll laugh because you'll know the truth. And each person you come across—they'll take away something they didn't have before—something pure, or joyful, a sense of control, something to grow on. At least one of those people will get on a plane. And then it'll spread to places you've never even heard of."

They stood there aghast. Michael stared at Dillon, slack-jawed. "You can see all that?!"

Then Dillon's straight face resolved into a wide grin. "Sucker!" he said.

Tory burst out with a relieved guffaw, and soon the others were laughing and razzing Michael, as if they hadn't fallen for it as well.

Dillon's grin faded quickly and that solemn melancholy returned to take its place. "You'd better all go," he told them. "You've got a whole country to get across." Then he glanced at Carter. "You can leave him with me."

Somehow it didn't seem fitting to say good-bye, so Tory reached out her hand to Dillon and introduced herself.

"I'm Tory," she said. "Tory Smythe."

Dillon smiled slightly, and shook her hand. "Dillon Benjamin Cole."

The others were quick to follow.

"Michael Lipranski."

"Lourdes Maria Hidalgo-Ruiz."

Winston kept his hands in his pockets, refusing to shake Dillon's hand. "Winston Marcus Pell."

Then the four who had come together turned and headed toward Michael's van, dissolving away from Dillon, the way they would soon dissolve away from each other.

Winston was the last to go. He stood there, a few feet from Dillon, a scowl well-cemented on his face. He looked Dillon over head to toe.

"You know you'll never be forgiven for the things you've done. There ain't enough grace in all the world to cleanse you of that."

Dillon had to agree. "You're probably right."

Winston studied Dillon a few moments longer, and his scowl softened. He shook his head. "I wouldn't want to be you," he said.

Behind them, they heard the others piling into the van. Winston took a step back, but before he turned to leave, he reached out and tapped Dillon on the arm, the closest he could bring himself to a friendly gesture. "Stay clean," said Winston. "Don't let the bugs in."

Dillon nodded, and Winston ran off to join the others. In a moment their minds were far away, their voices growing with joy and anticipation. Then Michael started the engine, and the four great souls ventured forth into the bright morning, ready to embrace their new, old lives.

It wasn't until lunch time that they spared a thought for Dillon again, when a coffee shop waitress told them their lunch was on the house.

· · ·

DILLON WATCHED THEM DRIVE down the dirt road away from Slayton's shack. The van's stereo was blasting, and Dillon could tell they were already soaring back into the world of love and life—a place where Dillon could not join them. Once the sound of their engine faded in the distance, Dillon approached Carter.

The boy still sat near Slayton's grave, doing nothing, thinking nothing. Dillon sat down in front of him and looked into the boy's eyes; the large back pupil of the left, the tiny pinpoint of the right.

Dillon gathered all of his attention, pushing out his own fear and confusion. He held this boy by the shoulders and looked through those empty eyes, until he found the impossible jigsaw of a little boy . . . mindless . . . patternless, splintered beyond any hope of repair, and yet Dillon set himself to the task of repairing it.

Dillon sat there ten minutes, twenty minutes, an hour, pushing his own mind into the boy's chaos and stringing a lifetime of thought and meaning. It wasn't as easy as destruction; it was a thousand times harder to re-create what was no longer there, but Dillon forced himself to do it.

When he was done, Dillon felt drained, cold and exhausted—but when he looked into Carter's eyes now, the boy's eyes looked normal. And they began to fill with tears.

"I done bad things," cried the boy, with a mind all too clear. "I kilt people. I done bad, bad things."

"It wasn't you," Dillon told the boy. "It was me."

Dillon took the sobbing boy into his arms and together they cried in the lonely woods. Dillon cried for all the souls he had ruined, for all the pain he had caused . . .

. . . And he cried for Deanna. Losing her was more than he could bear. If she had been here, she could have comforted this boy, touching him with her gift of strength and faith. She could have healed his heart just as Dillon had healed his mind. What a wonderful world this could have been if Deanna could still be in it.

So they both cried, and when neither of them could cry anymore, Dillon put the boy into the Range Rover and got into the driver's seat.

The boy, still sniffling a bit, studied him. "You old enough to drive?" he asked.

Dillon shrugged. "Not really."

The boy put on his seat belt, and Dillon started the car. The boy didn't ask where they were going. Maybe he just didn't want to think about it, or maybe he already knew.

INTERSTATE 84 CROSSED OUT of Washington, then followed the Columbia River east, along the Washington–Oregon border. Just before dark, they turned off the interstate, heading down a country road that wound through a dense forest. Less than a mile down, the road was blocked by a police barricade; only the truly determined would be getting anywhere near the town of Burton, Oregon, for a good long time.

Dillon stopped the car and took a deep breath as he stared at the barricade. In the distance, he could hear ghostly wails of the mad ones still lost in the woods—so many of them, it made Dillon wish he could turn and run, screaming louder than the voices in the woods. But then he remembered how bravely Deanna had faced things at the end. Certainly Dillon could find a fraction of that bravery now.

As they got out of the car, the boy looked at Dillon with trusting eyes, as if Dillon had all the answers in the world.

"Can you make it all better?" asked the boy. "Can you fix everything?"

Could he? There was no pattern Dillon could see that gave him an answer; there was only his will, the boy's hope, and a memory of Deanna's faith in him. But perhaps that's all he needed to begin the mending.

"I don't know," said Dillon. "We'll see."

Then he took the boy's hand, and together they walked toward the barricade of the shattered town.

Here's a look at the next book in

THE STAR SHARDS CHRONICLES

DILLON'S ARMS HAD GROWN STRONG FROM HIS LABORS.

At first, his back and shoulders had filled with a fiery sore-ness that grew worse each day as he worked. His biceps would tighten into twisted, gnarled knots—but in time his body had grown accustomed to the work. So had his mind.

He dug the spade in the soft dirt, and flung it easily over his shoulder.

The chill wind of a late-September night filtered through the nearby forest, filling the midnight air with the rich scent of pine. He shivered. With knuckles stiff from gripping the shovel, he struggled to zip his jacket to the very top. Then he resumed digging, planting the spade again and hurling the dirt, beginning to catch the rhythm of it, giving in to the monotony of spade and earth. He made sure not to get any dirt on the blanket he had brought with him.

He realized he should have worn heavy workboots for the job, but his sneakers, though caked with mud, never seemed to wear out. None of his clothes ever wore out. He had just torn his jeans hopping over the wrought-iron fence, but he knew they would be fine. Even now, the shredded threads around the tear were weaving together.

The fact was, Dillon Cole *couldn't* have a pair of faded,

worn-out jeans if he wanted to. He called it "a fringeless fringe benefit." A peculiar side-effect of his unique blessing.

The shovel dug down. Dirt flew out.

"I got a scratch."

The small boy's voice made Dillon flinch, interrupting the rhythm of his digging.

"Carter," warned Dillon, "I told you to stay with that family until I got back."

"But the scratch *hurts*."

Dillon sighed, put the shovel down and brushed a lock of his thick red hair out of his eyes. "All right, let me see your hand."

Carter stretched out his arm to show a scratch across the back of his hand. It wasn't a bad scratch, just enough to draw the tiniest bit of blood, which glistened in the moonlight.

"How'd you do this?" Dillon asked.

Carter just shrugged. "Don't know."

Dillon took a long look at the boy. He couldn't see the boy's eyes clearly in the moonlight, but he could tell Carter was lying. *I won't challenge him just yet,* Dillon thought. Instead he brought his index finger across Carter's hand, concentrating his thoughts on the scratch.

The boy breathed wondrously as he watched the tiny wound pull itself closed far more easily than the zipper on Dillon's jacket. "Oh!"

Dillon let the boy's hand go. "You made that scratch your-self, didn't you? You did it on purpose."

Carter didn't deny it. "I love to watch you heal."

"I don't heal," reminded Dillon. "I fix things that are bro-ken."

"Yeah, yeah," said Carter, who had heard it all before. "Reversing Enter-P."

"Entropy," Dillon corrected. "Reversing entropy," and he began to marvel at how something so strange had become so familiar to him.

"Go back to those people," Dillon scolded Carter gently. He returned to digging. "You're too young to be here."

"So are you."

Dillon smiled. He had to admit that Carter was right. Sixteen was woefully young to be doing what he was doing. But he had to do it anyway. He reasoned that it was his penance; the wage of his sins until every last bit of what he had destroyed was fixed.

The blade of Dillon's shovel came down hard, with a healthy bang.

Carter jumped. "What was that?"

Dillon shot him a warning glance. "Go back to the house."

"That woman won't stop praying," Carter complained, shifting his weight from one leg to the other, and back again. "It makes me nervous."

"You go back there and tell them I'll be back in an hour. And then you sit down and pray *with* them."

"But—"

"Trust me, Carter. You don't want to see this. Go!"

Carter kicked sullenly at the dirt, then turned to leave. Dillon watched him weave between the polished gravestones and slip through the wrought-iron fence.

When Dillon was sure Carter was gone, he took a long moment to prepare his mind for the task of fixing. Then he brushed away the dirt, and reached for the lip of the coffin.

Little Kelly Jessup, wrapped in a blanket, clung to Dillon Cole, shivering. Dillon braced himself as he carried her through the door of the Jessup home. Mrs. Jessup stood in the hallway, not quite ready to believe what her eyes told her, until the little girl looked up and said, "Mommy?"

The woman's scream could have woken the dead, if the job had not already been done.

DILLON'S DREAMS THAT NIGHT were interrupted, as they always were, by the green flash of the supernova—a memory that had seared its way deep into his unconscious. It was the first flash of vision that there were five others like him out there . . . and the first inkling of what they truly were; the most powerful and luminous souls on earth. Shards of the fractured soul of the scorpion star, incarnated in human flesh.

From there his dream took a turn into nightmare, and he knew where he would find himself next. The throne room of a crumbling palace, on a ruined mountain, within the red sands of what he could only call "the Unworld." That non-place that existed between the walls of worlds.

And before him stood the parasitic beast that had leeched onto his soul for so many years, its gray muscles rippling, its veiny wings batting the air, and its face an evil distortion of his own. It was a creature that would never have grown so powerful, had Dillon's own soul not been so bright.

I will be fed! it told him. *You will destroy for me. I will feed on the destruction you bring.*

In the dream, Dillon saw himself raising the gun to shoot it, knowing what was about to happen, unable to stop it. He pulled the trigger, the beast stepped aside . . . and there was Deanna.

The bullet struck the chest of the girl Dillon himself would die for.

He ran to her, took her in his arms, while the beast flexed its muscles, absorbing this act of destruction, feeding on Deanna's dying breaths.

"I'm not afraid," coughed Deana; "I'm not afraid"—for after she had purged the parasite of fear from her own soul, terror had no hold on her.

Suffer the weight, Dillon, the creature said, as Deanna died in his arms. *Suffer the weight of destruction . . . and every moment you suffer is a moment I grow strong. . . .*

Dillon was shaken awake by small hands on his shoulders. He opened his eyes to see Carter standing above him. By now this had become a regular routine.

"Dreaming about the monster again?"

Dillon nodded. The thing was still alive out there, Dillon knew. Both his beast and Deanna's still stalked the sands of the Unworld. The other four shards had killed their parasites, and Dillon suspected that if his were dead too, it wouldn't invade his dreams with such alarming regularity.

"My dog had worms once," said Carter. "They got to his heart and ate him from the inside out. Was that what it was like having that thing inside you?"

"Something like that," said Dillon. He sat up, taking a moment to orient himself. Where was he this time? What had he done here? He was in the Jessups' home. Yes—that was it. Kelly Jessup had been dead almost a year now, and her parents driven insane. Dillon had undone all that damage.

Dillon looked at his watch. Three in the morning. "Get back to bed," Dillon told Carter. "We need an early start tomorrow."

Carter returned to the couch across the guest room. "Who do we see tomorrow?"

"A family called the Bradys. There'll be more work than here."

"What about my father?" asked Carter.

Like so many others, Carter's father had gone insane, and

died a nasty death last year. Dillon's failure to find his grave was something Carter loved to hang over Dillon's head, and was a constant reminder to Dillon that there were still a million and one things and people screaming to be fixed.

"I'll find him," said Dillon. "And I'll fix him, just like I promised."

Carter shrugged. "No rush," he said, far too pleasantly. "I like being called Carter instead of Delbert anyway."

The thought unsettled Dillon. When the boy had been found, last year, wandering the streets, he had been a mumbling, maddened lunatic, just like everyone else left alive here in Burton, Oregon. He hadn't even known his own name.

"Carter was the tag on your T-shirt. Do you want to be named after an underwear company?"

"I don't care."

And that was the problem. Since Dillon had fixed the boy's mind, he had latched on to Dillon like a puppy. Dillon didn't mind the company, but he knew it just wasn't right. Life with Dillon was a poor substitute for life with his real family.

Dillon, knowing he would not sleep again tonight, turned to leave the room, but Carter stopped him.

"You were calling her name out in your sleep," Carter said.

Dillon sighed, wishing he could forget the dream. "Was I?"

Carter rolled over on the couch to face him. "You know," said Carter, "you could bring her back now. . . ."

Dillon grimaced to hear the words spoken aloud. When Deanna had died, Dillon had had no skill in bringing chaos from order, life out of death. All he knew was how to see patterns of destruction and act upon them. But a year had honed his skills. Now it would be so easy to take Deanna's broken body in his arms and bring her back to life, cell by cell. He imagined that moment when he could gather her life back and see her smile at him again. Hear the gentle forgiveness in her voice.

But he could not get to her. She was sealed away in the Unworld—a place Dillon could not reach. He was trapped in the here-and-now, and the people around him were constant reminders that he didn't deserve Deanna. All he deserved was the endless, exhausting task of fixing the disasters he had created—because he'd never be able to forgive himself for willfully feeding his parasite—until he had repaired every last bit of his decimation. From the moment the other four surviving shards had left him, he knew what his job was going to be. And one of the first things he bought was a shovel.

"Yes, I know I could bring her back," he told Carter. "Now go to sleep."

Carter rolled over, and in a few moments, he was sleeping peacefully. *And why not?* thought Dillon. He had repaired the boy's psyche so well, he never had nightmares, in spite of the horrors he had been through.

Dillon slid noiselessly out of the guest room. Downstairs he found Carol Jessup sitting in the family room. The air smelled of sweet cocoa and smoke from the smoldering fireplace. The woman lovingly held her sleeping daughter in her arms, absorbed in stroking the little girl's hair as she hummed a lullaby. She had been doing this for hours, unable to believe that her daughter was alive again. She stopped humming the moment Dillon stepped into the room. It took her a few moments until she could speak to him.

"I'm afraid to ask who you are," she said, "or how you did what you did."

"It's just patterns, Carol," Dillon answered. "My mind can see patterns no one else can see, and my soul can repair them. That's all I can do."

"That's all you can do?" she said incredulously. "That's everything. It's creation. It's reversing time!"

"Space," said Dillon calmly. "Reversing space."

The woman looked down at her daughter and her eyes became teary. "Maybe I don't know *who* you are," she said to Dillon, looking at him with the sort of holy reverence that made him uncomfortable, "but I know *what* you are."

Dillon found himself getting angry. "You don't know me," he told her. "You don't know the things I've done."

But clearly she didn't care what Dillon had done in the past. All that mattered to her was what he had done here, today. "When the virus came," she said, "my husband and I got lost in the woods, wandering insane like all the others in town. When we finally came out of it, we were told that Kelly had drowned in the river. I wanted to die along with her."

"What if I told you there was no virus?" Dillon said to her. "And that they call it a 'virus' because they don't know what else to call it? What if I told you that *I* destroyed this town last year—shattering everyone's mind—and that, in a way, I was the one who killed your daughter in the first place?"

Dillon thought back to the time of his rampage. It had taken so little effort for Dillon to shatter the minds of everyone in town. All he had to do was find the weakest point in the pattern, then simply whisper the right words into the right ear to set off a chain reaction, like a ball-peen hammer to a sheet of glass. Just a single whispered phrase, and within a few short hours, every last man, woman, and child in town was driven insane.

"In fact, what if I told you that I was responsible for the deaths of hundreds of people . . . including my own parents?"

"If you told me that," said Carol Jessup, "I wouldn't believe you. Because I know that a spirit as great as yours isn't capable of such evil."

"Bright light casts dark shadows," he told her, and said no more of it.

Dillon looked around the room. The furniture that had been well worn a day before was now in brand-new condition, and the carpet was thick and lush where it had once showed heavy tracking. Dillon wondered if Carol Jessup and her husband had noticed. He hoped they hadn't. Lately it wasn't a matter of him *willing* these things to happen anymore. Now they happened whether he wanted them to or not. He could sense his power was growing, and now his presence had its own sphere of influence, which affected everything around him. It made him not want to linger anywhere for long.

Little Kelly Jessup's eyes fluttered open for a moment, then closed again as she snuggled closer to her mother. She had already had a bath, but the child still had the faintest smell of the grave lingering behind the baby shampoo. But that, too, would be gone in a day or two.

"You need to leave here," Dillon told Carol Jessup. "Before anyone sees your daughter, you have to go somewhere where no one knows you. Where no one will ask you questions. You can never tell anyone what I did here today." Dillon knew there was still so much confusion in Burton, that one more abandoned house would not raise the questions it might raise elsewhere. It was that confusion which kept Dillon safely hidden from the view of the authorities . . . but the more he repaired, the less disorder there was to hide behind. Dillon knew his corner was getting tight.

"What if we do tell someone?" the woman asked. "What will happen?"

"You don't want to know."

The woman shrank back, and paled.

In truth, nothing would happen to *them* if she told . . . but if word of Dillon's deeds got out, he didn't want to think about what would happen to him.

"We'll pack our things, and leave in the morning," she told him. "And we won't tell a soul."

But it was clear from her tone of voice that she already had.

TWO HOURS LATER, THE town of Burton was swarming with police and state troopers, and Dillon knew they were looking for him. He had slipped away from the Jessups' at dawn, already sensing the world closing in around him. As always, they had decided to drive along the back roads. Carter sat silently in the passenger seat, impassive and unconcerned as Dillon managed to evade one police checkpoint after another, until he finally slammed the brakes on his Land Rover, and slammed his fists on the steering wheel.

"What'sa matter?" asked Carter.

Dillon shook his head to clear his thoughts. There was no way out of town—every road was crawling with troopers. The news of his feats must be more widely known than he had suspected, to mobilize so many troopers to ferret him out. Bringing back the dead must have been an offense as serious as mass murder in the eyes of the law.

A hundred yards ahead, the officers at the Harrison Street checkpoint took notice of Dillon's car stopped suspiciously a hundred feet away from them.

Carter yawned and brushed some morning crust from the corner of his eye. "We'll get away from them," said Carter. "You can get out of anything."

But it wasn't that simple. Dillon silently cursed his luck. His talent for seeing patterns in the world around him was as acute as ever, but when it came to his own life, he was blind. He knew someone would eventually give away his secret, but he had thought he would have more time. And it probably wasn't just the Jessups who had blown the whistle; other families must have come forward, too. He could imagine the most hardened of police investigators turned into blubbering morons when they saw the resurrected dead with their own eyes. No, they couldn't catch him, or he'd never be able to complete his repair work. He had to get away.

"We're smarter than them!" said Carter. "They'll never catch us!"

Dillon took a good look at the boy. Dillon couldn't remember ever being that innocent. That trusting.

"We're going to run, aren't we?" Carter's eyes were bright and eager. "Aren't we? You won't let them break us up—we're a team, right?"

Dillon knew what he had to do. Carter deserved more than an apprenticeship to a freak—Dillon owed him at least the *chance* at a normal life. And so, as the troopers approached, Dillon made no move to escape. Instead he quickly whipped up a new plan. A brilliant, brutal plan that would leave everyone better off.

Well, almost everyone.

THE TROOPERS DRAGGED CARTER, kicking and screaming, into one police car, and took Dillon off in another. Dillon offered no resistance. The two cars drove off, away from Burton, toward a saner part of the world where, presumably, Dillon would be "held for questioning."

The two state troopers in the front seat smelled of morning breath doused with black coffee. The older one, who drove the car, his graying hair cut in a tightly cropped butch, kept glaring at Dillon in the rearview mirror. His name tag read WELLER,

Dillon had noted. The stripes on his sleeve indicated that he was a sergeant.

"You've got the folks around here in one mighty uproar, son," he said. "We don't need any more uproars around here—the virus was enough trouble to last a lifetime."

"What are you charging me with?"

Weller laughed smugly. "Does it matter? You're obviously a runaway, and we're well within the law to bring you into 'protective custody.'"

Dillon broke eye contact and gazed out the window.

"Are you listening to me, son?" said Sergeant Weller.

Dillon still didn't answer him, but he did turn to catch Weller's eyes once more as Weller watched him in the rearview mirror. Dillon studied Weller—the way he moved, the cadence and inflections of his voice. Dillon noticed the way the man held his shoulders, and judged the way he aggressively changed lanes. To anyone else, it wouldn't have meant a thing, but to Dillon, the tale couldn't have been clearer if it were painted on the man's forehead. *I can see patterns,* he had told Carol Jessup. *That's all.* And the patterns of Sergeant Weller—each action, every word—betrayed to Dillon who this man had been, who he was, and who he was destined to be. It was not a pretty picture.

"Don't you talk, son?" Weller asked. "Or are you one of them idiot savants?"

Weller chuckled at his own words. Dillon paid particular attention to the methodical but nervous way Weller rubbed the fingers of his right hand, then clasped the hand into a fist. To Dillon, this man's life was easier to read than a street sign.

"Your wife wishes you would stop smoking," Dillon told him. "She wishes you would stop drinking, too."

Catching Dillon's intrusive gaze in the rearview mirror,

Weller's cold demeanor took a turn toward winter. "Watch yourself, son," he said. "You make up stories about people, you may find people making up stories about you."

For the first time, the trooper riding shotgun turned around. His name tag read LARABY. He was younger than Weller and to Dillon didn't seem nearly as unpleasant. He did, however, seem troubled. "People are saying you bring back the dead," Officer Laraby said. "You got anything to say about that?"

"It's all a bunch of voodoo talk," Weller sneered. "Mass hysteria—these people all think they got over 'the virus,' but I say some of their marbles are still lost in the drain pipe."

Officer Laraby turned to him. "So how do you explain all those people who turned up alive?"

Weller brushed a weathered hand over his butch and threw a warning glance at his young partner. "It's all hearsay. That's how a hoax works—hearsay held together by spit and tissue paper, isn't that right, son?"

Dillon smiled, all the while thinking how much he hated the way this man called him "son." "I suppose so."

The grin made Weller more irritable. "You think you're pretty smart, don't you? What did you do—take money from folks who didn't know any better, then bring back people who weren't even dead? That's the way you worked it, wasn't it, son?"

Dillon let the grin slip from his face. "You hit your wife one more time, and she's gonna leave you, you know?"

Panic flashed in Weller's eyes. His jaw twitched uncomfortably. Laraby watched the two of them, his head going back and forth like it was a game of Ping-Pong, to see who would speak next.

Weller hid his uneasiness behind an outburst of laughter. "Oh, you're good," he told Dillon. "You put on one heck of a show—but the truth is you don't know a thing about me."

Dillon found himself grinning again—the way he did in the days when the wrecking hunger had consumed him. "I know what I know," he said.

Dillon sensed the younger cop's growing discomfort, his confusion and uncertainty. Dillon also noticed the particular shade of the rings beneath Laraby's eyes, the faint smell of mild perfumed soap, and a handful of bitten fingernails. Dillon, his skill at deciphering patterns as acute as ever, understood Laraby's situation completely.

"Sorry your baby's sick," Dillon told Officer Laraby.

The man went pale. Dillon noted the exact way his chest seemed to cave in.

"Heart problem?" asked Dillon. "Or is it his lungs?"

"Heart," Laraby said in a weak sort of wonder.

"Don't talk to him!" Weller ordered Laraby. "It's tricks, that's all."

"Yeah," said Laraby, unconvinced. "Yeah, I guess. . . ."

In front of them, the car that carried Carter had pulled out far ahead of them. If Dillon's plan was to work, he knew he would have to strike now, with lethal precision. He leaned forward, and whispered into Sergeant Weller's sun-reddened ear, hitting him with a quiet blast of personal devastation in the form of a simple comment.

"*Sergeant Weller,*" he whispered, "*no matter what everyone says . . . it* was *your fault. Your fault, and no one else's.*"

A subtle hammer to glass. Dillon could feel the man's mind shatter, even before there were any outward signs. Weller gripped the steering wheel tighter, his knuckles turning as white as the cloud-covered sky. Dillon could hear the man's teeth gnash like the grindstone of a mill, and then, with a sudden jolt, Weller jerked the wheel.

The car lurched off the road and careened down a steep wooded slope. Pine branches whapped at the windshield, and a single trunk loomed before them. Then came the crunch of metal, and the sudden *PFFFLAP!* of the air bags deploying in the front seat, while in the backseat, Dillon's seat belt dug into his gut and shoulder. The car caromed off the tree, skidded sideways another ten yards, until smashing into another tree hard enough to shatter the right-side windows before coming to rest.

Dillon was stunned and bruised but he didn't take time to check his own damage. He climbed through the broken window, falling into the thick, cold mud of the woods, and for once the deep, earthy smell was a welcome relief. He stood, and quickly pulled open the passenger door of the ruined car. Officer Laraby was pinned between the seat and the firm billow of the air bag. The bag had knocked the wind out of him, and his gasps filled the air like the blasts of a car alarm. Dillon pulled him out of the car, and he fell to the ground.

Meanwhile, Sergeant Weller didn't seem to care about any of it. He just sobbed and sobbed. Dillon didn't dare catch his gaze now, for Dillon knew how his eyes would look. One pupil would be wide, the other shrunken to a pinpoint. They always looked like that when Dillon drove them insane.

"It's my fault," sobbed Weller, deep in a state of madness that went miles beyond mere guilt. *"It's my fault my fault my fault my fault. . . ."*

Laraby turned to Dillon, just beginning to recover his senses. "What's his fault?"

"I don't know," said Dillon, "but it doesn't matter now." And he really didn't know—all Dillon knew was that every pore of that man's body breathed out guilt that he was trying to hide. Very old guilt, and very potent. All Dillon had to do was tweak it to shatter his mind.

Up above, the other car, which had doubled back, had pulled to the side of the road. Doors opened and closed.

"Listen to me," Dillon told Laraby. "The boy in the other car—he says his name is Carter, but it's really Delbert. Delbert Morgan. You and your wife are going to take him in as a foster child. You're going to volunteer to do it."

The officer squirmed. "But—"

"You *will* take him in, and take care of him until his father comes for him someday"—and then Dillon added—"or else."

"Or else what?"

The answer came as another incoherent wail from the insane cop, still in the driver's seat pounding his fist mindlessly against his air bag. It was evidence of the destruction Dillon was still capable of when he chose to destroy—his ability to create chaos still every bit as powerful as his ability to create order.

Dillon could hear shouts on the hillside above them now, and people hurrying toward them. He tried to run, but Laraby, still on the ground, grabbed Dillon's shirt as if he were sinking into quicksand.

"Can you save my son?" asked the officer. "Can you fix his heart?"